fish

Grooming
and other stories

Joseph Powell

fish

Grooming
and other stories

I would like to thank the editors of the following magazines in which some of these stories were first published:

Trestle Creek Review: "The Iron Horse," "Red Geese"
Crabcreek Review: "Green Eyes"
Full Circle: A Journal of Poetry And Prose: "The Oddest Thing"
Talking River Review: "Fish Grooming"

Sincere thanks to the Artist Trust of Seattle, for their support.

Thanks to my wife, Judith Kleck, for decades of patiently reading rough drafts and for suppressing all snickers.

To my dear friends and generous readers who offered suggestions, many thanks—especially to Donald King, Bobbie Halperin, Paulus Pimomo, and Mike Lancaster.

This is a work of fiction, the characters are wholly invented, and the situations are derived entirely from the author's imagination.

Seven Kinds of Kisses

The Far-Off Herd

Fond Desire

To Donald King,
whose enthusiasm for the story
was contagious.

Seven Kinds of Kisses

"Let our scars fall in love"
—GALWAY KINNELL

THE ODDEST THING

The woman on the radio was talking about love when Dawna came in, but with her in the room, you can kiss whatever's on your mind goodbye. She had an unlit cigarette in her mouth, her long nails trying to get a paper match out of a new book. First thing Dawna says is that Terry's fat Lover Boy is sitting in her chair.

Dawna's blonde hair has tints as pink as cotton candy and more sweep than a broom. She wears false eyelashes, black mascara, and blue eye-shadow. The foundation on her cheeks is as thick as spray paint on a store going out of business. But she has beautiful brown eyes. There's green in them, and she walks straight-legged, head and neck poised like a llama.

"Which 'Lover Boy,' I thought Ray was my one o'clock," Terry said, getting up. "Oh, the fat bald one, I don't know why a person like that even needs a haircut. I think I'd get me a little electric razor, one of those cute enameled ones, and just do it myself," Dawna let out a long satisfied puff of smoke. "Damn lighter gave out on me this morning. I've only had it for a week. I bought it in that new candle shop on Eighth, next to the old watch-repairman's place? It smelled so good in there and that Mrs. Minor's so nice. I couldn't resist." Dawna could say less about something than anyone I ever saw.

Terry drank the last sip of her coffee and brushed past Dawna on her way to her 1:00 o'clock. That left me alone with Dawna. I brought my lunch today. Usually I go to the Fifth

Street Deli for a salad and tea, maybe some toast, and meet my girlfriends. Dawna works the lunch hour and takes her break at 1:00, so that left me with Terry. Terry doesn't talk much, so I caught most of the autistic lady's interview on the radio. She said her mind worked only in pictures like a video camera. She wrote a book about slaughter houses from the steers' point of view. She got in the pens and was herded around just like them. She crouched down and turned corners, walked up the chute, on into where they shoot them or whatever it is they do. She designed a whole new death system and goes around the country getting paid to talk about it. But here's the funny thing. She can't think in words so hate and love and jealousy might as well be green dogs and pink chickens. She has no concepts. Imagine! So how does she write a book? I used to think love was nothing more than a song you can't get out of your head. And I'd walk down the streets singing it until one day the song just stops. Some are top-forty for a month and some last about twenty-five minutes. And they're all better on the charts than in the kitchen.

Now, Terry she likes men. As customers, I mean. Some of our ladies have to wait, sometimes half a day, just to get in because the men are all stacked up in front of them. The ladies don't like that, but that's the way Terry is. She just says they'll have to wait. Dawna has her men too, but they're not the same kind if you know what I mean. I prefer women. When a man's in the chair, I usually don't know what to say. I usually just don't say anything, except to ask what he wants to look like, where the part is, how long the sideburns, that sort of thing. Then I spin him around at the end to see if it all matches. He pays and doesn't complain. Now, a woman can talk about anything. You name it and we can talk about it easy as pie. I might have to cut theirs twice and maybe see them in four days because they don't like their bangs, but I don't mind.

Dawna microwaved a cup of soup and sat in the floral armchair. She had an ashtray on one side and the soup on the other. I've told her a thousand times she doesn't eat enough to keep a lizard alive, but her figure's more important than her health. Her men come for a show. They're the ones with a wife whose stardust is all on the floor to be swept up. Or maybe it's just a look they are after, stars or no stars. Dawna knows what they want and she gives it to them. Her low-cut blouses and push-up bras are enough to make their minds wander in every three weeks or so. Dawna loves to talk and doesn't care who she talks to. Which is just fine for her men because they only have to chuckle now and again, say uh-huh, and slip back into whatever is on a man's mind when he's seen her cleavage. But Terry's men are different. They're odd-ball mechanics, repairmen, grocery managers, a few dentists, waste management engineers. It's like they have ten speed minds and like to go through a few gears each time you see them. Some of my ladies are like that too, I can spot a smart one by the way she parts her hair, but any woman can talk. They just know what to say. We have that gift.

"Alice, would you hand me that magazine, I think it's a *Self*, there's an article about garlic pills I want to read. They're supposed to be good for reducing cholesterol and your heart," Dawna said putting her ashtray on the counter.

"I don't think your heart needs reducing, Dawna," I said, handing it to her.

"I said I'm trying to reduce my cholesterol. Of course,

my heart's been broken so many times it's been reduced already." This was a topic Dawna and I were experts on and almost any conversation seemed to go there.

"I had better get to my 1:15, Madame X and her blue hair."

"Oh, it feels so good just to give my feet a sleigh ride," Dawna said.

Janet was sweeping up hair, and Terry was still trimming the sidewalls of the fat bald one. He had brown polyester pants and a blue-striped cotton shirt with an anchor on the pocket. I saw it when he reached under the cape to pull out his glasses. Terry could have been done with him ten minutes ago, but she's giving him the whole show even if he doesn't have any hair. Janet had been stuck all morning doing an extension on a black woman who had more hair than a caterpillar. I had three cuts and a henna, so I was feeling good.

Madame X was in the waiting area reading a magazine. I escorted her to my chair and gave her a shampoo and rinse. She was a hairdresser in Phoenix in her youth. She has large, flat lips. Her red lipstick made her look like Martha Raye. Her hair's so thin it hardly takes a curler. She wore mascara and her powdery cheeks were caked with wrinkles. She had a pale, creamy look like she'd fit right into a wax museum. She laughed a lot. She had heavy rings on her fingers, probably from all her dead husbands. I toweled her hair and combed it out. Terry was shaving the fat one's neck with an ivory-handled straight-razor. He just leaned forward, sleepy-like, as if a slip of that blade was the furthest thing from his mind.

"Doll, there's a drip going down my neck, could you catch it," Madame X said pointing to her right ear. I caught it.

"Did you hear that LeTourneau woman was caught again?" Madam X asked.

"I think they ought to leave that poor woman alone. I believe in love. As long as they aren't hurting anyone we ought to keep out of it. Women are different than men. We believe in love, and men believe in sex. It's as simple as that."

The old woman was watching me in the mirror. Her head shakes just a little bit, and I have to keep one finger on it to keep it steady.

"I believe in sex," the old woman said, grinning with her wide red mouth.

What does this old prune know about sex anyway, I thought.

"I'll bet you were quite the heart breaker in your day," I said, snipping a few thin strands above her left ear.

"Listen, Doll, my day ain't over yet. I've had four husbands and I'm working on the fifth. And I loved them all, the dears. They were as different as mongrel dogs. That LeTourneau woman wanted a boy so she could raise him right, if you know what I mean. Men are already raised so they won't do. Now that she's famous for it, she'll love him till she dies. And get holier about it all the time. My second husband was like that. I thought he was the smartest man alive until he failed. Then he was the dumbest one I ever met."

"What'd he fail at?"

"Life," the old woman said with a huff.

"I believe God is love and love between any two creatures on earth is paying respect to God."

"Oh, Pooh," the old woman said as she climbed out of the chair and brushed off her sleeves and shoulders.

"Thanks for coming in, Mrs. Donovan, it's always good to see you."

"Well, I'm still keeping the dead alive. Bye now," and she shuffled to the counter to pay.

Terry had finished with the fat one, and was working on a skinny little man in bib overalls. He had a trim mustache and high cheekbones. His hair was black as a skillet, but grey was coming out his ears and streaked his mustache. They were talking about raising cattle, probably from that interview on the radio. I couldn't imagine what Terry knew about that, but she's a surprise. I've heard her talking about newspaper editorials, flyfishing, beekeeping, the stock market, the global village, whatever. Terry's been here for about six months and I still don't know what makes her mind tick. At lunch she'll read the weirdest things, about how batteries work, Taoism, how to make stone walls, horse grooming. There's no reason or rhyme to it. She has short dark hair and when she's reading she leans into her right hand with a finger pointing at her temple like it was a gun. She's thin and has hazel eyes and a dark complexion like maybe she's French. She wears jeans with a silk blouse and a vest. She likes jewelry, looks good. She gets all done with the skinny guy and he pays her instead of Janet at the counter. She puts the money on her scissors and sweeps up the rancher's hair. When she turns around her next customer is a cripple who just strolled in, or rolled in. He's got a tattoo of a black leopard's head on his right forearm, something underneath it I can't read from where I am. His hair was past his shoulders, and he wore gold-rimmed glasses. He had a graying blonde beard and wore a flowered shirt and black pants. A thin gold chain was around his neck.

"Say, lady, you got time for a haircut?" he asks Terry.

"You got an appointment?" Terry asks, smiling.

"I do. You can check at the desk if you like."

"So, what's your pleasure," she says, like there's a nasty joke in her voice. When she puts the cape around his neck, she bends down and kisses him right smack dab on the lips.

Well, it turns out this cripple is her husband. Terry introduced us. His name is Tom, and he has a wide smile. He had just gotten his first interview for a teaching job and he needed a new look, a responsible, every day in the salt mines look. It was his way of saying he had to make an appointment with his wife to get his hair cut.

I saw him again two days later at the Fifth Street Deli. Dawna had called in sick, so Terry took her noon shift. For a surprise Tom had come down to have lunch with her. Terry told him I was at the Fifth and if there was a cancellation she'd join him. Over soup and a sandwich, I talked to him for nearly an hour. He had gone to school and majored in history. He's a Viet Nam vet who had been "sideswiped by a M-79 launcher—that's one of ours" which is what put him in the wheelchair. He chose history because he wanted kids to know what a war means, what can happen. That's why he got a teaching certificate. He was almost-living proof that ignorance is deadly. He wanted them to see that flesh was bartered for oil, that the causes of war come down to things like tobacco, gold, cotton, sweat, and backing up some old bastard's word. He wanted them to taste the salt of freedom, feel the nap of history, to really sense the lime-taste of terror. He said these things and I just listened to his words, but they were words he meant, earnest words. His voice had something in it that just made me want to hear more. It was a soothing puzzlement. The nap of history? The lime-taste of terror? He said he wanted them to know what a farm boy from Kittitas was capable of, that in a few months they could be killing machines who cried at night for their girlfriends, the steady sploosh of sprinklers in their backyards, and then slice the throat of a fellow human being while eating a sandwich. Thrill to it, even, like a football game. His vocation had come as a kind of revelation after years and years of therapy and VA meetings and dope. After two years of daily breakfasts with other Nam Vets more fucked up than he was, he made his decision. And did you know that twice as many vets had killed themselves after the war than were killed in it? He met Terry at school. She had been divorced from her first husband when she was in her twenties, and now in her late thirties she had married him. He was forty-seven. Terry was still going to night school and had another year to go.

As I watched Tom shift around in his chair while he was talking, while his arm rose and fell like an empty pillowcase in the wind, I kept wondering why a woman like Terry would marry him. But he is handsome in his new haircut and shave. You could see his dimples when he smiled. His eyes were gray and tarnished as silver but polished around the edges, the shine came from underneath somehow. When he left he shook my hand, but it wasn't a normal shake. His right hand took my left, and he said, "Pleased to get to know you." It was a gentle, soft shake, like a father taking the hand of his child. There was nothing in it but a courtesy, some pleasure like us being alive at the same time.

I can't in God's name explain this, but for over a week now, I can't keep my mind off him. Those eyes, that handshake, the eager rush of his words. And what he said about the war. It was more the feeling behind the words and the way he said them. I think about my father who was younger than I am now. I think about the Kittitas boys I knew from high school and I'd see them waist-deep in rice paddies with guns on their shoulders. They weren't geeks and cowboys but killing machines. They were men who could be damaged into my father. They looked at me with the coldness of professional card players, picking their teeth with dried blood on their hands, their eyes drilling into me like icepicks. It was like a memory of a scary dream, and then I would wake and go back to Tom's flowered shirt and his eyes.

I also think about his body, the mechanics of their life together. How he could manage his wheelchair down the hallways and turn into a room. How he could reach a book on the top shelf. How he could cook his own dinner, how he took a bath or a shower, how he made love or if he did, how he got dressed, how he would change a lightbulb. Those kinds of things. I found that as I walked through my day I began to notice curbs and steps and narrow passageways. I began to see danger everywhere. So I invented things. A wheel-chair with height hydraulics so a person could cut hair or work behind a counter. A stick with a little basket and a squeeze handle that tightened and released the webbing so a person in a wheel chair could change light bulbs or adjust a curtain. A short refrigerator with pull out shelves, a remote control vacuum cleaner. It got to be an obsession.

I have always felt guilty about the war. For twenty-five years my dad said zip about it. Silent as a tomb, his own I'm sure. Sometimes he snaps and screams, throws something. Then he leaves. Drives, he says, anywhere, just him and the miles out in front of him. His boss is a vet too and they have an understanding. I never knew my dad, what he went through, what help he needed. I just tried to duck at the right time.

At night, as I lay in bed, I ran my hand over my body as if it were Tom's body. So help me, I can't explain this. My mind broke its leash and just kept on going. I wondered how much he could feel and where, how Terry and Tom made love. On my day off, I deliberately went to the library at 8:30 in the morning before people got there and looked at a book on male reproduction and abnormalities. I read about injections with vasoactive drugs, intracavernosal injection therapy with drugs like papaverine hydrocloride and phentolamine mesylate. I saw a diagram and found where the cavernosa was and how it resembled a cavern or cavity. I read about prostheses, inflatable and non-inflatable, and how they were wired and implanted. I wondered what Tom's was like and whether Terry had to give the injection or help with the inflation. Then I felt embarrassed for even thinking this way and I put the book back where I found it so it wouldn't have to be reshelved by one of the librarians who saw me come in.

That afternoon the oddest thing happened. A house two blocks from my apartment was having a yardsale, and in the garage was a wheelchair. It had $10 on it. I don't know why but I bought it. In the elevator, the landlady asked what it was for. I told her I had an elderly aunt who was going to visit and she wasn't getting around as well as she used to. I practiced around my apartment. It is an old apartment house with oak wainscoting and wooden floors. The halls smell like old paper and Pine Sol. Each unit is two bedrooms and identical in floorplan. The wood threshold was hard to get the wheels over, and the door opened into the living room. Leading out of the livingroom was a hallway to one of the bedrooms. I wheeled it down, but couldn't turn it through the bedroom door. I backed it up and maneuvered my feet, until I finally made it. I thought I would change clothes and tried to get out of the chair onto my bed without moving my hips or legs. I pulled my bedspread off the bed and the blankets ended up in a heap. I was lying face down on the bed when I realized my clothes were in the dresser and closet. I couldn't even reach the housedress I wanted to change into. I gave up and did some ironing and baked chocolate chip cookies to take to work. I read the paper, but that night I tried again.

Every day I spent a little more time in it. One night I decided to cook dinner this way. I got the chicken out of the refrigerator, but that was easy because it was in the meat compartment at the bottom. I cut it up, put lemon pepper and salt and garlic on it, and baked it. My herbs and seasonings are in drawers and easy to reach. Then I peeled some boiled potatoes and put them on to fry. I like to make a large dinner and then eat leftovers for several days. I started to make a little salad when the phone rang. My answering machine had already started by the time I wheeled my way to the phone. I have a cordless but keep it in the livingroom. My wheel had caught the kitchen door, and I had to back up and start again. It was Dawna. She wanted me to take her noon shift the next day because she had a date. She said she thought she was in love and told me all about him. They met in the Laundromat, she liked a man who washed his own clothes. She told me his name, where they were going, how nice his butt looked in jeans as he bent over the washer. I couldn't hardly get her off the phone. Her talk jumped from her date to a movie, from popcorn to saturated fats, from Janet's scheduling to the prospects of hiring someone else. When I hung up, my elbow hurt from being crooked so long.

I wheeled back out to the kitchen, and it smelled like

scorched hair. The pan was smoking. I wheeled over and grabbed the handle and pulled it off the burner, but just as I did the smoke alarm in the kitchen went off right over my head. It buzzed right through me like an electric shock, from my heart on out to each finger. There was a little spasm like that jolt you get as your body clicks into sleep. And when I looked up into the white mesh of the alarm, I had the sensation of looking down the barrel of a gun. It was yelling at me like some torture specialist. And here's the thing. My body went numb from the waist down. I felt paralyzed. My feet were lead. My legs were water-soaked rags. The panic of helplessness surged through me. I couldn't shut it off and it was yelling and yelling in my face. And here's the strange part. My heart was thudding, and the walls were echoing. In the middle of my panic, I almost yelled for Terry. The word actually came into my mouth, but I didn't say it. My whole body went limp. Then I struggled to my feet. Picked up one foot and shook it, then the other. I pulled a chair over from the table. I stood on it and switched off the alarm.

THE LIAR

That summer my older brother Frank was sledding hay for Jake Wainright, but knew about the job with Leonard. Although Frank was only four years older, he seemed to know everything that happened on our side of the valley long before I did. He would come home with little projects that someone had told him about and get paid to do simple things like feeding two bulls on Watson's patch of sagebrush or pitching some pellets to Morrison's trout. Of course, when he went to the pond he'd bring his pole and come back with three or four. Or he'd get free pasture for changing sprinklers, or barn wood he'd tear apart and sell for decorating someone's rec room. He told me I was too young for the Leonard job, but he said it with a sly smirk as though I were missing something big. The more he said I couldn't handle it, the more I hounded him. Then he'd say Leonard was too nice a man and paid too well for me to mess up a good deal.

For Frank, truth was merely the backdrop for his stories and his brand of bluff. As a child he was a ham who liked to sing and swagger with both hands on his six-shooters, but he had graduated to telling the most bald-faced lies with the earnestness of an altarboy. It was nearly impossible to tell when he was lying and when he wasn't. It's not that he was malicious; it was all just a game of pulling chains and swaggering. He usually endeared himself to new friends by telling stories about the malarkey he gave to gamewardens and reporters. Once he was pictured in our paper with a string of huge fish and a wide innocent grin. He told the

15

reporter he caught them in a high mountain lake using white corn and a glow-hook. That the reporter could believe glow-hooks and corn were common supper fare in high mountain lakes was the true source of his mirth: the dance of fun was all about that exact point to which gullibility could be stretched. He'd really caught the fish by sneaking into Olsen's pond at night and using worms. Another time a game warden stopped him with an extra limit of ducks in a cardboard box in the back of his Willy's jeep; he had a blanket over the box, a silver crucifix on top. The warden inspected the three birds behind the seat and bade him a good day and happy hunting.

But it wasn't so much the poaching or the lying that interested him; it was the way his mind could lean into the wholly imaginary so gracefully and dip out something beautifully preposterous. It was like screening for hellgram-mites in the river for whitefishing: onto the window screen tumbled crayfish, shiners, dragonfly larvae, caddisfly larvae, sculpins or bullheads, worms, any host of squirming sub-aquatic things. He never knew what might leap out whole and strange and wriggling with life. This thrilled him, but the amazing thing was he could tell his fantastic tales to anyone without even so much as a miscalculated blink. Two days later it would be so funny in the retelling that tears would come to his eyes, and he'd slap his knee to keep from falling over with laughter.

So when he discouraged me from working with Leonard, I thought of two possibilities. Either he was plotting some scam, or he was saving me for work he wanted done but I'd never get paid for. I pestered him, called him a few choice big shot names, then launched into the econom-ics of the situation. If I worked for Leonard which would probably pay $1 a ton, I might make a hundred dollars in a week, and he wouldn't have to lend me any money for the rest of the summer. I really had no clue how much I might make or how many tons per acre might be in a field, but the numbers seemed round and sufficient and sturdy.

Finally, he said I might be able to do it because Leonard had bought a new trip-sled. The old sleds were made of four long wooden planks nailed together and bolted to a metal plate that curved up in the front so the sled could slide behind the baler. Welded to the metal plate on the right side was an upright length of two-inch pipe that held a long metal bar. A three-inch gap ran down the center of the sled, and the haybuck took the bar and speared the moving earth under the sled, the bale stack slammed into the bar, and it was pushed off the sled. If the haybuck didn't brace himself well, the jolt could swat him to the ground and the bar would disappear under the sled. Level fields were manageable, but steep fields forced you to push the bales off uphill. You needed to be part gorilla to do that. These sleds were about three times as long, holding 16-22 bales, but the new trip-sleds held 5-7 bales, which were picked up by a squeeze on a tractor and arranged in the middle of the field so the trucks didn't have to go from stack to stack over the entire forty acres. The trip-sled had a metal lever on the side that when kicked caused the sled to buckle in the middle and the hay-load would tip back, catch on the ground, and slide off. Leonard wanted a 3-2-1 stack for his squeeze, so I only had to buck one bale two-high. A breeze, he said. I eagerly signed on.

The next day Frank dropped me off on Brown Road. Leonard was already there. He was a tall thin man with thick black hair and bushy eyebrows. His face looked as if someone had grabbed him at his hairline and pulled up: the center of his eyebrows arched, the corners of his eyes curled up, one side of his upper lip, and the corners of his mouth. He was quiet and answered every question with a grunted monosyllable. His laconic wit and pulled-up face made him seem mean. When it came to farming, it was difficult to determine whether he was ambitious or just liked speed.

We started baling at two in the afternoon and opened up a forty-acre field. It was about 95 degrees in the shade, and the baler's dust wrapped around us like wool. Chaff and dust were so thick that after about ten windrows my eyes were burning, and I was spitting mudwads the size of fifty-cent pieces. Leonard had the tractor in high gear and never looked back. I knew then why one of my brother's friends called him "Crazy Leonard"—though I imagined other fine reasons as well, including a stint in a mental hospital where the electro-shock treatments had tweaked his face.

We'd been baling hay for about two hours when the baler ran out of wire and the loose hay chunked out of the machine for an entire windrow. I was giving him gasping mud-muffled yells about every fifty yards, but he couldn't hear over the roar of the machines and his own daydreams. And I was too tired to try to outrun his speeding tractor. He didn't see what happened until he turned the corner at the end of the field. He cursed and glared and muttered as he rewired the baler. I was grateful for the reprieve and weakly sat on a bale, praying for rain. I knew why the last guy had quit and figured my brother had had his little joke and had made his point.

To make up for lost time, Leonard made the bales spit out of that baler even faster. The sixth bale was getting harder to place, and a new one was always dropping onto the sled. The extra bale was making the use of the trip lever difficult—I usually had to move it before I could step on the lever. Occasionally, the load wasn't far enough back and the lever didn't release it, so I had to get off the sled and stamp on the back. That would release it, but a second bale was dropping about that time which would often nudge the first one off or roll off itself, and I had to hook it with one hayhook and pull it back onto the moving sled. To make matters worse, if we happened to hit a large rock, it would trip the sled and all the bales would either tumble into the field or I would try to hang on with my hooks while I snapped the sled back in place by jumping on the buckled edge. With the heat and the dust and chaff and hell-bent speed, I was drenched with sweat; mud and chaff were in my eyes and ears, the corners of my mouth and down my neck. Yet Leonard blazed on trying to beat the weather. I had no saliva left and my mouth felt like it was full of baby powder. I would have given my entire sex life for a drink of water, but Crazy Leonard didn't carry a burlap waterbag on his tractor like most farmers, nor would he have even considered stopping.

Finally, one of the wires broke, and he heard my shout. I trotted over to the irrigation ditch and drank a few handfuls and threw some in my face. We lived near that ditch, and in it I had seen dead cats, dogs, a cow, fish, and floating cowpies, but nothing could have persuaded me from that drink. The mudwad dislodged, and I blew my nose on a shirt-tail which looked like a mudflap in spring. I looked up into the sky: clouds were just beginning to gather, and far to the west I could see a gorgeous gray curtain sliding our way.

After a few more hours, the first drops fell. A

thunderhead swept a black squall of rain along Manastash ridge, and the storm it was part of promised to pass right over us. This new hope was enough to keep me slamming my bales into place. There is nothing quite like a vision of the end of hard labor to bring on a spurt of energy. The sky finally broke. I looked up and let the water sprinkle my face. Never was I so glad to see wet hay. I was absolutely convinced there was a God. Crazy Leonard was forced to call it quits because some of the bales were getting "slugs," dense moist balls of hay that could cause a barnfire.

He took me home in his battered white pickup full of empty baling-wire boxes, cutting-pliers, wrenches, popcans, a chain, and a scratched-up black lunchbox. I don't remember us saying anything. My eyes felt like I had brushed them with a thistle; my nose was so stuffed that I had to breathe through my mouth and that made me thirstier. When he dropped me off, he said if it didn't rain too much we could probably start about noon the following day.

At noon the following day, I planned to be about two miles from home on my horse, Popcorn. I would be catching horned lizards or sitting on a hilltop watching the clouds coil and spool away, redtails swoop easily across the sky and calling in that haunting scream-whistle that gives you shivers if you let it—and I planned to let it. I would be sitting on that grassy sagebrushed knoll where the only human thing amid the miles and miles of hills and valleys and deer and chukars and coyotes and stinkbugs and lizards was me and the part of me the horse knew.

That afternoon as I stood in the shower, I imagined it all down to the lunch I would take and the waterbottles in the saddlebags. I let the showerhead spray into my mouth and would spit and spray it until the tight clog seemed to loosen. When I got out, I dried off and blew my nose again which was still full of mud and particles of hay. With warm water, I filled a glass eye-cup and washed out each eye. On my bed in the back bedroom, I was sore and tired, and lay like a defeated thing, my limbs sprawled loosely, floating away, dissolving into the bedspread.

I thought about my brother and just how to handle this latest episode: "Leonard is such a nice man and he pays so well." He had played me like a fish. I plotted revenge. I could pour some oil under the engine of his Willy's pick-up and keep it up for a week or two. I could smear Red-Hot in his baseball cup or, better yet, put some on his fingers while he's sleeping and when he went to scratch his balls in the morning, he'd apply it himself. Of course, then he'd know immediately who did it. I could take one of his girlfriend's notes and have my friend Kathy Drexall forge a note saying that she's pregnant and what in the world were they going to do about it and fold it the way she always does. I could dump a bottle of Ex-Lax into a brownie mix, his favorite, and give them to him when he plans on spending the day in his buddy's boat on Lake Sullivan. There was a peculiar and durable pleasure in this reverie, and I got up feeling almost refreshed. I discovered that these imaginary retributions could lend the body a savory lightness like finding a twenty dollar bill on the sidewalk. I decided I wouldn't give him the satisfaction of my reaction, that I would tell him the day went fine, but because of the rain we couldn't work tomorrow, damn the luck. I would slip out right after breakfast, saddle up, and be gone.

Mom was cooking dinner when I went back out into the

kitchen. Stacks of white laundry made little moguls on the couch. New jars of strawberry jam were laid out on the counter beside a wooden bowl of fresh butter with a paddle leaning into the crosshatched design she'd etched on the top of it. Pot lids bubbled on the stove and elk cube-steaks sizzled in the frying pan. When my brother came in still stitched into his leather hay-apron, the metal snaps jangling, the hooks still in his hand, she told him to take those boots off outside, she didn't want any more hay and dirt on the floor. She never looked up as she set the table. He came back in: his shirt and socks off, a collar of dirt around his neck and bits of hay caught in his chest hairs.

"So, how was your day with Leonard, Squirt?" he asked walking toward the bathroom, his voice full of brotherly concern.

"Great, if it weren't for the damn rain, we'd have finished that field," I said, not taking my eyes off the TV, though Walter Cronkite could have been uttering obscenities for all I heard.

"Watch your mouth, Todd, you don't need to talk like that," Mom said, looking up and frowning significantly.

I sat there wondering whether Frank had thrown Leonard at me just to see if he could stir up something for Mom to pounce on, then I thought I was getting paranoid, giving him way too much credit. He was merely twisting his little knife, saying gotcha buddy in that brilliantly casual way of his.

When my father came home, I shut off the TV, and we all sat down for dinner. "Bless us, our Lord, and these Thy gifts which we are about to receive. . ." my father said with a deliberate slowness as if his memory had to scoop out each word like chunks of beef in a stew and place them into the bowl of the evening. Perhaps it was just the strange syntax of that prayer which seemed so foreign and God-like and thus true that caused the hush to go deep in us, but tonight through the lashes of my squinting eyes, all I could see was that fluffy mound of mashed potatoes and the steak steaming its incense into my nose. The pleasure of eating well after a sweat-filled, exhausting day is like a soul-massage, a conferred grace; it can fill up your body and make it glow like headphones filling your mind with music as you lay in bed.

Yet like most pleasures, it is brief, for when we were finished, the empty plates pushed back a bit, the glasses filmed with milk, the used silverware smeared and useless, the table looks like an arrangement of artifacts from some already distant joy.

"That rain was nice this afternoon, wasn't it?" my mother said, leaning back in her chair.

"It wasn't so good for the hay," I said, a little sharply, for my brother's benefit.

"It just smelled good and I like it when the clothes come in after they've dried and the sheets are so fresh. Everything smells clean. You could bottle and sell that smell." She said this to no one in particular, her voice soft and tired.

"How long do you think it will take the hay to dry out?" I asked Frank.

"It didn't rain that much—probably by one or two if there's a breeze and the sun's out. What did Leonard say?"

"Sometime after noon, but I'm not sure I want to wait around for him." Because Frank had gotten me the job, I thought I had better lay a little ground work for the great horse escape.

He pinched a toothpick from the white and red woodpecker dispenser at the center of the table.

"If you want to clean out a shop in the morning and maybe cultivate some corn, I can set that up," he said stretching out, the toothpick wobbling between his lips.

Cleaning out somebody's shop didn't sound like a job worth giving up a horse day for, but driving a tractor for money was a new and tantalizing prospect. It seemed like just the thing to rescue me from Leonard's wild and woolly windrow. I was two years away from a driver's license but you didn't need one to drive a tractor. The rain hadn't soaked in enough to keep a tractor out of a corn field. And if I got some driving experience here, then I might be able to drive a swather for second cutting or maybe even the Massy Fergusson with the squeeze that gathered the small stacks the trip sleds made. Yet this was my brother talking.

"Whose place?" I asked warily.

"You don't know him, lives on Strande Road, needs somebody for a couple of days."

"What's he pay?" I didn't want to sound too eager. He knew I'd do just about anything to get a chance to drive.

"Oh, I think he said $1.35 an hour, a dime over minimum wage, pretty good for just driving and doing a little cleaning."

"Sounds fine to me," I said, though my horse fantasy was almost as big as that tractor.

The morning sky was clear, the sun warming the windowseats. Mom had our lunches on the counter and milk-toast on our plates when we were dressed and ready to go. She was dressed in blue jeans, a western shirt, and old tennis shoes, and had already collected the eggs and fed the chickens.

"I'll drop you off, but you might need a ride home

because I don't know how long I'll be this afternoon," Frank said.

"I know, you told me already," I said, a fine wave of spite curling over the words "know" and "already" just to show him he didn't have to try to manage every moment of my life. His right eyebrow arched then relaxed, but he didn't say anything.

"I want you boys to carry that table in the garage to the back patio for me before you leave," Mom said from the stove as she buttered more toast. "We're having Father Bernard over for dinner tonight and we might sit outside." She was such an inveterate peacemaker that it was almost an unconscious reaction, but I suppose she did need the table moved. If we forgot, she'd find some way to move it herself.

Although I chose the end that allowed me to walk forward rather than backward, by the time we got it out the side-door, the positions were reversed, and I had to walk backwards all the way across the yard, taking baby-steps like an old Chinese woman with bound feet. I somehow always managed to get this end of things. Of course, he kept the pressure on so that I had to walk as fast as I could or get my shins banged by the leg-supports. He enjoyed steering me into the shrubs and flowerbeds or a pile of dogshit. I could see the outline of a grin on his face even when he wasn't grinning.

Driving toward Strande road, he casually pointed out where he'd worked or where some cute girl lived or which streams had fish in them. When we passed the Ackerman place, he pointed to the barn and said that was where he first had sex with Lucy Ackerman. He merely moved his thumb in its direction and said it as carelessly as he named a fish stream. As I look back on it now, I think it too was a rock dropped in the pond of my mind to set the ripples in motion, widening on the infinity of my inexperience, sensation upon sensation in concentric rings. I barely knew Lucy, but I couldn't imagine her with my brother, handsome and entertaining as he was. She was the only daughter of the man who owned the cement company in town. She drove a new red Camero and stood erect and poised as though she perpetually walked a fashion runway through an audience of boys. Undressing her in my mind so that she could lay on a blanket in the loft of that barn with Frank seemed a violation. It was like goosing the Queen of England or watching the sway of a nun's breasts beneath her habit. It was impossible, but something in my mind could not leave it alone and I'm sure he knew it.

When he dropped me off at the driveway, he told me to walk over to the shop and knock on the door, because I was expected. The ruts in the road held a thin plate of mud; whatever water there was from the rain had already evaporated. Lilacs lined one side of the road, apple trees the other. The trees were old and unpruned. A blackbird in the lilacs dove at me several times, squawking and looping over my head until I had passed out of range of its nest. From the shade of a combine, a tri-colored blue marl barked and trotted toward me, his guard duty executed and dissolving into the possibilities for a friendly pat and ear-scratch. He wagged his bobbed tail and his clean shaggy hair rippled with the pleasure of my attention. The main shop doors were open. I peered into the shady recesses and saw a man in coveralls with his legs sprawled out as he lay underneath a baler.

"Hellooo," I said.

When the man pushed himself out from beneath the baler, I don't believe he saw the desperate sinking shock on my face. In Leonard's hands were a greasegun and a shoprag. His green baseball cap was turned sideways. A small black streak of grease cut across his left cheek. His pinched face had a ruddy hue as he got up.

"We've got a few things to do before we can bale this afternoon. I'd like to grease the swather too. You can clean up the bench and put the tools away. You can tell where they go easy enough. Greaserags are in the bottom drawer on the right, there. I need to go to town and get some more wire. I'll show you around before I leave."

I was so dumbfounded that I followed Leonard around the shop like his Australian shepherd. It took everything I had within me to put a lid on the boiling, seething pot. This last trick had gone beyond the confines of practical joke. Strangulation—a slow death by torture—a baseball bat—were all that seemed to enter my mind as Leonard told me what needed to be done. He had a tight way of speaking which made the words seem labored and jerky like a rusty chain over a bike sprocket.

"I'll be back in a couple of hours," he said, stuffing his rag into the back pocket of his coveralls as he walked toward his house. He straightened his cap as he took a wide step over a dying puddle. I watched as he and his dog got in the white pickup I hadn't noticed was parked beside the gas tanks.

As he disappeared down the road, it was not revenge that preoccupied my imagination this time but murder. I began to think of possibilities: outstretched, naked to the open sun, Frank's wrists and ankles bound to stakes; chained to Leonard's sled, bucking bales until he dropped; lowered into a tank of piranha; dumped in a locked room of angry black-faced hornets.

Interesting, though, imaginary murder has no refreshing effects. It makes you feel tired and small and stupid. Perhaps it is the weariness of the emotions required to keep the vile visions going, or anger is simply and flatly exhausting; it is like dragging a great weight rather than using the wheels of humor. I got little work done in that first hour. The swather had about a thousand zerk fittings on its rotary blades, and little globs of grease would hit the floor when I got distracted and pumped too much in. I had to crawl between the blades with a grease rag to clean them up. The bench was a mess: pliers and screwdrivers and tape measures and levels and squares, paper bags and cellophane wrappers and bits of cardboard, oily greaserags and shop towels, lengths of wire and spools of twine and tape, pencils and sandpaper. The man hadn't put a thing away in months.

I had just finished sweeping the floor around the baler and swather when Leonard returned. He said it was still too wet to bale, but he wanted me to go to the barn and arrange some bales before the new hay was brought in. It was an old barn with a dirt floor, feeding mangers along the side, a loft in its upper section from which a flock of parti-colored pigeons flew out when we opened the large front doors. The barn was empty except for a narrow stack of hay at the back that was six or seven tiers high and five bales wide. Leonard wanted me to knock the stack down and arrange the bales as the bottom tier to protect the new hay. The bales on the bottom usually mold and collect dirt, so if he put the old unsold ones on the bottom, fewer of the new bales would be wasted.

"Come to the house when you're done," Leonard said, digging something from the palm of his hand, speaking like he was talking to it. He was bracing the doors open with pieces of wood when I pulled the first row over, two bales deep. This first part of the stack hit the floor with a whooping thump, a few rolling and bouncing to the middle of the barn. Just as I began to drag the bale closest to me toward the outer perimeter, I had an odd sensation. It was an instant of almost detached awareness, like a leaf must feel just before the wind strikes it from the branch. It was a taut, paralyzing flash of time, a segment suddenly dislodged from linearity, suspended. I had only enough time to glance sideways before I was slammed to the ground and buried in bales of hay.

What I remember next is a flickering of strobe-like images shrouded in fog: the tired smell of car-seat vinyl, streaks of traveling light and pole shadows, my fingers in the dust of what I think is the floor of a car, a whistle from a cracked window, white uniforms, a soothing voice as fingers undress me, red lipstick on an old face surrounded by black and grey hair, but it is only the lips I really see moving in a timeless space talking but no words are reaching my ears, and a greenish arced lamp with vertical ribs above me.

But the next images are more complete and start to take a solid shape. In the dimness, a little hissing exhalation to my left comes and goes like a mechanical snore. Using my eyelash trick, I see a tray with a water glass and a white bent straw through a fretwork of grassy shadows. Thin horizontal bars of light peek through the partially drawn white shades. I can just feel a lightness cross my forehead, a touch so soft it is almost not there so I have to concentrate on it. I roll my head to the right very slowly trying to imitate the natural movements of a sleeper. I try to keep my face completely relaxed, to let my eyes sag and roll like a marble in the toe of a nylon.

Suddenly, I'm aware of a sharp pain in my upper chest so I stop, but I have turned just enough to see a hand stroking my forehead. I can smell the heat of dried sweat, the must of damp dirt. It takes a moment for me to realize it is Frank sitting on the edge of the bed and his thumb is stroking my forehead. I see only the right side of his face. There is a clean penny-sized oval under his eye with a thin dried streak below it. He is wearing a look I have never seen before. His face is whiter, and all the smirky, cocky play has been drained out. His head is bowed slightly and his shoulders curled inward. I feel his thumb come to rest just above my cheek.

And I am almost embarrassed to say what happened next. I was not ready for it, and if it were not for whatever drugs were coursing through my veins, I may have flinched, spoiling it. He bent very softly and kissed me on the forehead, his lips just brushing my skin like my mother used to do when she tucked me in at night. It was like two feathers in the air touching and floating off.

GREEN EYES

Today for the first time in two weeks, I packed my lunch and spent the noon hour with my feet on the desk reading the *Tribune*. It was a dark day, sporadic rain, a little wind, so the thought of staying in with my answering machine seemed like a good idea. I read about the usual squabbles between the city council and the county commissioners, rate hikes for electricity, the assault charges against a football player who is the starting linebacker for our college team, what the local scores were for the weekend, and then I came to a picture of Marlene Gunderson on page 14. It was her high school picture from ten years ago; her mother must have sent it in. I cut it and the obituary out and was thinking of sending it to Bruce.

Marlene was a thin blonde with eyes so green they seemed fake the minute you saw them, but they weren't. She had a freckled nub of a nose, and teeth that were straight and white as a model's. Marlene sometimes talked with a bad Western drawl and exaggerated even the smallest details. If you asked to borrow her eraser, she'd squint her eyes, say something Western, wink and produce a pink cowboy-hat eraser with the brim chewed off. When she drank, the exaggeration got even worse and the words rolled from her mouth in slow motion. Bruce, my best friend then, loved her and followed her after school. She usually walked down 3rd street, crossed over at Washington where the Washington Mutual Building is, then went into the Magnolia Mall to the Cinnabun store where her sister worked. Walden's was across the aisle from Cinnabun's, and Bruce used to fake like he was some whiz-kid who couldn't wait to read every book in Walden's. Once a lady who had seen him there several times said, "I sure wish my son loved to read as much as you do. How did you become such a good reader?" Bruce looked at her through the cokebottles he wore but didn't get from reading, and said, "Green eyes." The lady, who was wearing a jean outfit whose vest had little bells sewn into it, rang slightly and said, "Isn't that sweet."

So from then on "green eyes" became a kind of motto or code we used in all kinds of situations. When Mr. Lyons, our health teacher, asked for one of the causes of early heart failure, Bruce raised his hand and said "green eyes"; when a waitress with wrinkled lips and silver hair with pink tints in it took her pen from behind her ear, tapped it on her packet of checks, and said, "What'll it be, boys?" Bruce said "green eyes," and we'd laugh until the waitress's mouth puckered into a withered kiss and we ordered hot dogs.

Bruce had thick dark hair and one eyebrow that went all the way across his forehead. He was almost blind without his glasses, so his eyes are a little magnified when you look at him. Although short, he was tough as a weasel. He was on the wrestling team and state champion in the 148 pound division. One ear has been ground into the mat a few too many times. The upper part swells out like dough in a pie crust that wasn't quite forked all the way around. He talks like he'd whip anybody's ass if they looked at him wrong, but he's all talk. Our junior year, he took his sister to the Senior prom because she didn't have a date. He didn't let the jokes about their retarded children get to him either, he just danced right in their faces. Once he missed meeting me at the mall because his cat got beat up by his neighbor's dog. He waited at the vet's for three hours then took her home. Marlene wouldn't wait for him longer than a yellow light. I saw a hurricane coming and no way to stop it.

I liked math and my war of wit with Mrs. Connolly who was the teacher for my Math Analysis class. She was a large no-nonsense woman who wrote numbers so they looked like bouquets of flowers on the board, except "5" which looked like a little Japanese junk that bobbed on the black water. She held the chalk when she talked like it was a cigarette, and I would look for a chalk ring on her lips because her hair always smelled like smoke when I went up to ask a question. I never saw her smoke, though. Her smell is a mystery, maybe her husband smoked in the car on their way to work. Bruce had her for a different class, Algebra II. He thought it was Algebra II because you had to take it twice until he found out it was a sequel that starred Mrs. Connolly. He wrote an anonymous letter to the school board about our dismal lack of math teachers but nothing ever came of it. Marlene was in my class. When Bruce finally talked to Marlene, they started exchanging notes. Bruce would ask me to give them to her during second period, to tell him what she did or said, how she talked about other boys.

One day as I was rubbing some artist's rendition of a penis off my desk, I looked up and Mrs. Connolly looked like she'd accidentally walked by a fan, one of those heater-fans in the gym. Her green dress was slightly crooked, and when she finished what she was saying, her eyes looked like she had X-ray vision and she was examining something in the next room. Because each number was like a flower to her, which is what she said to us one time, she hardly ever made mistakes.

She could talk and write at the same time and the little bouquet would take its perfect shape. But this day, she was introducing the idea of imaginary numbers. She drew a horizontal line and intersected it with a vertical line. She put 0 at the point of intersection. She said that there were four classes of numbers: positive real numbers (she marked these to the right of the zero on the horizontal line); negative real numbers (she marked these to the left of the zero on the horizontal line); and positive imaginary numbers (she marked these on the vertical line above the zero); and negative numbers (she marked these on the vertical line below the zero). Marlene, who had been told by Mrs. Connolly on a number of occasions to please take her feet off the back of that chair and that this isn't a theatre and to please act like a lady, shot her hand in the air like a harpoon. But Mrs. Connolly didn't even seem to notice. She went on talking about possible uses of a grid like this, how it was first devised in the 1770's by a Swiss man by the name of Leonard Euler, that he was the one who introduced "e" as the base of a natural logarithm, "I" for imaginary numbers, and f () for functions. She also said that he lost his right eye looking at the sun through a telescope while trying to study time. finally, Marlene, who sat in the back of the room by the row of drawers where the slide rules and old calculators were kept, said, "Mrs. Connolly, I think you're wrong." Now, Mrs. Connolly's class was as tidy and predictable as the periodic table, yet she slowly turned and looked at Marlene as if she wasn't even there, as if her X-ray eyes saw right through her face and into her brain. It was like she had snapped open a pocket-watch and stared into the crowd of tiny inter-locking wheels all working diligently, stupidly, second by second, minute by minute, and was struck by the profound simplicity of it all.

When she spoke it was with a voice that seemed to be asking about some other question: "About what, dear?"

"It's negative imaginary numbers."

"Didn't I say that?" she asked the smart girl in the front, Zoe Bennett. Zoe looked down and shook her head.

"Well, thank you, Marlene, I'm glad you were listening. I'm sorry I left out the imaginary."

"So are we," said Marlene, just loud enough for her to hear.

Then, Ms. Connolly told us to do 1-4 of Exercise 10 in our math books for tomorrow. The metallic smack of the chalk as it hit the tray and the click of her heels toward her seat were all we heard until the bell rang about eight minutes later. Marlene was just pushing open the door to the science wing when I caught up with her.

"Marlene," I said, "what do you think's wrong with Mrs. Connolly?"

Her green eyes seemed to narrow and her hair swung around to her cheek then back to her ear like a large fishhook.

"That old bitch. Who cares?" She pushed the door wide and rushed into the breezeway, crowded with kids hurrying to classes.

Bitch? The word worked like an elevator in me. It was a basement word that had suddenly come up to the top floor with no stops in between. It was dark and gloomy and smelled like a damp mattress yet here it was, bare and ugly as a bone.

Now Mrs. Connolly was no bosom friend of mine but we walked around each other like dogs checking things out. She was the big dog and let me pass anyway as if the snarl was for the neighbors and not between us. We had an understanding as my father would say—he was a realtor and said that a lot. So when Marlene's "bitch" came out, my heart somersaulted like I was hearing something I shouldn't. I knew Marlene had to have seen that edge Mrs. Connolly had, like someone she loved had given her the heave-ho, and yet Marlene went for it, tooth and claw.

Marlene was beautiful, I'll give that to her. Her parents were divorced and she lived with her mother who had to work all the time. This left Marlene to come and go as she pleased. I had my first drink of bourbon at her house. Marlene was arrested for shoplifting when she was in the eighth grade, so her mom put her in a Catholic school, but she was so rude to the nuns they kicked her out. The Talking Heads were her favorite band, and she would write their name on everything she owned and on quite a few things she didn't. She liked a brownish-red lipstick that she outlined in black. On these days she would wear a black lace glove with the fingers cut out. This outfit seemed to exaggerate her sneer. I'd seen her look at people like she could see their low IQ's.

Bruce was standing by his locker waiting, his English book under his left arm, tossing a hacky-sack with the other. When he saw me, he asked if I gave the note to Marlene. I told him I did. He said he had to go over his vocabulary words for his English test and he'd meet me after school.

I went to history class where Mr. Haskill got very excited about the Bedouin way of life. He thought carrying everything you own on three camels, having a portable dairy, and betting on horse races while eating figs and rice was what Thoreau meant when he said "Simplify." Sleeping on goat hides, going from one water hole to another, not having to pay taxes or mow lawns or prune trees or weed the flowers or wash cars was his vision of ideal living conditions. Mr. Haskill was short, balding, and fat around the middle, and we could just see him after he'd milked the goats, dug for water, fed the camels, picked up dried dung for their fire. Roughing it did not seem like his cup of coffee, but I liked his funny enthusiasm anyway. I missed Bruce after school, so I assumed he had found Marlene somewhere.

That night after dinner, I was sitting at the kitchen table reading for my history class about Ibn Saud and the assimilation of the nomadic tribes into a single Arab nation when my father laid his paper down and looked at me over the top of his reading glasses.

"Isn't your math teacher florence Connolly?"

"Florence? I have Mrs. Connolly but I don't know what her first name is."

"Well, it says here that her mother passed away last night at the Jazz Festival the college puts on. Of a heart attack. She was 85. One minute she was clapping and the next she isn't." My father picked up the paper and continued reading as if sharing that information was our father-son interaction for the night. I sat quietly and tried to read but I kept thinking of Mrs. Connolly. Florence. Florence Connolly. It's strange but I never even thought about her first name. Then I thought about all the other things I must not know about her. Her husband, what he does, what he looks like. Her kids, her parents. Her house. How would she decorate her house? I saw numbers on her wallpaper then erased them. Then tiny roses, pictures of her family by the entryway, bookshelves full of books, a TV room with a beige recliner for her husband and a blue rocker for her so that she could grade homework. When I thought of her bedroom, I quit thinking about her house. I thought of Marlene instead, and Bruce.

I decided to call him. He was helping his dad put a new clutch in his car and couldn't talk long, so I said I'd see him at school, it wasn't important. I could see his dad in his blue coveralls with "Jim" on the lapel, though his name wasn't Jim. It was Sean. He had gotten the coveralls from a garage that went out of business. He made Bruce wear a pair, too. His name was "Bill." I used to call him Bill when I needed help with my car. His father thought he should take things apart and put them back together again, that it was spiritually healthy to work with your hands. Bruce was good at mechanical things and could take two broken lawnmowers and make one good one or listen to an engine and go straight to the problem. Though I loved math, mechanical things to me were like animals who bite. I decided to see Bruce before his second period class and set something up after school.

Bruce gave me a note for Marlene. I set it on her desk when I went to get a calculator. She put her hand over it and slid it into her pocket. Mrs. Connolly looked bad again. There was a coffee stain on her beige blouse the shape of florida, and she looked like she didn't finish putting on her lipstick. Her eyes were kind of puffy, and her hair was pulled tight against her head and pinned in back with a green comb. The gray in front was more noticeable and seemed to be in an even streak around her head as if she had a gray halo. Usually she wore her hair combed out and kind of curly. We corrected 1-4 of Ex. 10, and she worked out the answers on the board but her voice was detached, as if it came from some other place. That no-nonsense tone was still there, only quieter. Marlene asked two questions just to slow her down but otherwise things went okay. Mrs. Connolly reviewed what we'd done that week and assigned 5-10. Ron Wilson, who belonged in a milk commercial because of his good-boy look and clean hairless face, announced that our annual, *Zanadu*, would be ready next Monday and people should bring their $10 to Room 112 to pick them up. Mrs. Connolly said, "Thank you, Ron," like she was a newscaster signing off the weatherman.

After the bell rang, I was the last one out and saw Mrs. Connolly standing in front of the window with her arms tight across her chest, covering up the coffee stain. I felt like saying something but didn't know what to say. When I walked by the wastebasket on the way out the door, I saw Bruce's note, still folded into the triangle he thought appropriate for math class.

When I found Bruce after school, he said he had to see his dad downtown, so we planned to meet the next day, Saturday, in the corner of Memorial Park to shoot some baskets. I wanted to talk to him about Marlene and warn him about sticking his neck out too far. My fears for him flashed in red neon when on Friday night I saw her outside the mall. She got into Calvin Hines's car, the quarterback for the college football team. She scooted over beside him, and they kissed. Calvin was nearing a school record for TD passes completed in a single season, and had led his team to the quarterfinals in the national championship. I wondered how Marlene might have known him. I only knew him from the sports pages.

Bruce showed up for our one-on-one game just after 11:00. I was sweating the time and kept going over how to say what I wanted to tell him. We played for about an hour and Bruce won two of the three games. Even though I am taller and could beat him at H-o-r-s-e, he was a good dribbler and could toss any kind of lay-up, left-handed or right, and it would go in. When we finished our third game and sweat was running down both of our faces, I suggested we sit on a grass hill and drink some water I had brought. Because the tension was getting to me I decided to plunge right in.

"Bruce, I gotta talk to you about Marlene."

"What do you want to know, studless."

"Well, I just don't think she has your best interests in mind."

"What do ya mean by that?"

There was a little anger in his voice, and I could tell he didn't want to have this conversation. The red blotches on his neck from playing basketball began to spread into his cheeks. I reached into my pocket and pulled out the note Marlene had thrown in the wastebasket. He looked at it and all the red drained out, I saw his jaw muscles flinch, and his eyes glaze then narrow.

"Damn you, Scott," he said, getting up. "I knew there was something wrong. You didn't give it to her, because you're in love with her too. I can't believe it, you jerk." He grabbed the note from my hand, walked towards his car without turning back.

I sat on the grass, stunned. I knew he might take this the wrong way, but not this way. It hadn't even occurred to me that he might think I kept the note as some kind of sabotage. I heard his car back up and squeal away. I just sat there, embarrassed, guilty, stupid. My hands shredded the grass and made little piles of it between my legs. I did think Marlene was beautiful. I had loved her green eyes and blonde hair, was intrigued by who she was and what she must know about sex, had responded to her flirtations by flirting back. And that one night at her house drinking bourbon with her and her friends lingered in my imagination as some kind of initiation into a world I was on the edge of, peeking in. Nothing happened, except she put her hand on my knee as she poured me another shot of bourbon, and she looked directly into my eyes and paused as if to tell me something but I didn't know what. She just smiled, kissed the air, winked, then left. The rest was all in my imagination. There was a sick hollowness in my stomach that was spreading and I dreaded the idea of meeting Bruce and trying to explain what I had meant. And now I didn't know how clean my motives were. Was I trying to save Bruce or fulfill some dark wish of my own that I hadn't even thought of yet?

I was sitting, picking grass stalks apart, when I noticed a line of cars with their lights on led by the blue flashing lights of a police car. At the intersection another policeman was directing traffic. A lavender hearse followed the police car, a black limousine followed the hearse. I was close to the street and could see the policeman as he drove by, then the driver of the hearse with a little chauffeur's cap, and then I saw Mrs. Connolly staring out the window, crying, daubing her eyes with a white handkerchief. She looked like she had been crying for a long time. As I watched the line of cars go by, I couldn't help myself. I started crying too. I just sat there with my hands over my knees, crying. I didn't know why. I thought it was for Mrs. Connolly, but I think now it was for all of us on that fall day when the leaves were blowing off the trees and the air was colder. Bruce was in love with a girl who hardly knew he existed. I was in love with experience because I had none; I was afraid I'd die a virgin, never see a Bedouin or even a camel, never see the Eiffel tower, never do a damn thing but watch other people do what I wanted to do. I loved Marlene because she was living, she was in the race and I was in the grandstands. She was full of danger and mystery, and herself. But the truth was I knew deep down that for me Bruce was more important than Marlene. For Marlene, I'd just be another bottle she tossed when she was finished drinking. She saw Mrs. Connolly as the enemy, a policeman eager to write her up and off, yet Mrs. Connolly was solidly there, because we needed what she had to offer. I was more innocent than guilty and felt betrayed because I had worked so hard to remain neutral, to keep my hands to myself, to be honest with them even if I wasn't entirely honest with myself.

After all the cars had passed and the policemen had gone away, I got up and walked back home, leaving my car at the park. I kicked the leaves, feeling the cold air on my face, knowing it was only going to get colder.

On Monday we had a substitute in for Mrs. Connolly and Marlene looked hung over and reeked of pot. She sat quietly with her hands folded and whenever our gazes crossed she would grin and put on some expression as if to prove she could change her mood at will. She was wearing a tan leather jacket with fringes across the chest and a blue dress. The substitute assigned more math problems but didn't know how to do any of them herself so we got to roam around and talk as if we were getting help. I got up to ask Ron if he received his yearbook for free because he had his picture in it so many times, and when I went back to my seat I noticed Marlene outlining in purple a name she had written in large ornate letters: Marlene Hines. She saw me looking, put her elbow over it, and opened her eyes like she was trying to see underwater. I winked, knowing that in her state I had the advantage. She went back to doodling and I decided to confront Bruce at lunch time.

When the lunch bell rang, I went to Bruce's locker, then to our usual lunchroom table. I finally found him sitting alone on a bench beside a sculpture that looked like a giant cement tooth.

"Hey, Bill. Care if I join you?"

"Free country, studless," he said, unwrapping the wax paper on his roast beef sandwich.

"I want to talk to you about that note," I had to get it out before it hardened in my throat. I could feel drops of sweat sliding down my sides. "I gave that note to Marlene and she threw it away. I only picked it up so somebody else wouldn't stick their nose in it. I don't even know what it said."

"Forget it," he said, his gaze passing through the tooth and beyond the cafeteria.

Although I tried to patch things up, I always felt that Bruce never trusted me like he did before. But maybe that was only my own guilt working. He went to a state college, and I went to the university. Whenever I saw his parents, I asked about him, got his new address. We exchange Christmas cards. He's living in Denver and is a mechanic for United Airlines, has two children I have never seen. Mrs. Connolly is still teaching at the high school, and I think she was one of the reasons I became a CPA. I stop by occasionally to give her some vegetables from my garden and she brings me her taxes. Her hair has turned completely grey but her face still looks the same. I call her Florence because she asked me to, but it has a strange effect on my tongue like words from a foreign language. I looked at Marlene's black and white photo in the paper and I could still see those green eyes, could still feel them, their defiance, their beauty. I wondered what her life had been like for the last ten years, what those eyes had seen that mine had been too cautious and safe to.

Although I was going to send this clipping to Bruce, my hands started to fold it, first lengthwise, then again, and again, until it was a long narrow strip. Then I folded it into a triangle that I turned over and over. I got up, put on my coat, stuck a note on my secretary's computer screen that said I was going to be out for the rest of the afternoon. The day was still rainy and cold, so I took my black umbrella from the stand near the door. On the way out, I tossed the little triangle, folded like a flag, into the wastebasket.

●

THE KISS

My brother, Sid, arrived home from Viet Nam exactly three days after Grandma died. Dad had left Sid's car at the airport in Yakima because mom had to go to Spokane and back, and we didn't know exactly when he would arrive. I was in the driveway shooting baskets when his car pulled up, a blue Studebaker with so many miles on it he didn't know how many times it had clicked over. He was in his uniform, the last day I ever saw him wear it. I stood with the ball under my arm, grinning. I was a junior in high school and on the basketball team, a uniform of quite a different color.

"Hey, Bro," I said, though this was not a term I'd use on him before he left, "welcome to the home zone."

"Hey, Danny-boy, you're taller than I am," he said, dropping his duffel bag and giving me a hug. The basketball fell and dribbled towards the lawn. "I'm going to have to whittle you down to size." I thought he held on just a little too long, and when he let go, his hand remained on my shoulder in a long firm squeeze.

"Fat chance, soldier."

When Dad came out, Sid gave him a hug too. Dad stood stiff but something wavered across his lips like he didn't know if he could control it so he just stood there, nodding. I carried the duffel bag into the kitchen where mom was already crying, though I didn't know if it was for Grandma or Sid. Her hug was earnest and easy, one hand rubbing his back, the other around his waist like they were dance partners. When you're sixteen, a hug is a thing to consider—you don't

45

know where to put your hands. To me, nothing ever seemed right about a hug, even from my mother.

The next day Sid and I got up early to drive to Spokane. We didn't have to be there until 6:00 that evening, so Sid thought we'd make a loop and hit the potholes for a little fishing. The season had just opened and the fish were still bright; they only had about a month before the lakes took on a tainted smell. It was warm. Some of the balsam and lupine were still blooming in the sage and along the road. We took the old way to Vantage, Sid's idea. He said he wanted to breathe deep, feel time on his hands. He rubbed his fingers together as if he could actually feel it there like talcum powder. As we approached Ginko State Park, he slowed down and pulled in.

"Let's take a look-see at the petrified world," he said.

"I thought you wanted to go fishing?"

"You know, all the time I spent in Ellensburg, I've never been here. Have you?"

"In third grade at Lincoln, we came down on a field trip, but not since."

We walked by the little stone house and its gate. A sprinkler ratcheted over a rocky plot of flowers, but no one was around. The path was wide and graveled; winter run-off had cut some grooves across it, but the slope was easy like it was made for retired folks with nothing better to do but hit all the historical markers and points of geographic interest on their way to old age. The tree stumps were in excavated holes with locked screens over them. Gum, ginko, hemlock, spruce, and fir trees rose out of the earth like old hippo teeth. The bark formed a creamy gold rind around a black translucency.

There was a tight silence as Sid squinted at me. "Do you know what your life is, Danny?" There was a luxurious sadness in his voice as if he'd traveled a long way to ask an important question to a deaf person. This was not the first of his elliptical asides that seemed to have no context. It was as if he had something on his mind, and a fragment of it just popped out.

"What do you mean?"

"Two hundred and fifty million years ago, these trees were breathing, producing pollen, putting rings on year after year." He tied a piece of grass into a knot and continued, " We're a geologic burp, a bubble in frogspit, a little waterbead dripping off a leaf. Get me?"

He turned and walked through the sage toward the Quilomene. Many of his comments seemed to have behind them a yearning to say something profound, but piddled off into this kind of cliché. I felt there was something else, like the build-up of heat that sends a lonely plume of water geysering into the air.

The sage and rabbitbrush had an acrid smell like a smashed fireant, yet sweet too like a smelly person wearing perfume. In the soft green under the sage, there were purple onion flowers, widowgrass. The old cheat stuck like blond feathers in the sage branches, and the tops of bunchgrass clumps were all that remained of last year's growth. I followed Sid's back over a couple of hills and coulees until he finally stopped on the crest of a ridge. On the other side of the ravine, a group of magpies squabbled and hopped. We decided to see what they were working on. When we got close, the smell slapped us. A deer lay on his side, his head turned toward us. His eyes were empty sockets; his tongue hung from his mouth, a cartoon of death. A rectangle sawn out of the top of his forehead exposed a dried pink mash of blood and brain. His forehead was broad, a black brow, his front legs crossed. The hindquarters had been eaten by coyotes and the birds. His guts had spilled out, staining the ground a dark olive green. His back legs were scissored open, exposing a white scrotum. flies murmured, ants trickled in and out of the eyesockets. The stench seemed to swirl up and out, a lazy dust devil.

"Low-life bastards, killed him for his antlers," Sid said, shaking his head.

"By the size of him, probably a four or five point, maybe more. It's hard to say out here."

We climbed the ridge behind him and stopped near an outcropping of columnar basalt. These rockpiles rose up in varied patterns, jointed like fingerbones. We sat on the top of two looking at the spring desert whose green vibrancy belied the heat and crackle of summer, the stink bug trails in the dust, the pudgy scamper of horned lizards. The sky was open and the sun ignited the blond tufts of bunchgrass.

My brother sat, his shoulders hunched slightly the way they were when he was pulled from his high-school basketball game and had to sit on the bench. As one of the starting forwards, he had quick hands that were good at stealing the ball, blocking shots. His specialty, though, was baskets from the baseline. He broke his wrist as a sophomore and turned out everyday with his cast on, shooting this one shot over and over again until he could almost do it blindfolded. He wasn't a good dribbler, and his left hand was almost useless, even with a layin. He was a jokester, a class clown, and he loved scaring me by driving fast around corners or popping out of a closet with a nylon over his head. Once he gave me a pinch of Copenhagen and told me to chew it like gum. In less than ten minutes, I puked all over his Studebaker. He thought it was hilarious and slapped his steering wheel half the way home. Yet when he was pulled from a game for some mistake, there was a smoldering defeat in his shoulders that always made me look away. And after his two years in Viet Nam, I saw the same smolder, the shoulders curved as if they just wanted to collapse upon themselves, and disappear. He wasn't good in school, but he got A's in shop and made beautiful bowls and goblets and an endtable out of mixed woods. I still have his cup made of birdseye maple with a ring of ebony around its base—my birthday gift. The hands that shaped that cup did not seem the same as those now hanging loosely in his lap.

There was a question I was afraid to ask for a long time, but something was on his mind, and I thought maybe this was it: "You ever see someone die in Viet Nam?"

"Dan, what do you want to know that for?"

"I just thought you might want to talk about it."

"It was a war, man, you eat death for breakfast, lunch, and dinner, and if you've been a really good soldier, a fine up-standing human being, you get it for dessert, too."

"What was the worst thing you ever saw?"

There was a hard fix to his face, like he was waiting for a punch. "I'll say this once and then I don't want to talk about it again. Okay?"

"Sure," I said, looking down into the rock I was sitting on.

"And I'm only telling you so you can be smart, and know what you're getting into, which I didn't, by a long shot. You know what I mean?"

"Yeah," I said, though I didn't.

"I never killed anybody, at least I don't think so, but I saw enough bodies to fill Holy Cross Cemetery, men with their legs blown clear off by a claymore, arms and legs in trees after the B-52s dropped the 'ordnance' on a village. But the worst of it, the goddamn worst of it, was this ten year old boy, about two years younger than you when I left. Me and my buddy, Steve from Shreveport, Louisiana, were cutting elephant grass with machetes behind a MASH unit. 'Securing the perimeter,' standard procedure. It was outside Khesanh. This boy jumped out of the grass and started to run. Steve took the top of his head off with a machete. But he had to, see. That war was fought with kids. They'd put grenades in the gas tanks of our jeeps. When we drove away, the vibration dropped them into the tank and blew everyone to smithereens, to fucking kingdom-come. This kid was helping to plot coordinates so the Viet Cong could shell us at night. He had an American grenade in his pocket. Took the goddamn top of his head clean off, like it was an apple."

Tears dribbled down his face, and his hands shook, but he was looking at me, staring like I was that kid, lying in the grass, not even embarrassed about the tears or his shaking hands.

"Jesus, Sid, I'm sorry." I didn't know what else to say, or even what I had expected when I asked. Perhaps it was only a vague curiosity that had no beginning or end. It was like wondering what a girl's breasts looked like but not having a clue about what would happen next if you found out. I picked at the dry and flaky lichen stuck to the side of a basalt pillar.

"Forget it, kid, just count yourself lucky."

Although we stopped at the potholes and wet our lines, we didn't catch any fish. We sat in the sun and listened to the yellow-headed blackbirds call and chase each other among the cattails. They made a strange unearthly sound, a mellow knock, a watery clunk like hollow bamboo, then a spray of blended "e" sounds. It's tropical and nothing like other blackbirds, some evolutionary throwback. And when they all go at it, it's pure chaos. Something was brewing, building. We felt a sense of imminence without a tangible cause. We were simultaneously separated, attracted, isolated, drawn together, repulsed: a welter of brotherly regard separated by the gulf his four years away had made. We saw bluegills and squawfish in the shallows, a painted turtle on a muskrat mound. Sid sat in the grass and then lay down, his arms out.

"This is the life, Danny boy," he said just before he dozed off.

On our way to Spokane, Sid wanted to know about me, what I'd been up to in sports, in school, the usual. I could tell he cared about what I said, but not always in the way I meant it or said it. It was like the story I told was not always the one he heard. Sometimes he'd look out the windows at the miles and miles of dryland wheatfields, some lonely little house with a few trees sitting in the middle of it, somebody's life like a speck among the converging sections of wheat and dirt. And I would wonder where he was, where was the Sid who left our house in a creased uniform, the jokester, the deadeye from the corner, the craftsman. I felt there was a large empty place in him, and he didn't know where he stood in it or whether he'd blink his eyes and it would all disappear. I watched him as he looked at that deer and sensed he felt as though a piece of his own head had been sheered off, taken as some kind of ransom so that I could stand in the driveway shooting baskets, skip school, pop the starlings in our cherry trees. I think he envied my easy innocence, and felt he was somehow paying for it.

I felt as though we were stalling for time, avoiding the scene at Grandpa's: all the aunt-hugs and handshakes, the useless milling about in their tiny living room, the kids shooed to the basement. The little windows of lost time on the walls: my mother and her brothers and sisters as babies and high school graduates, Grandpa on his horse, Grandma's thirty-pound salmon, wedding anniversaries, reunions, all our baby pictures at the far end of the hall beside the bookcase. It would be so useless and forlorn.

All day Sid and I hardly said a word about grandma. She was not a likeable woman. She was rough and opinionated and smoked any chance she got. She didn't care whether or not smoke blew in your face. She ground out her cigarettes with her right foot like she was crushing the head of Satan himself. Once she called me a little bastard for walking in on her while she was on the toilet. She never locked the door. I didn't like the way she treated Grandpa—ordering him around, never letting him finish a sentence. I remember watching *American Bandstand*, the Beachboys I think, and she came into the room, slapped me on the head, and said, "They don't do anything but wiggle their poop. You get on outside now and play." But she could be nice, especially when you were alone with her. She bought me a pocketknife once, saying a boy my age should have one. I still have it, a yellow Buck knife with two blades.

We got to the church in plenty of time. Sid was to be a pallbearer. He hadn't seen Grandpa or Grandma in two years.

It was a simple funeral. The preacher spoke, Mom's brother said a few words, someone played some old songs on a piano while we sang along. At the end of the service, people filed past the open casket. We were in the family section, curtained off to the side. We watched people pat her hand, make a sign of the cross, bow, or stoically walk by, their hands folded in front of them. We were the last ones to leave. I couldn't get closer than six feet. She had red lipstick on, a pinkish rouge, her gold-edged glasses, an orange satiny dress with a matching belt and buttons up the front, a white silk scarf around her neck. It seemed odd to me to think of all the clothes we go through in a lifetime, and of one thing we wear into our underground eternity. Was orange satin her choice? Orange satin with a white scarf was nowhere near who I thought Grandma was.

Her face looked cold and pasty; there was a yellowish pallor like candlewax. Her eyes were sunken, her nose slightly collapsed. Her white hair fluffed out against the white pillow. She gave me the creeps—lying there in her fake sleep.

The family filed by, touching her hand or cheek or dress. Sid was the last one. He walked right up to the edge and looked in. I saw tears dripping off his cheeks. He bent down and gave her a long kiss on the forehead. When he was done, her head fell a bit to one side. He readjusted it and her glasses, stroked her hair back in place. Then he left, his hands loose at his sides, his head up. I felt like I was going to get sick, my legs were weak. I could not fathom what that mean old woman had meant to him, nor the differences that seemed to be defining us. We had had other relatives die, and he had been as aloof and unsettled as I was, but now there was a fearlessness, an abandon as if he'd be perfectly happy as an undertaker. I was chilled by this new knowledge.

The next morning we drove back home in the Studebaker. Sid chain-smoked and fiddled with the radio dial, mumbling about the choices. We used the main highway this time, the wind whistling through the wing window on my side because it couldn't close properly. The cigarettes trembled as he brought them to his lips, ashes fluttering like gray commas to the floor. He couldn't seem to quiet his mind. His chin and lips were fixed tight like when he used to shoot foul shots during the game, but this went on for miles. The day was beautiful, the winter wheat was a deep green but you could still see thin lines of dirt between the planted rows as if the field had been combed. Distance put things into neat squares and rectangles, soft swales and curves, that up-close were always contradicted. I wondered if Sid would ever have that kind of distance on what he saw, whether the edges would or could blur and soften.

From the corner of my eye, I watched a fly that must have been in the car when we started. The heat from the back window made it more active. It flew to the seat behind Sid and began to crawl up his shirt. As it sat on his collar, it rubbed its front feet together, then walked across his neck and onto his cheek, but Sid didn't do anything. He stared straight ahead, the cigarette burning in his left hand so the smoke went out the window. The fly crawled slowly across his face. When I reached to shoo it away, his head jerked back and his right hand, in a spasm of recoil, hit me with so much force, I lost my breath and clutched my chest. He'd hit me in my left pectoral, grazing my arm. His own hand went back to the top of the steering-wheel, his knuckles white and his arm tense.

"What'd you do that for?" I finally wheezed out.

The look he gave me was more frightening than his hand

slamming my chest. It was a millisecond of white-hot seething, like glimpsing instinct uninhibited by any twinge of human conscientiousness, any language with its network of modifiers, codifiers, and quantifiers. He was like a man who suddenly sensed he was falling and reacted to catch himself. Then his eyes refocused, his face muscles and eyebrows relaxed. A mild confusion followed as if he didn't know whether to be angry, to cry, or laugh, yet having to turn and watch the road gave him a moment to adjust, to find some composure.

That was our last trip together. Twice we had fishing days planned, but he'd call the night before and say he couldn't make it. Something always came up. During phone conversations, gaps stretched between his sentences until I couldn't stand it and had to lie to hang up. I'd sit leaning away from the light on my desk, among the shadows, and all I could see was his kiss, his hands stroking her gray hair back into place, readjusting her glasses.

THE IRON HORSE

It didn't look like a very bad wreck. I couldn't see any dents or scrapes, and the sun shined on the roof making the yellow even brighter. The snow was beginning to melt, and Dad just kept whistling to himself like he knew something I didn't. When he stopped alongside, I couldn't see anyone, though the glass was fogged. The car was down a ten-foot bank and about twenty yards from the road. The rear lights stuck out like red eyes making the back-end into a big flat face. Dad opened the door and said, "Go down and see if anyone's inside, I'll radio it in."

"What if there is?"

"Just get goin'."

I walked to the edge of the road which was kind of slushy, and for a second looked down at my boots, the ice crystals stacked on the toes. God, what if there really were someone in there, and bloody. Maybe it was nothing vital, only an arm or leg or something. I tried not to walk too slow, I knew he would be watching. Maybe it was one of those things he thought I had to do. A shiver ran through me and I tried to step faster, but the car-trail was slippery and I kept sliding into the soft bank of snow, and each time I did the car joggled a bit as if it was the one moving. As I got near the back, I reached out and touched the fender to steady myself, my heart pounding so hard the top of my chest hurt. I strained my eyes through the steamy back window but couldn't see anything that took up much room. When I got near the front door I could see through the water-drips that no one was inside. The doors were locked, two Rainier bottles and newspapers were on the floor, a man's hat in the backseat. I stood there for a few minutes, but my heart was still wobbling a little, like a jumping bean after a jump.

"What the hell you doin' down there?" Dad yelled from the pickup.

"There's no one in it."

"I know, it's already been reported. Come on, let's go."

The bank was steeper than I thought. My fingers got cold and the wet gravelly dirt under the snow got under my fingernails. When I got back up to the pickup, I asked Dad for his pocketknife.

"What's in it?"

"In what?"

"In the car."

He stretched back, the brim of his hat curled against the roof of the truck, and pushed his hand into his left front pocket, his leg stiff against the floor, making the bulge at the center noticeable.

"Oh, nothing, just some bottles and stuff, nothing worth taking if someone wanted to. There aren't many cars that use this road anyway, are there?"

"No. What ya gonna do?"

"Clean my fingernails. Got some dirt under them coming up the bank."

"Little dirt never hurt anybody."

"Never helped either."

"Hey, watch your mouth. Your mother'll take it but I'll be damned if I will."

I hate to have dirt stuck under my nails; it makes my hands feel thick and clumsy like they aren't exactly mine though I have charge of them. I always think of that torture where small wedges of wood were driven under the prisoners' nails. For what I don't know, but I shuddered when I pictured the poor guy all bound and screaming. I always cleaned my dirty nails as soon as I could. It never seems to bother some people though, just go on like it was natural, eat that way too. Like Uncle Jim who's a mechanic, not only his nails but all the little creases in his hands. I always wondered how Aunt Gladys stood it. She never said anything, never seemed to mind. One time at dinner he reached for the bread and left a little smudge of grease on the slice under the one he took. I sat for the rest of the dinner waiting to see who would eat it, but no one did. Maybe they saw it too, I don't know. I wished Dad would have eaten it, if it never hurt anybody.

Dirt, a funny word. It stopped him cold when Mom found those magazines under Dad's mattress. Dirt, she called them, filth. He said a friend left them in his car, and he just thought he would take a look. Anything that looked naked was devil-sent, and anybody who looked was "eatin' of the apple," as she called it. I felt kind of sorry for Dad, though, maybe that explained why he was so ornery sometimes and left for the bar. Or why he came home stumbling and laughing real queer under his breath like some private magic show was going on behind his eyes and he was the one picked from the audience.

"What you so quiet about?"

"Just thinking."

"About what?"

"Oh, about how I'd like to go to the movies tonight."

"What are ya doin' for money? Think your mother'll give ya some, and who's to take ya? You always think everything should be done for you when you want it. Jesus, when I was a kid if I asked for money I'd get slapped down, no matter what it was for."

"I wasn't askin' for money. I've got some. Where are we going anyway?"

"Home."

We stopped in front of the house. I could see Mom standing in front of the kitchen window, probably peeling potatoes or skinning apples. Dad got out, slammed the door and said, "Take that bucket by the gate and catch Spider. The horseshoer is coming out this afternoon."

"Today is supposed to be my day off, but I have to work harder than if I were in school."

"Oh yeah, you really have it rough. Hurry up, lunch is on soon."

The bucket was by the gate all right, but the halter was in the barn, which was in the opposite direction from the horse. He always acts like he's doing you some big favor with some little thing, and it usually turns out not mattering in the slightest, or something he was going to do anyway. Like Friday night, he said he would take me to the movies, but what he really wanted to do was go to the bar. When I got out I saw his pickup down the block at the Iron Horse, and had to call Mom to come get me. She wanted to go in and get him but I talked her out of it. He came home, though, about an hour afterwards.

The halter was hung up where it always was, between the saddles and the grainbox. The horse was easy to catch, stupid thing always thinks there's grain in the bucket and comes running. You'd think it would learn, or at least be more cautious. Birds are smart. They'd never let you do that. Even the ones on the nest never let you get too close, unless it's at night, and that's really unfair. I mean just think if you were in bed sleeping, and someone grabbed you. You wouldn't have a chance.

When I got back to the house, I felt kind of lousy. I walked in on what sounded like another argument and shut the door quietly so that I wouldn't be noticed. My dad shouted, "When they catch that bastard, they oughta let'm rot. I can't understand what moves a bastard like that. Can't understand it."

And my mom, all sullen-like, but her eyes not narrowed to points like usual, beating the potatoes as if they had done something, said, "I don't know what it's coming to. A small place like this too. You might expect it in a big town where things are bad anyways, but here . . . I just don't know."

"Don't know what?" I asked, passing through the kitchen on my way to the bathroom, realizing that it wasn't really an argument, but moving so that I wouldn't get caught between them.

"Oh, it's that wreck we seen this morning," Dad said with disgust.

"Ted, now I didn't tell you so that you could tell the boy. He doesn't need to hear." She was looking at him square-on and she had stopped thrashing the potatoes. I could see it rising, so I stepped into the bathroom, but didn't turn on the water so I could hear.

"Oh shit, Gracie, he's old enough. Hell, he's probably seen more at those movies he goes to than this'll call to mind."

"I don't care what he sees or hears outside of this house, but he'll not hear it in."

"Just don't see the difference myself."

"Well, you wouldn't, you don't have the nature."

It was then I turned on the water. I have heard all the rest before. The "nature" as she calls it, or the inclination, is for the religious turn. Because he doesn't go to church, and doesn't have the nature, he doesn't see things the way Mom does. For her everything is mapped out, and if it doesn't fit, then it's to be hushed. I *have* seen lots in movies too. I always got into the PG's when I wasn't supposed to.

I finally got the smell of the horse off my hands and could hear that it was quiet outside the door, so I came out saying, "What's for lunch?"

"Hamburger steak, mashed potatoes, and string beans." Mom said it like a waitress, so I knew things must have cooled down some. Dad was sitting on the edge of the chair with the paper rolled up in his fist. He was looking out the window like he was absorbed in something outside but I don't think he was.

"You gonna eat?" Mom asked.

He slapped the rolled paper on the chair, and said, "Yup," like he was answering some other question.

Lunch went quickly, and no one said much. I don't like string beans very well, except with big chunks of meat, so I gulped it all down, including my milk, and got up to leave. Dad suddenly said, "Where do you think you're goin'?"

"I told Vince that I would walk down to his house this afternoon to listen to his new stereo."

"Oh no you don't, I got plans for you. You're gonna clean the tool shed while I go look at a bunch of cows Burt has for sale."

"But that'll take all afternoon."

"You can do what you want tomorrow."

"Why can't I clean it then?"

"Because Pete's comin' over to work on the welder tomorrow morning and I want it clean."

I spent the rest of the afternoon out in the shop. Dad left to check on the cows, and Mom went shopping for most of the late afternoon. I worked for about two hours steady and could see that the sweeping and the arranging of the screwdrivers and wrenches wouldn't take past dark, so after Mom left I shot baskets till I was tired of it. I only had one corner to do when I could see Dad coming up the lane. He was moving very slowly, so I knew he must have gotten the cows. I heard him pull into the field behind the house, and was thinking that he might need help, when I heard the heavy rattle of the wooden tail-gait. I kept at it then until I was finished, and it was getting dim when I walked in the door. Dad was watching TV, Mom was already fixing dinner, and I caught the smell of cornbread.

"Smells good. What's for dinner, Mom?"

"Chicken and cornbread. Did you get all your work done?"

"Yeah, just finished .... Hey Mom, will you take me to the show tonight?"

"I don't know. I have a pile of sewing to do for the church bazaar next Sunday."

"What time did you want to go? I could probably take you in," Dad said, leaning back in his chair and talking out of the corner of his mouth.

"Well, the movie starts about seven-thirty, so we'd have to leave about seven."

"Ok."

"You men wash up, dinner's almost ready."

We both washed and sat down for dinner. Although the conversation lagged sometimes, it was better than at lunch. Mom told about all the gossip she had heard in town, and Dad about what he saw on his drive. When we had finished, Dad told me to hurry with the shower because he wanted to take one too: "I don't want to smell like a truckload of cows all night."

We were ready to go out the door when Mom yelled from the sink, "You watch your wallet in the crowd tonight."

Dad was already out the door and to the pickup. When I stepped out into the clear night, the cold air washed my face and I suddenly felt refreshed after the hot shower and warm house. The ground was starting to firm up, and the gravel made a slight clicking noise as I walked. The pickup seat was especially cold. When the cold air from the heater went up my pantlegs, I shivered.

"What're you squirmin' about?"

"Oh, nothing, just a little cold."

"Should've wore more clothes."

"I'm OK. The theater will be warm anyway."

We were out the lane and headed toward town when I remembered about the wreck and wanted to ask Dad about it, but I wasn't sure how he would take it. I tried to ask very casual-like, as if it didn't matter to me, and I was only making conversation.

"Hey Dad, think that woman ever got her car back this afternoon?" I didn't know for sure if it was a woman, but the way Mom acted I thought it must have been.

"I suppose. It wouldn't 've taken much to pull it out."

"What happened to her anyway?"

"Hey, you know what your mother told you .... Well, I suppose it can't hurt none. Don't you tell her I told ya now, or else I'll make them pants a little thinner."

"I won't, you know I wouldn't." Dad wasn't really afraid of Mom, he just wanted to avoid the argument. He gets mean when he gets mad, and Mom knows just how far to go. His face turns red and a vein on his right temple pops out, and his ears kind of lay back like a horse's.

"I guess it was late last night, maybe even early this morning, say one or two o'clock. A woman was stopped to change a flat, and some weird bastard stops by to help her. Well, I guess after they got it fixed, he beat her up, pushed the car off the road, and raped her. Somebody found her about an hour later and she was still in shock, couldn't even describe him."

"How did Mom find out?"

"One of her friends who's helpin' her with the sewin' for the bazaar."

"Do you think they'll catch him?"

"Shit, he's long-gone by now."

I didn't talk much for the rest of the ride in. Just kept thinking about that woman, how bold the man was, taking off his clothes in front of a total stranger, and doing what he did. I wondered how old he was, and what might have led him to do it. I imagined a big slack-jawed man who smelled like a goat, and was missing some teeth in front. He wagged his head as he talked and his eyes drooped real sad like a bloodhound. It was when I saw a grimy hand with long dirty fingernails suddenly grab the white of her neck that I scared myself and gave up thinking about it, or tried to.

I was glad to get to the theater, its soft light, the people crowded into the outside glass lobby. As I climbed out of the pickup, I said, "It'll probably be over about ten."

"Just call home, someone'll pick ya up."

"OK, thanks," I said as I leaped onto the street. Dad raised his thumb from the steering wheel to say goodbye, and rolled through the light as it changed.

After I paid, I hurried in. I like to sit down near the front and in the center. I would like to have had some popcorn and a coke, but I didn't have much money. I was still spending what I got for my birthday from relatives. I found a good seat in front of an older couple. They're usually quiet and don't crinkle cellophane or eat peanuts. So I settled down in the seat with my coat draped over the back and waited for it to start.

In the opening scene there was no music, only the occasional sound of metal sliding on metal, and everything was dark. Then a light grows in the corner of the screen, and a man appears bent over something, working very carefully. Then the metal slammed hard with a sliding click, and I could feel my heart jump. The man stood up. He was dressed in black, even had on a black stocking cap. He took several steps over to a table and the linoleum creaked under his boots. The sound gave me the spooks. He then slowly put on gloves that squeaked like wet rubber, and I saw his face for the first time. It was dark and handsome though his forehead was wrinkled up like he was thinking real hard or worried about something. Then he is walking down the dark fire-escape stairs, his shoes making a dull ringing sound over the flat iron rungs. You follow his feet along through a back street, until the scene suddenly changes to an older man in a hospital bed. It is very dim except for a small circle under the bed-lamp. The man seems restless; his face is stubbly, but his well-styled hair and his watch make him look like he might be important. He looks at the face of his watch and frowns. Glancing up at the window through which we are looking, he sees that the blinds are open too far. Painfully, he rises to pull the white knob on the curtain cord. Suddenly a knife swipes through the dark and the man falls kicking and writhing in a pool of his own blood. It was then that I shut my eyes, shaking inside like I was going to be sick, my heart wobbling in my chest. When I opened my eyes again, the music had started up and there was a garden full of people having a good time. The rest of the movie wasn't nearly so bad. The lights came on during the credits, and we filed out not saying much.

It was cold. The windows on the cars in the parking-lot had a thin glaze of frost on them, and the centers of the leaves in the gutters were starting to turn white. I could have called from the lobby, but I felt like walking around a bit before going home. I headed down the street toward the Iron Horse half expecting to see Dad's pickup parked outside. As I approached the door I saw two dogs lying with their heads on their paws: one was a big black Labrador, the other a mangy collie with dirty mats of hair on the side facing me. I wasn't sure if I should go too near the door, so I looked through the window. It was awfully smoky inside, and I could see it rolling through the lights that hung over the pool tables. I kept looking to see if I knew someone, when all of a sudden I saw Dad with a woman at a table right in front of me. She was standing up and had her hand cupped around his neck. She bent down and kissed him on the forehead, and when she raised up again, I thought for sure he was looking right at me. It scared me so much I just took off walking as fast as I could. When I got to the corner I ran hard for two blocks and ducked up an alley. I walked through the dark, weaving among large garbage bins and empty cars. The street I came out on was the one that led out of town toward home, so I decided to walk the mile and a half to the service station that had a phone outside. I would call my mom from there because I didn't want her to see Dad's pickup and want to go get him. Then Dad would think that I had told her and I would really get it.

I had walked nearly a mile cursing Dad, wondering what he would do to me in the morning, when I finally stopped and asked myself what I was doing so far from anywhere and in the middle of the night. The wreck popped into my mind like something out of the dark, and I began to get real scared and started to run. The cold air made my eyes water and my face hurt. I hadn't run fifty yards when I heard a truck behind me. I started to walk again so whoever it was wouldn't stop. I moved to the far side of the road on the edge of the short bank. Turning my head slightly so that I could see out the corner of my eye, I saw the truck slow way down. Suddenly it stopped and when the door opened I could see a man inside, so I took off running. I ran towards an open field. I ran and ran without looking back. The image of that flashing knife and the old man's bony legs writhing in blood made me run faster and faster without worrying how hard it was to run through the snow. The cold air that ballooned in my lungs hurt only for a while and then burst into a warmth that took in my whole body. Even in that cold, my face was pouring down sweat and my shirt was clinging to my back. I ran through the dark, crunching through the thin crust of snow, threading through the bare trees. finally, I spotted a huge old haybarn on a knoll ahead of me and ran to it panting and steaming. It was not until I stopped and leaned on the door, my lungs gulping in the cold air, that I turned and looked in the direction I had come. Like a slap, I realized I could be easily tracked to this very spot, but I was too exhausted to go on, so I decided to go inside and figure out if I was being followed.

Inside it was damn dark, except for an occasional long, thin shaft of moonlight that came through the holes in the roof. There was a layer of musty haybales on the floor, and as I walked over the top of it I could feel and hear pigeon-droppings crunching under my feet. Once I fell in a hole between the bales and scraped my shin against the prickly dry grass stalks. I swore out loud and I heard a rustle of tiny feet above me. I thought of rats swarming through the rafters, their black beady eyes on me. I shut my eyes and started to pray. I said the same words over and over again, not caring what they meant.

When I finally stopped I felt tired, my shoulders ached and my feet were numb. The only thing I could think of then was what a bastard my dad was, what a goddamned bastard. I kept saying it over and over like it was a prayer. I was sitting on a hay-bale feeling the cold leak into my clothes, watching the moonlit holes in the barn's roof when I thought I heard something outside. Then I saw a light at the door and just when I thought I was going to faint for lack of air, my dad walks in, shining his light and calling my name. I sat there stunned. I tried to speak but only hushed words came out like somebody else was saying them.

"What the hell are ya doin' in here? What got into you, boy? I been trackin' you for a mile. What made ya take off like that?"

"I was scared. I didn't know who you were."

He stood, then, catching his breath, letting the relief trickle out. Circles of light pooled at his feet, yet I could see his face, the change in it.

"Jesus, boy, you're gettin' awful damn skittery. What the hell you sneakin' around for anyway? Didn't I tell ya to give a call when you was done? You're liable to get yerself killed. What'd you do, forget the goddamn phone number?"

"I didn't know who you were."

"You can see well enough. I think ya could use somethin' to help ya think straighter." He bent down and picked up a long piece of wood and broke it over his knee. He came at me with his flashlight in one hand, the stick in the other. I ran to one corner of the darkened barn, and he followed, his arms spread like he was chasing a cow, the light bouncing crazily around. He started to run and I heard a small, choked cry like a goose grabbed by the neck. Then he was moaning in the old hay-bales, his feet in the air. He had run into a guy-wire that supported the walls. He was holding his throat, his legs moving in slow-motion like that old man in the movie. I ran over to him and he was clutching little beads of blood on his neck. I reached down and asked what I could do. I picked up the light. His eyes were shut, and there were little prints of blood on his fingers. The stick-end was half-buried in the hay and was just outside the light's edge. His hand reached up and caught my shoulder. It rested there until his eyes opened upon a faraway look, drained of their anger. He just lay there for a few minutes, and then sat up, strands of straw clinging to his wool cap and coat. I started to brush them away as he moved his head slowly back and forth. There wasn't a sound I could hear but his breathing. The rats and birds had vanished.

Moonbeams still poured through the holes in the roof like tiny spotlights.

"God damn," he whispered, "never saw that comin'." He sat there looking into his empty lap. "Help me up, John," he said, and I put my hand under his arm and lifted as hard as I could. When he was standing up square, he reached for the light and said, "Come on, let's git on home."

As I passed in front of him to go out the barn door, his light swirled around my legs so that they made long thin shadows, and I saw his arm reach out like he was letting Mom through a door, but it stopped mid-way and hung in the air like it couldn't decide whether to come down or not. I walked out into the night and the moon on the snow turned everything a deep white and the few trees stood up tall and shadowy, the snow in their arms shiny. When we walked under one, a large bird flew out clapping his wings. I watched his dark shape weaving over the snow with the moon on its back, and saw how the tree stood like something important had left its body. We walked back over the fields not saying anything as our boots crunched through the snow, my feet stretching to reach each footprint.

The pickup was cold and dark. During the ride home, the dashlights lit up the lower half of his face. His mouth was pulled tight like he was a million miles away. Somehow, everything I wanted to say to him, or have him say to me, seemed just as far. It was like he was driving the tractor and baler and I was on the haysled. The wires were busted but he was driving to beat the rain, hay chunking out every which way and he can't hear a word. We go on, leaving a trail of mistakes behind us.

Once his hand brushed my knee when he was shifting, and he kept it on the gear-knob as if he needed something like that to hold on to, the edge of his palm touching my knee. And I couldn't even look at him, except at a glance. I stared into the tunnel of light the pickup made through the night, not knowing what to do with my own hands. We rode home in this charged darkness. Telephone poles and fenceposts flared, cast long shadows, then disappeared again. The large chunks of ice from other people's cars and trucks joggled us a little until we got home.

My father died three years ago of an aneurysm in his brain. He was standing by a gate watching some steers he just released into a new pasture. He fell and never got up again. My older brother, whom I rarely see anymore, gave a speech at the funeral about the love between a father and son. It was a touching speech about a man I can't say I knew. My mother gives her free time to the church now, and for all the years of their determined opposition, their cutting silences and glooms, she took his death very hard. She wept and wept, and my brother and I had to practically carry her to the gravesite, each hooked to an arm. I can't say I understand it.

When I think back to that night in the snow almost six years ago, my mind can't get past the arm hanging in the air, the blood on his neck. I never found out about the woman, who she was, or how he knew her. Last winter trying to find out what all this meant, I walked back to that barn in the daylight and I couldn't get over how small and lonely it was. It was as if the daylight had squeezed a continent into a tiny island. As I entered, a cross-bred pigeon spotted with all kinds of colors flew out a broken window. I watched the sky close around it until it vanished. I stood for a long time. I began to think about the way we went about our lives together. His little tests to make my hide tougher, maybe so I could stand and hold my mother up at the gravesite, maybe for something else too, still to come. I thought of the way he moved to the brink of some strong emotion and then stepped back almost puzzled or confused. The way my anger and hate hardened around me, closing me in. This dance between the father and son had no music or steps to go by. We had only the faintest measures to guide us, a hand on a gearshift knob, the worry that took us miles through the snow together. We hung on to the small revelations where what we spoke of was really something else. And yet underneath it all, steady as an engine, was the unrealized knowledge that the hand and the shoulder matched, that the words and the deeds would know each other at last. At least that is what I felt at that moment, standing there looking out the broken window.

THAT SUSPENDED SUMMER

Aaron made a nice dinner because this was his week to cook. Given his effort, Anna felt she had to linger in her praise of it. She thought there was something small in this praise, yet it seemed as expected and natural as answering the telephone with a "hello." The faint whirring of the ceiling fan was like a clock in fast motion.

"This is delicious. Is there anise in it?" she asked casually, though she knew it wasn't because she saw the plastic packet in the wastecan.

"No, it's fennel. It's supposed to help prevent prostate cancer," he said, musedly forking a speck of it out of his quiche.

She thought of telling him it was the glycyrrhizin in licorice root that seemed to work on mice, but she didn't want to get into an argument or endanger the compliment about his cooking.

"What time are you meeting Sally?"

"7:30, but you know Sally, probably about 8:00."

"I still have piles of poems to read. The Poetry-On-The-Buses committee meets tomorrow and I have a lot of work to do. Never volunteer—my new motto."

She watched the concentrated way he ate. He had a round, freckly, wholesome-looking face. His white teeth, high cheekbones, and sturdy build made him seem virile, but his eyes had an opaque earnestness which at first was attractive because they seemed guileless, but after two years of living together, they were fading into dullness.

He had graduated with a drama degree three years ago and was working on a play in his spare time. He drove a city bus and would bring home stories about the loneliness of some passengers, how the bus absolutely filled up with it like a noxious vapor spilled along the roadways. He would describe his passengers to her in excruciating detail—the way a bent old woman stared out the window and her special quality of sadness, how a man rubbed his umbrella handle in an oblique, friendless way as if he were trying to conjure a genii out of nothingness. She found it tedious and abstract compared to what she saw every day at the hospital.

She thought, though, that his dullness might just be their pattern of predictability—of habit blending so surreptitiously into habit, of today so easily moving into the contours of yesterday—that caused her to feel a stifling anxiety. She slowly spooned a strawberry from the dish of sliced fruit. It had been dusted with powdered sugar, and its cold sweetness saturated her tongue.

When Nile had called and told her that he was going to be at the theater this evening with a dance troupe from Russia and would it be possible for her to meet him at the Bayview afterwards, she had flushed with a busy confusion, yet finally said, "All right," without really knowing why and felt remorse immediately after hanging up the phone. She had wanted to seem independent, and casual to Nile, but she did not like deceit, and had a particularly keen nose for it when Aaron appeared evasive or overly solicitous. It's just that she and Nile had such a mysterious and ineffectual relationship during school. In a way it had been an affront to her inner assurances that privilege and beauty had conferred so casually as to seem natural, inevitable.

In high school, she had waited with her friends as he entered the school, and she gave him a note wrapped into a little square with a flower drawn on one side, his name on the other. The note was ceremoniously presented, and the girls stood reading his reactions, aloofly superior.

The note had been direct: she liked him and wanted him to take her out. Beside the "Anna" signed at the bottom, she drew a winking face. The knowing, mischievous grins on the faces of her companions, the wink, and his lack of confidence were enough for him not to act, so he went on fearful and inaccessible, and all the more charming because of it.

Nile had managed an enigmatic charm that was as fragile as a bubble, yet it floated along with him and he was popular, girls often sent notes and cards on holidays. He was handsome with soft eyes and an engaging smile. His skin had a healthy coppery hue that made his eyes seem darker, deeper. But that small transparent bubble broke when he was faced with a real emotion, a direct demand for action.

His father worked at a motel that just managed to stay in business. The manager's small apartment had the TV on behind the reception desk, a stack of towels and sheets on the shelf behind the counter, penciled notes about delivery times or recipes for stain removal, a cat in the windowsill, keys hung on hooks under the cupboards, the register a maze of erasures and scribblings, an ashtray with a cigarette burning. Nile never had enough money to go skiing with his class, or to camp, or to dinner before a prom, or to pay the insurance on a car if he'd had enough to buy a car like most of his friends. This undertow of denial, of being persistently pulled back, kept him from venturing very far.

At one school party they had danced, slowly, sensuously, their hands telling more than their mouths believed they had a right to. They fell into a tandem rhythm of body realizing body, fitting into a dizzying warmth. She leaned into him and kissed his neck. When the music ended, they disentangled in a blush of cordiality. He felt like running away, and she wanted to turn and walk back, take his hand, reassure him. But the lights came on and the music ended. The spring night was cold, and they bundled into coats and scarves and gloves, and the fullness and promise of the dance had dissolved into the padded mechanics of departure. They became little engines chuffing white clouds into the darkness.

There were lingering glances, gossip, and notes. But to get him to act, she finally started dating another boy, a college freshman, someone he didn't know. He felt betrayed, hated himself for being so shy and fearful and possessed by some ambition he couldn't even name himself. The college boy had a car, and he and Anna seemed to spend much of their free time together. He was miserable, yet rallied that misery into calculations, graphs, and the writing of essays.

Nile had chosen for his university the one that had the best business school in the state. He was a gifted student and had no trouble getting in. In his junior year, Anna had transferred to his university, and they met one afternoon in the Student Union Building. They had lunch in the cafeteria which led to a weekend date. They had gone to a spacious cabin on Camano Island that belonged to the parents of one of his best friends at the university. There was a bonfire and wine. They spent a good part of the night talking about their goals and ambitions, some of their friends from high school and what they were doing or not doing. The night was warm and forgiving; the restless surging of the surf swelled into their chests.

They ended up in bed, but they had no contraception, and she did not want to make love without it. He had not been insistent, but had been swept into the numbingly sweet pleasure of one touch ramifying gently into another, of the soft snuggling, of the electric pings that ignited whole regions of feeling and allowed the mind to lie down, to float, dissolve. They lay naked together for some time until she suddenly removed his hand.

"If you respected me you wouldn't do that," her voice was soft and calm.

"Do what? I was. . ."

"Men never know when to stop, and it's really a matter of respect," she said with a mildly reproving smile.

She got out of the bed and pulled a green and blue nightgown out of her small suitcase. She put it on and buttoned it almost to the top button, then got back in bed. It wasn't the sexual refusal; it was the unconscious motherly condescension with which she handled it that kept him awake.

For much of the night, he lay there thinking about this defect, how it might limit what he wanted to be, how it might compromise everyday life. The next day she was soft and nuzzling and acquiescent. The more remote he became, the more solicitous were her gestures, and the more remote that center inside him. The drive back to the university seemed engulfed in silences. She thought he was dramatizing the importance of this lost sexual adventure and was glad they had not made love. It would give him something to look forward to, to strive for, to lead him slowly into the relationship she wished to have with him. Part of the patronizing edge in her voice came unconsiously out of her knowledge about his past—his shyness, his uncompromising fixation on academic success, his father's shabby motel.

Her father was president of the major bank in their hometown, had a large house, and knew the wealthiest people. Her speech about respect had in it a mild reclaiming of ground that the admission of her feelings had lost. On the drive home, both sat mining their own privacies, convinced of the rightness of their actions, though a little suspicious of their own motives. When he dropped her off at her apartment, they kissed, and she winked a goodbye that was supposed to be full of mysterious and complicitous understanding, but Nile immediately added it to the column of patronizing attitudes on the tally sheet inside his head. He hated her superiority and was, in fact, afraid of it.

This weekend occurred near the end of spring quarter, which meant that he was soon preoccupied with final exams. He also had a summer job with a construction company in another town that started the day after his last final. He was to work with a crew making forms for concrete. Though he had applied for many construction jobs in the past, he had never gotten any, but his friend's father owned a construction company. He had gotten the job without even submitting a resume. This experience solidified in his mind the effects of privilege: how the world was divided by it, how arbitrary its exclusions were, and what he had to do to succeed. He needed to make a good impression, so he worked hard and neglected all other aspects of summer life. Then in the fall, he went to study abroad on a scholarship. He spent the next quarter in youth hostels and cold hotels trying to make his construction money last as long as it could. He came back with ten dollars in his pocket and twenty pounds lighter, from bread and tomatoes and sleeping in the gloomy, winter-damp hostels in southern France. Yet he had seen the major museums, cathedrals, and tombs of famous men he had read about. His appetite to belong to that world, to be a part of it, to sit at the table of Western culture and take a few sips of its wine, break its bread, had been at least temporarily satisfied. He had climbed the iron steps of the Eiffel Tower, the wooden ones into the belfry of the Notre Dame, had squandered a whole afternoon in the gardens of Versailles, seen Neitzche's and Keats' and Newton's and Shakespeare's graves, seen the Prado, the Louvre, the Sistine Chapel, Westminster, the Alhambra, and the Parthenon. That intrepid restlessness and pride that pushed and prodded him had eased in the Mediterranean sun where the deep blueness of time wrinkled in on each wave and crashed and rose in a white feathery spume of release. It was as if some constriction in his throat that had impaired his breathing suddenly vanished and the ancient air slid freely and fully into and out of his lungs.

In those long months, she pursued a nursing career, and grew to hate Nile for not calling, though it would not have occurred to her to call him. Her disappointment had gradually subsided from fantasies of revenge to a dull disregard. His name only occasionally came into her mind like a breeze suddenly filling and lifting a gauzy curtain. If she were alone and it were evening, she let the old feeling wash over her. She might pour herself a glass of chardonnay and sit while the curtain swept lazily away and back. The old hurt was back there still and she felt it the way a healed bone-break sometimes throbs in the dead of winter.

Even as she started the car, she wasn't sure why she had agreed to meet him. Perhaps it was a test to assure herself that she was finally free. Perhaps there was a residue of that curiosity which anger had slowly burned away, some ember that could finally be stamped out. It was a warm June evening, and the Seattle skyline stretched into the water. A blood-orange sun shone boldly from behind the Olympics like the globe of light rising with Jesus in Grünewald's *Resurrection*. This light was tinged with the same blue-green nimbus that now surrounded the evening sun. It was one of her favorite paintings, and she had a reproduction in her bedroom. She had bought it while on a ten-day European tour sponsored by the Lutheran church. She loved the way Christ seemed to be ascending into a golden rush of radiance and was himself becoming light, his shroud unspooling magnificently upward, the stigmata glowing like tiny oil lamps from their red wicks. And the men, the metal-plated, earth-numb Roman soldiers, were struck blind, fallen and falling.

This evening glow lit up the sides of houses which ordinarily seemed dreary and pathetic; it gave them a softness and depth that rose mysteriously out of the paint. Children rode on scooters and skateboards or bounced balls in driveways trying to catch that last bit of the day before it sank behind the mountains. When she got to 50th, she sensed how long her drive would be. The traffic on I-5 was the usual wild rush, and she had to concentrate on driving. The Russian troupe was performing in the Coliseum. She was going to meet Nile in the bar of the Bayside where he was staying, so she took the Mercer exit. She and Aaron had lived in an apartment near Ravenna Park for the last two years, so it was a short trip down I-5, but crossing all those lanes in this light and against the impatience of people speeding toward the thousand events in the city was both a physical and moral challenge. Anna had difficulty with interstate travel. She often missed her exit because she let others cut her off or get in front of her. When this happened, she cursed her own passivity and goodwill. She encouraged herself to be tougher, to be like the Romans when in Rome.

Off the freeway, the traffic was immediately more tolerant. There was a recognizable grid of protocol and sequence which she much preferred. The sun had slipped beyond the mountains, but against the orange afterglow the mountain range loomed even larger and more ragged, its snows cloaked in shades of pink and streaks of blue. The glass of the skyscrapers absorbed and bounced back a diffused glow. The bay was glossy and golden. A white and green ferry towed a pink line like frayed ribbon through the water. Anna loved the ferries and the little pockets of time they promised travelers who were asked to do nothing but watch the water, its yellow disks of jellyfish, aerobatic seagulls, diving ducks, mountains and forests and sailing ships, all the lazy sunlit commerce that naturally evaded the working eye. They reminded her of those hometown days where time hung heavy in the summer air, and her thoughts could drift like blown dandelion down. She felt herself driving back toward that time, that suspended summer.

The bar of the hotel was low-lit and plushly carpeted. Men in dark business suits with bright ties and expensive women were scattered here and there. Boats, wooden piers, and lights posed outside the windows. The water wavered restlessly, litter washed back and forth on its surface. Anna was not sure she would recognize Nile in this place. The waiters wore white shirts and dark slacks and carried wooden trays with green felt on the bottom the color of pool tables. The bartender was young with a black mustache that drooped at the corners just enough to suggest a prodigal resistance to his humdrum job. As she walked around one corner of the bar, she saw a hand wave and beckon her toward a corner seat.

Nile wore a dark pinstriped suit, a white shirt, and red tie dotted with tiny blue rosettes. His hair was shorter than when she had last seen him, and the coppery skin had darkened a hue, but his eyes still had a lively intensity. He stood up, shook her hand.

"You look as great as I remembered," he said, smiling.

"Thank you. You're looking good, too." She took off her jacket, giving her long hair a casual flip.

"These are my work clothes, I didn't have time to change."

"So, what are you doing with a Russian dance troupe, sounds awfully mysterious."

"Actually, I'm merely indulging my artistic side. I'm on the board to raise money for our theater, so I volunteered to go along with the troupe to find out how the business works. I'm on the road a lot. What about you? Still at Harborview?"

"No, I'm at Virginia Mason, now. But we do rotations, so I'll probably end up back there before long."

"I just wanted to see you again. I feel like there's about ten years of unfinished business between us, most of which is my fault, and. . . I just had to see you and try to talk about it."

"Just another business deal, eh?" she said, not letting him push her where she wasn't ready to go.

The waiter put a cardboard disk in front of her, and asked what she'd like.

"Chardonnay, please."

"Another for you, sir?"

"Yes, please."

Nile continued, "Anna, you know I didn't mean it that way. It was a figure of speech." He put his hands flat on the table. "I mean you've been on my mind for the last ten years, and I'm embarrassed by who I was, then, and want to, if I can, somehow, find some. . ."

"Just like that?"

"No. I just wanted to explain. I never meant to hurt you. I was afraid, and stupid, and full of myself."

"Afraid of what?"

"Afraid of ending up in a grimy motel. Afraid of watching other people lead their lives while I followed mine around like some puppy on a leash. I know you probably can't understand that."

The waiter returned with the drinks. He set them down gently, flipped his tray under his arm, and left.

"Life probably seems more sensible to you, all laid out in streets and avenues with a light on each corner, but I always felt one step away from . . .failure."

"And I was in the way?"

"You weren't. That's what I'm trying to say. I was afraid to love you, and I don't think you knew how to love me. I don't think you understood how easily the wrong word, or a look, sent me down some dark alleys." He loosened his tie. "I guess I called you because I wanted to apologize, to say something honest, for once."

She sipped her wine. "I'm getting married this fall."

He unbuttoned the top button of his shirt. She waited, observing him coolly.

"So, who's the lucky man?"

"His name is Aaron McPherson. He's a playwright. He's a wonderful writer. You should see some of the things he's written."

"Yes, I should," he said, suddenly getting up. Before she could reply, he had walked away. She watched him pay on his way out. He didn't look back.

The music which had struggled to stay in the background now felt like the soft beginnings of rain falling. The cones of street lights seemed more artificial in the way they tried to use the dark, to portion it out into trim aesthetic patterns. Suddenly, that voice inside her that had wanted an explanation, a full accounting, seemed weak and mean. Why had justice not felt better? Why did she now feel empty and remorseful? And why did Nile always make her feel this way?

On the drive home, the city was alive with light: bustling cars had somewhere important and romantic to go, and the moon, in its descent, had cast a white veil across the bay. The west-facing walls of the buildings were painted with a pale light. There was something personal and sufficient in being in her own car, yet when she parked behind her apartment house and turned off the motor, the dark was flat and pervasive. The parkinglot with its yellow stripes and cement barriers, the overflowing blue garbage bin, the torn thread-bare sofa beside it, were contemptible. She felt time had lurched awkwardly forward. Why had Nile left so suddenly? He'd planted an emotional bomb but didn't stick around for the explosion. Was it truth or nostalgia? She opened her purse for a packet of Kleenex. She ripped it open and wiped her tears, blew her nose.

Aaron was watching television when she entered the apartment. She walked through the living room and into the kitchen. The light over the stove was on. She poured herself a glass of wine from the bottle he had opened.

"So, how's Sally?" he asked, when she came back into the living-room.

"Oh, she's not doing so well. Did you finish with the poems?"

"Almost. Why, what's she up to?"

She sat beside him and patted his thigh. "She and Tim are having problems, and she doesn't like her job, same old stuff. Did you find any you liked?"

"Yes, a good bunch, really, though I don't know what everyone else on the committee will think."

"Well, you can be persuasive when you want to be. What are you watching?"

"An old movie with Jimmy Stewart. I just turned it on."

"You know what I was thinking on the way home?"

"What?"

"We should get married."

"You know we can't really afford that. Not now."

"I don't care about a big wedding anymore. I used to want one with a huge cake, a white bouquet of roses on every pew, that sort of thing. But it doesn't make any difference, I don't care, really I don't," she said, putting her arm around his neck.

"But even a small one is expensive. I always thought that after I got my first play produced, that would be a good time. I mean…"

"Forget it, just forget that I said anything," she said, abruptly rising and walking toward the bedroom.

"Anna, come on, what? I thought we were having a discussion."

But the brisk smack of the door was all the answer he got. He knew better than to try to placate her in this state. If he went in now, all his pleading and justifying would only make it worse. She would get sullen and rigid. Even if he said he wanted to fly to Las Vegas tomorrow and get married, she would see him as patronizing and insensitive. He settled back into the sofa watching Jimmy Stewart who was witty and gallant and not at all misunderstood.

Anna undressed and got ready for bed. She washed her face and brushed her teeth. She sat on the bed and combed her hair. She found no solace in Christ rising in his golden ball of fire, the Roman soldiers awestruck and blinded and falling. The bedroom seemed small and cluttered. The dressers were messy: each with their collection of bottles, change, magazines, and clothes. There were shoes carelessly arranged along two walls. She thought of Nile undressing in a clean hotel room, folding his shirt, hanging up his coat, stretching out on his bed, watching the chandelier lights of ferries slowly crossing the bay, pulling a gauzy train of moonlight behind them.

SPACE
WALKING

I had just come from my mother's bedside where the consequences of her stroke, after long hours of waiting, were revealed. The right side of her seventy-nine year old mouth moved only in a kind of reluctant obligation to the emotions of the left; the right hemisphere was not amused or sad or angry, but merely tagged along like a kid brother whose dogged decision to follow had superseded any purpose he might have begun with. Her right hand was thin and curled. Her eyes seemed sunken, her face more placid than I'd ever seen it. I was assured by this apparent composure. She lay quietly under the white clean sheets. It was not until she began to speak that I felt the dread. Her words came out, syntax and rhythm were there, as well as the urgency of some intention, but nothing made sense. It was if all her words were in a giant fishbowl and she pulled them out and pronounced them with absolute surety, but nothing belonged together. I didn't know how much of this she herself recognized, underneath that stream of language, and how was I to tell her? I kissed her on the cheek and walked out to find a doctor. I was told I could confer next Tuesday with a brain specialist who worked exclusively with stroke victims. And it was in this context, this anxious hiatus, that I ran over Willy Jordan's tricycle.

Despite the red welts on his face or the dirty half-moons under his fingernails, the man grinned in almost any situation. He peddled a large tricycle with an array of colorful plastic ribbons dangling from the handles; his bell sounded like a telephone going off every five seconds. He began sentences that faded into a puzzled silent wheezing, but he was accepted by all of us who knew him or saw him every day on the streets.

We would like to say our town, full of cheerful exteriors and easy kindnesses, embraced him, for we are like that—the way we feed the three-legged stray who makes its rounds from Safeway to Carlyle's to The Honeyrest Cafe, living off handouts and tidbits, that veneer of charity we find for misfits, beggars, and loons so that we can feel better ducking down the next aisle. But the red welts, the deep vacancies, kept me dodging him until that one moment of our meeting when communication was mandated.

I backed over Willy's rain-rusted tricycle in the Safeway parking lot with my pickup. The tricycle looked as misshapen and purposeless as all dead things. I can't explain it except that when I turned the key a tape of the Rolling Stones blared on, attuned to the volume of the road and not the parking lot. Willy was talking to the driver of the car next to me. I was looking at the red welts on his neck which seemed to catch the sun when the bike's metal made a sad crumpling sound. And then Willy cried out, his hands and shoulders began to tremble. I got out to apologize and explain what happened, but his sobs broke heavily through my sentences. The other driver shook his head and glared as if he'd never seen a more despicable fool. While I talked, I saw the stern end of his car leave the lot, the way his back tire clipped the curb and jostled his Jeep and was gone. I was relieved no one else had seen what I did. The empty vehicles sat like blind witnesses in even rows. Finally, I took Willy by the arm like an usher at a wedding, and we walked two blocks to the bike shop, the spectacle we were, rippling out.

I usually see myself in complete opposition to the gaudy emotionalism of the media—the *Pretty Woman* syndrome of seducing the poor with wealthy, handsome salvation and "meaningful" love relationships with soft lighting and calculating music, the mind-numbing simplicity of Hollywood men who are eagerly taught the excellencies of the emotional life by prostitutes, children, and the family dog, the syrupy sighing and ooohing of laugh-tracks on sit-coms telling us to applaud their pedantic platitudes about love and other matters of the heart—but when faced with the wailing and blubbering of the village mascot whose soul-ache I had just caused, I was silenced into a sizzling embarrassment. I could do nothing but look at him, and avoid making eye-contact with others.

His eyes had a subtle twitch. He was clean-shaven, his hair was combed back and short at the sides. It was the sudden thought of the razor in his hand, his image looking back through the mirror each morning, that struck me—what he sees there, his slightly trembling hand razoring over the welts. At the bike shop, I bought him a large tricycle in the exact shade of red as the one he had. It even had the same rims and spokes. He seemed to like it, and we began to talk. He works at the recycling center on Tuesday and Wednesday afternoons, sorting cardboard into sizes. An orange stain on his white shirt was the shape of Italy without the full toe. He told me he lives by himself. Our talking distracted him until it was time to push the tricycle out of the store.

When he grabbed the handlebars, he didn't grin as I thought he might, but touched up and down the bars haltingly. Then he asked where the plastic streamers were, and the bell, why the pedals had a different shape. He didn't want this one. The welts seemed to redden, his face sunk, and all he could say was "not pretty, not pretty." He was stuck on this phrase. I explained that we would order the plastic streamers, the bell. The dark haired boy in the Padres hat who sold me the tricycle didn't know what to do either and backed away from the street and slid inside his shop. I knew Willy's mother died a year ago. Her name was Beatrice, a school teacher before she came here with Willy. They lived together on Sprague. His deep empty look made me think of her, the way she glared at someone who had made a remark about Willy. Her hair was grey, and she wore it short. With high cheekbones, blue eyes, full lips, she was still attractive, but wore glasses decades out of date, maybe back to her husband's death. Sometimes she would stand in her small yard with a rake while Willy was swinging in a rubber tire suspended by a rope from their elm tree. She was ready to deal with any child who might stare at him through the fence because often he'd hoot and make animal noises as he swung. She would have known what to do about the bell and streamers.

My mother would have used her wits. She's Irish and inherited a love for jokes and stories and could make anyone laugh, even Willy. She had never been to Ireland, but still had cousins there from her father's sister who did not want to go to America. She sent Christmas cards, but never saw her grandparents except in photographs. When I was young she threw parties frequently and was a graceful hostess—freshening drinks, passing platters of hors d'oeurves, resting a hand on a shoulder in intimate welcome, negotiating bits of conversation fluently. She would tell a story about trying on dresses and stepping out in her panties before the Superior Court Judge, or her Sunday school student who said "the Catholic Church just inferiorates me," or about a man named Rick Shaw who sought opportunities in China, or joke about the sign in the podiatrist's office that said "Time wounds all heels." She laughed with her whole body, and one humorous encounter seemed to bubble over into another as if she were transporting this warm coal from person to person. Yet she wasn't just some feather-headed ninny good at parties. She volunteered at the church, organizing social events. She worked for seventeen years in the lab of a vegetable cannery before marrying my father who was divorced and owned a chemical fertilizer plant called Chemco. His money enabled her to wear large hats and gloves when she wanted to.

I am an only child, and my father was almost twenty years older than my mother. I never knew him well. He died of cancer when I was ten, and I became the focus of her attention. She was not overly protective, though insane with worry when I was out late during high school. She was generous with her time, stingy with her money, and volunteered at the museum and the Centennial committee that produced a local history.

But it is her voice I think people will remember, the way she sometimes seemed to laugh and talk at the same time, zipping off to hyperbole or understatement with equal ease just to lighten the mood. She is, or I should say was, a person for whom language was the element she lived in, like the bird's air, the worm's dirt. To see her now making sentences that were nothing but shaped air, hollow sounds, pinpoints and musical ridges, was like watching a plucked bird try to fly, again and again.

I did meet with the neurologist on that Tuesday. He said she had a cerebral infarction caused by an embolism or arteriosclerosis and wondered whether she'd experienced any transient ischemic attacks, that is any impaired brain function like loss of vision, numbness of the face, dizziness, hearing loss, or temporary paralysis. While he talked, his hand adjusted the right side of his glasses or rubbed his knee. He did not look at me, but off into some space beside me, behind me. When I told him I wasn't aware of any symptoms and that she was a person who kept her medical difficulties to herself, he nodded, slightly closing his eyes. He explained that her aphasia or speech impairment was probably permanent, that the loss of her motor skills were, perhaps, repairable with therapy. He brushed the baldness of his head as if to suggest the visitation was over, then told me his nurse would give details about an agency that would help me with the next steps.

I didn't even know what an infarction was, and why didn't I have the presence of mind to ask? Cerebral infarction=dead brain tissue, I looked it up. Did dead brain tissue automatically suggest black spots of memory, lacunae, vacancies, whole hemispheres of experience had been swallowed up into a void as irrevocable as the past? Or did the important events of one's life sidle over, hop on board a train that was actually going places? My mother was not able to read or write or speak with any intelligibility. It was a kind of imposed autism after a lifetime of operating an exquisitely well-tooled machine. She could understand what was spoken to her but had no way of responding in turn. How is it possible to live when you feel your own mind is your enemy? And how many people got out of bed every day ready to begin this battle anew?

When I'm asked about my occupation, I say I'm an interpreter, but that is only partly true. I majored in Spanish,

lived in Mexico for several years, and like Spanish literature
or literature written in Spanish, Neruda, and Lorca particularly. However, I work as an interpreter for the courts and
businesses like motels and the vegetable cannery who run
into difficulty communicating with their employees. I also
work part-time for Culligan's, delivering Purified Water in
18.9 liter jugs to businesses on a weekly circuit. I own a
pickup for hauling these plastic containers of "Calcium
Free" water to our patrons. I mention my interpreter job as
an example only, to show how language has so thoroughly
seeped into the interstices of my being. Inner talk is the
essential element of my work day, reading is the solace
before sleep, crossword puzzles are inextricably entwined
with my coffee, words are the coinage of the day, the
passport from one moment to the next. The healthy,
lambent coursings of my mind, for all its casual speed and
agility, are absolutely unable to imagine the cages Willy's and
my mother's minds have been locked into. It's the
claustrophobe's nightmare visited, the cord cut on the
astronaut's spacewalk.

About a month after my mother's stroke, I asked if she
would like to go to the hairdresser's. She said "I believe about
your cake climb the wall." I assumed that she did not want to
go, that the prospect of re-entering the world in her condition was too daunting. But she soon began to cry and beat
her good fist on the table, upsetting a water glass and soaking
the TV Guide. She was desolate. When I tried to decode
what she had said, I thought the hairdresser's would "take the
cake" because she was "climbing the wall" to get out, but
when I took her there, she refused to go in. Perhaps she

changed her mind on the way over, perhaps I decoded erroneously in the first place, I didn't know. Our transmission lines were down, and there seemed little I could do to repair them.

The Sunday she refused to go to church, I got scared. She could see and hear the priest, accept communion, pray, enjoy the Catholic panoply of hymns, gold-brocaded vestments, solemn silences and murmurs. She has always been a pious woman, dedicated to her church. But perhaps she now feels too much like the spectacle, the welted Willy in the pew. Had Willy eaten his pride until there was nothing left? How much can we eat at the end of our lives when things go sideways? Could my mother swallow enough to find some joy? I didn't know because she can't tell me and the signals I get—the tears, the sudden sweeping of books and papers onto the floor, the lethargic submissions—are too broad to be interpreted into change that might help.

When I went home one evening, mother was lying on the sofa in the dim livingroom light. I greeted her nurse in the driveway, but she didn't respond. We hired Gladys because she could stay late on the evenings I made some deliveries. She was a retired nurse who lived alone. She was kindly in a stern, quiet way, would do little things for patients to make them comfortable, but her face was impassive.

I was a little late, and she must have been waiting by the door. Photo albums were on the table, pictures of me when I was young, friends of hers I had never met, a few of my father in hats now distantly out of date. Many had been taken out and were piled in the center of the table. The nurse must have been trying to make her feel better. The room felt cold, so I got a blanket and put it over my mother. Her eyes were set in dark circles, her mascara was smudged. The TV was on but the sound was off. An almost full cup of tea and her glasses were on a low stand beside the sofa. She could not remember the word for pillow and pointed at the small one beneath her shoulders. I got one from the linen closet, put a case on it, and then stood for some time in the dim light with the pillow in my hands. There was no word for this kind of pillow.

When the plastic streamers and bell came into the shop, I had almost forgotten about them. I'm not sure why it took so long to get them in, perhaps they arrived and sat on the counter till the boy finally remembered what they were for. I had no idea where Willy lived after his mother died and the house was sold. I got the directions to Willy's place from the manager at Safeway, for he has had to take Willy home a number of times. His apartment was on the ground floor. Torn green fiberglass awnings covered the entrance, and outdoor carpet ran from the patio into the hallways. The doors were scratched and scuffed, some with dents and multiple locks. The walls were a dirty pale-green. It was ten in the morning when I rang the bell. He answered the door naked, a towel over his shoulder, his hair wet. A pyramid of empty pop cans stood against one wall, all the labels turned exactly the same way. He had an orange vinyl chair, a TV, the tricycle I had bought him was parked in the living room.

"Willy, I brought these over to put on your bike. Is it okay to do it now?"

"Yes, good, come in. Those Seahawks are going to get kicked again. Goddamnit, the bastards. What do they make all that money for?"

"You go ahead and get dressed while I do this, okay?"

"Ya, ya, I was just going there."

I got a good look at his welts. They were primarily on his face and neck, some sprinkled across his shoulders, but none extended below his nipples. I wanted to ask him about them, but didn't want him to have to recall something so unpleasant, though they might have been a natural pigment malfunction. Seeing them in their entirety, their random speckled pattern, made them seem less grotesque, less the product of some malevolent intention.

The boy at the bike shop told me how to put on the streamers. The bell was easy. I also brought over several reflectors for the spokes. I had brought my few tools and the job was almost done when Willy came back out, fully dressed, except for his shoes.

"It's going to rain today and there's traffic backed up on the interstate. Thirty percent chance. Goddamn Seahawks, goddamn it."

"Do you like your bike now, Willy?"

He walked over to it. Put his hand on the seat, patted the handlebars, pulled the multi-colored streamers falling from the handles, allowing them to brush lightly across his hand like a woman's hair. He clicked the bell. It had a different sound from his last one, but the more he clicked it, the more he seemed convinced that this was going to work. He grinned, ringing the bell, nodding his head like a fan at a rock concert.

"Ya, ya, ya, it's good," he said, ringing it, then smiling brightly.

I thought of the pictures on my mother's table. Perhaps Gladys didn't get them out. Perhaps mother was reading the only texts left her to read that related significantly to her life, unlike the television which was a world of orchestrated, charmed moments full of expensive interiors and model faces whose problems were neatly solved, comically shriven, every half hour. Her own world was now a collage of pictures she had to try to put into a sequence that paid some homage to order. They were her passport into the world of intelligibility, where she could still wear a large hat and tell a story, and her friends and husband brushed the dust off their shoulders and smiled back into the long-forgotten lens.

I had left my mother alone. She is quite capable of taking care of herself for short periods of time. She can't cook and is in fact dangerous around the stove, and I worry about her attempting the stairs alone, for they are metal and slate and a fall would be trouble. But if she knows I am coming back soon, she is content to watch television or knit. Her right hand has recovered enough agility for her to do that. Our first visitors were surprised when she came to the door. She used to wear her hair in a loose bun, but since the stroke she wears it long and straight and it appears much grayer. She doesn't often wear her bridge and the gaps in her teeth are unsettling when one remembers her old vivacity, the prim and exact outfits, her bubbling charm. And her languagelessness makes her seem grief-stricken and more aged.

When I arrived back at the house, I was thinking of the pictures, how I might try to understand, through these windows to the past, a way into the future. It is strange how one thin ratchet of time can so change us. It's like passing through a portal or tunnel into an utterly altered landscape. My mother's house, the house of my childhood, with its slanted drive and sloping lawn, its picture windows and flagstone walkway to an ivied door is now strangely alien. The place that holds my memories, the thousand secrets of my childhood, is now but a house of dangers on a cold and friendless street. Visitors have stopped coming by because the rush of unintelligible words is more than they can bear. They listen and talk and soberly pretend that their conversation has some purpose and direction, but the experience is so unnerving that they do not wish to repeat it. When I think of my divorce and the way my wife and I only pretended to understand what we were saying to each other for the last few years of our married life, I believe that conversation with my mother is a metaphor for all our communication, that only a few words out of whole paragraphs actually leak through in a way that seems to matter. That all of us are Willys on our tricycles, ringing our bells, cursing the Seahawks and the news. That we can't listen because the machinery of our own lives makes such a racket in its daily functions. But this is a glib metaphor constructed by a mind still capable of glib metaphors. For my mother the ground for language's metaphors has dropped away, has become loose and chaotic, as ambiguous and ill-defined as a moonscape.

When I walked into the kitchen, Gladys and my mother were sitting at the table. I was surprised to see her, for this was not a day Gladys had been scheduled to work. She was wearing jeans and a light green sweatshirt with three little bears on the front who danced above three pink hearts. Her blue eyes looked up at me, and she said Sit down, have some pie. From a lidless cardboard box, she pulled out a boysenberry pie with a perfectly embroidered crust, a five-pointed star of purple holes forked into its face. My mother sat in sweatpants and an Irish cardigan with wooden buttons, a sweater she'd favored for the last week or so. Her hands were folded in front of her and her face seemed illumined from within. Her grey lank hair fell from the part, covering one side of her face. I wondered how Gladys knew boysenberry was mother's favorite. My grandmother had raised these berries and sold flats at Presley's Grocery. She also sold pies to Carlyle's. She achieved a local fame and the berry-raising and baking had been mentioned in her obituary which my mother had cut out and kept in a scrapbook that also included pictures and postcards. How could Gladys have known? She's not even from here. She came with her husband four years ago and he died of cancer soon afterward. She could not have known about my grandmother, and that scrapbook is in the drawer under the TV.

When Gladys cut the pie and eased out the wedges and placed them on the plates, my mother's eyes followed each movement like a cat watching the twitches of a string. The berry filling was almost two inches deep and thickened so that a wedge rested on a knife without leaking berries. My mother clapped her hands silently, her mouth wide open, as the slack skin around her eyes aged backwards and seemed to gather color.

"Oh, my, oh my," she said, "thing wonderful."

Gladys did not take a piece for herself but sat and watched us. The pie-face seemed to be eating its own past, a stain of sweet berries on its lips. My mother was genuinely happy. Her lips smacked as she ate and a dribble leaked out of her mouth on the stroke-stricken side. Her eyes had a faded alertness which did not seem real to me, having known the old vivacity they once admiraled with such adroitness, such tactical cleverness. The powdery wrinkles, her hair, her exaggerated happiness, the gapped empurpled teeth exposed in her wide smiling, seemed pathetic and awful. The purple dribble on the right side of her mouth widened and elongated until Gladys, without missing a word in her lopsided conversation with mother, leaned over the table and wiped it off casually. Gladys talked seriously, allowing the nonsense, the swells of incomprehensibility to slide by. To me this kind of conversation with my mother was maddening, but Gladys seemed to sit in the sun and let these insects buzz imperturbably by.

Last week my mother was stuck on water. She kept saying she needed water, but when we gave it to her, she shook her head, and said no, no, and cried. She needed water all week and nothing I tried worked, nothing satisfied that simple subject-predicate equation. At first I thought it was like Willy's "not pretty," some emotion-meter stuck at a particular reading, but it was deeper than that, wider, more encompassing, more exasperating. Before that it was shoes, and before that pants. Language is like our hands, without them you have to learn everything anew: scratching our noses, feeding ourselves, buttoning a shirt, opening doorknobs and windows and pill bottles, putting on socks, wiping our asses. What is water in this new language, or pants, or shoes? It's like getting a prosthesis that never fits. This kind of interpretation is beyond me. It is like trying to sculpt with mercury, any movement modifies the medium and shapes shift.

"I saw Willy's new bike and he likes it very much. It was nice of you to think of the streamers," Gladys said suddenly turning her attention to me. My mother was through with her pie and I had barely touched mine.

"How do you know Willy?" Of course, most people

know who Willy is, he's a town fixture, but how did she know about the streamers?

"He's my nephew. I've known him since he was a baby. He's one of the reasons we moved here."

"You must be Beatrice's sister?" I said in that way small town conversations both seek to understand connections and make in-group validations. I could see the resemblance now, in the cheekbones and lips.

She was Beatrice's younger sister, and after her own children were raised and off to distant states earning a living with their spouses, she had moved to be nearer Beatrice and to help out with Willy, for she knew he could be a great worry for her. She now checks on Willy every other day and has found a "renewed resolve," an underlying purpose for the "bounty" of her "mature years." I found this language quaint for someone who had worked in nursing homes and could cleanup shit while eating a sandwich. How does one adhere to personal codes of decorum that are sweet and uplifting and at the same time function so adroitly in the messy world of sweat, cries, and bedsores? It occurs to me that we are opposites: I am all educated doubt, with a library of historical injustices for every color of man and woman on earth, have seen the awesome pettiness and cruelty at the center of the human heart, but am protected by a "supersensible soap bubble," as Schopenhouer has said, refracting rainbows, sunny smiles, earnest handshakes. Gladys, on the other hand, willingly reaches into the rot of everyday life and pulls out pies, lotions, backrubs, and dancing bears with hearts.

Eight months later when my mother died, I was not at home, and for that I felt a chillingly deep gratitude, both for the death itself and also missing the awful moment when her heart failed and her face shuddered and fell into that inert opacity of the end, where finitude and infinity become one in the blinklessness of an eye. Gladys was there and was famously discrete about details of my mother's passing. She said my mother felt uncomfortable, had a headache or what she deciphered to be a headache, and after Gladys called 911, mother died in her bed. According to Gladys, it was "very peaceful" and a "nice way to go."

I became immediately preoccupied with the arrangements: the cremation, funeral, contacting the old priest to say the mass, food preparations, writing the obituary, flowers, contacting our relatives, cleaning the house for our visitors after the funeral, choosing Biblical passages. This carried me all the way to the hour of the funeral. It is customary at most Catholic funerals for the family to stand in the foyer and welcome guests as they come through the door. I did not feel like doing this and, besides, I had some last minute duties to complete before the mass started. I had asked a cousin to carry the cruets of wine and water to the altar before communion, but I needed to show her where they were kept and tell her what signal the old priest would give her. I also had to go over the cues for the readers and organist. We were to sing "Ave Maria," "When Irish Eyes Are Smiling," and "Amazing Grace." At first our parish priest, who is French, objected to "Irish Eyes" as being too secular, but the old priest finally talked him into it.

I don't, now, remember much about the ceremony itself, other than it seemed to go quite well. In the morning the day was gray and a light rain fell, but it stopped before the funeral started. Everyone hit their cues perfectly, the readers didn't stumble or mispronounce anything, and the singer had a particularly fine voice. He had been requested by my mother several years ago, but I had forgotten the aching melancholy he could find inside himself for "Ave Maria" and "Amazing Grace." He was a small, thin, bearded man in a long-sleeved plaid shirt, black dress jeans, and a large western belt buckle. He folded his hands, palms up, like a choirboy. The old priest had had a stroke himself and the right side of his mouth hardly moved when he spoke. He looked as if he had been to see a Novocain-happy dentist. Yet his speech was clear and measured with that Irish roll of the r's and that slight hesitation on the strongly accented syllables. His deep voice was soothing and sincere. His homily was about the "mystery of suffering" and how it is a call to witness Christ's sacrifice for us, and by suffering we enter the holy mystery of God's love Who does not punish but merely allows these opportunities to happen, and we are brought closer to His side the way a mother is closer to her sick child in those deep hours of sleepless worry and concern, in those quiet countless ministrations to bring comfort and solace to the ailing one. Suffering is a beautiful mystery where we witness Jesus, the blessings of the church, and the full power and glory of Love itself. The priest's own stroke seemed to give resonance and vigor to his little essay, and he sprinkled details about my mother's difficulties through his text to ground it in pity and wonder, but I felt it was mostly colorful wrapping and bright bows on the box that contained my mother's ashes. My mind drifted during the mother metaphor to the story in the newspaper the week before about the mother who couldn't stop her child's crying and shook the poor thing into paralysis and ultimately its death.

But when I looked up from this guilty vision, I saw how many people were in the church. Several hundred had come to pay their respects to a nearly eighty year old woman. I saw my cousin, Alex Dillinger, the sports psychologist, with his wife and two kids, all looking neat as needles. Claire Wilson was there with her twin Maribelle; they lived together on Sprague and used to work with mother on the Altar Society. The Goodrows, the Benders, the Smiths were there. I saw Gladys and Willy in the east wing of pews near the back. Willy was nicely dressed and played with the red felt pagemarker in his hymnal. Gladys's hands were folded and her head was bowed as if the homily were a prayer the old priest was chanting. Many people I didn't recognize were there, and I thought about how attracted people were to my mother's good humor, her chronically uplifting cheer, that self-critical hyperbole that rendered the fantastic and absurd with a serious poise. I have been to other funerals of people in their eighties where you could count the mourners on one hand. Humor is a balm to the tribulations that daily beset our best intentions, and people tend to honor the voice that lightens, at least temporarily, their burdens.

In the Catholic funeral tradition, the family members are escorted out first. As I walked out into the foyer, distant relatives and friends I hadn't seen in many years came forward. As they began filing out, many hugged and kissed me on the cheek, and offered condolences. After the third or fourth one, I suddenly began to cry. At first I tried to discretely wipe the tears away with a sleeve, but as I leaned into the shoulder of one man or woman after another, something inside me broke and ran like the waters of Meribah. When a close high school friend, now an English professor, seemed to seize up and blush as my arms reached out to his shoulders, past his outstretched hand, I held him there, leaving a dark blotch on his blue jacket. Tears were dripping off my cheeks, and in that helplessness, I crossed some inner threshold that was beyond language or explication, beyond solace itself, and into a segment of time and space from which there is no advance and no returning.

When I came out of the church to go to the interment at St. James Cemetery, it was warm and the sun made the tops of the cars shine. The streetlamps in the parkinglot dripped beads of brightness. Steam rose off the asphalt and smelled like hot wet sauna cedar. A black limo waited at the curb, its chrome decorations glistening. The driver was in a black wool suit with a red tie, a black overcoat and gloves, standing at attention beside the door, waiting for me. On the sidewalk leading toward the town soccer fields and playground, I saw Gladys and Willy walking home. She was carrying his sport jacket over her left shoulder, her right hand was waving him back. He was on his tricycle ahead of her, ringing and ringing his bell, leading the way into the mystery.

The driver opened the door with his black gloves, and it snapped shut in that secure, satisfying way of solidly made vehicles. The ashes were to be buried near my father in a private ceremony. The driver sat upright and spoke in a serious, formal tone as if decorum had a very narrow band-width. The long, roomy car was empty and black with silver handles and window-buttons. I watched the people on the street as we passed. A retired philosophy professor in orange slacks and a brown plaid sport coat was pulling a wagon loaded with bound newspapers. A boy in loose pants and sneakers was riding down the street on a skateboard, bouncing a basketball. A pair of German shepherds was stuck together in someone's yard enclosed by a pink picket fence. I remember a middle-aged man sitting on a bench in front of Winegar's Drive Inn eating a hamburger very attentively, which made me, suddenly, quite hungry.

After the graveside service, the limo was taking me back to the church.

"You ever been asked to pull into MacDonald's after one of these things?" I asked the driver.

"No, Mr. Murphy, I haven't. Are you hungry? I have a sandwich under the seat here."

A lunch was being served at the church, and I knew we didn't have enough, given the unanticipated number of people at the funeral. I asked him to pull over at a drive-in on the edge of town which advertised DAGWOOD BURGRS & FRIES, inside blinking blue lights. The parkinglot was oiled gravel, and chainsawed bear and eagle sculptures were for sale on a grass island. I couldn't help but think that mother, the one before the stroke, would have found the polished limo at this drive-in and the amorous dogs funny, would have found a story they could fit into at a party.

I ordered the burger special.

"What kind of drink would you like with that, Sir? It comes with a medium-sized soda." I guess my black suit and red tie made me look like a Sir. I thought of ordering a boysenberry milkshake, but then said, "Water, just water."

The Far-Off Herd

"The heights of heaven were no safer than the earth."
                    —OVID

THE BLOOM'S PRIME

I.

Avery sits on a bench near the bridge watching the pattern of light and shadow the willow casts on the water. There are lanes in the grass along the ditch-bank: one bright green, the other brushed with silver. A robin near a molehill tugs on a worm. Avery is an art history major and is, at the moment, charmed by the Viennese of the 19th century who painted peasants in their elaborate and colorful costumes. Her father has a fine art collection, and the book in her lap, one of his, is turned to Waldmûller's "The Interrupted Pilgrimage" where a sick girl lies in the grass on top of a pass and the mountainous panorama, the faces and costumes, are exquisitely rendered. She likes the classical sense of composition, the order and perspective. The writer had been criticizing the "sentimentality and opportunism" of the painters, and she stopped to wonder why. The painters had preserved a now lost era, their technique was flawless, their palettes bold, and each character fully individualized. But were they peasants or friends of the artist posing as peasants? She didn't know. But "opportunism," wasn't that too harsh? Was this Mrs. Boye in Jacobsen's *Niels Lyhne* who while in Naples posed wearing an Albanian peasant's costume and was painted with an urn on her head and a little brown boy holding her hand? No, nothing so silly. They were real peasants in real houses. She is sure of it. Besides, she loves the beautiful costumes and Waldmûller's tribute to peasant art. As her hands rest on each page of the book, the water slides amicably by.

Through the leaves of the willow, she sees a man sitting in the grass. He is wearing light-blue jeans and a green long-sleeved shirt, rolled above his wrists. He has long curly hair and glasses, his legs are crossed in a lotus position. She watches him stare into the water. Is he meditating? Does she know him, has she had classes with him? From this distance, he looks faintly familiar.

She is about to turn the page back to "The Man With The Magic Lantern" and the gathering of peasants who marvel at the new device when the first rose floats by. It is near her side of the bank, but out of reach. A just-opened bud, deep-red like the apple she ate at lunch. Its stem is cut at a diagonal, the leaves pruned to a delicate pattern. It must have come from William's florist; she has seen that pattern before.

Who threw it in? Avery imagines a woman standing on the bridge where the water enters campus. The bridge is arched and narrow, for foot-traffic only. The concrete walls are topped with rows of bricks on edge. The woman leans on the bricks watching the water pass beneath her. Is the rose a kind of prayer? Has she just gotten news that her old high-school boyfriend was killed on a motorcycle, the crazy-man, the snowboarding maniac, the adrenaline addict who got drunk at a party and headed off angry because his friends told him not to ride his new bike, tried to take his keys? Her flower trades waste for waste, a song in a windstorm. Avery thinks of Jace, her old boyfriend, his eyes, the way he used to look at her when she stepped back from him, slowing his momentum, that head-long on-rush of energy and certainty. She had seen death in them, and it had scared her. She had stepped further back.

When the rose and chrysanthemum came by with crossed stems, she shut her book, turned it, and pressed the spine into her lap. She could see other flowers further up-stream, the beginning of a cryptic message. The woman on the bridge was symbolically relinquishing, exorcising. She saw it clearly: he wishes to make up for some misperception or misdeed—a kiss at a party, say—and she hates that he believes she can be so easily mastered by trite tokens, yet secretly she wishes she could be, that she could allow herself a luxuriant forgiveness, to give in to the free-falling ease that this leap of faith requires, but she's a hard student of human nature and knows one lapse foretells another, one acquiescence or capitulation narrows the necessity for the next until she sees herself bereft of herself, a discarded flower floating down some canal, too far from shore for anyone to retrieve. The crossed stems, an admission that what they have is impossible to sustain.

Avery smiles at herself. Perhaps all the flowers had been thrown in together and the arrangement was merely the accident of current and the interference of grass along the bank. She almost laughs at the drift of her mind that runs out into the ocean of possibility and must always come paddling back to shore. What a quicksilver thing it is!

When the last rose comes by, she cannot help but fit it into the plot she had spun: it was the last lonely gesture, the period to the sentence, a blown kiss at a blown kiss. She smiled again. Why is tragedy the first picture in any mental album we open?

Perhaps the explanation of the flowers was quite simple: this was Friday, the woman was going home for the weekend, she had been given a bouquet, they'd kissed, set their next meeting. So the flowers would either embalm an empty room for three days, their water thickening and stinking, or they would spend hours in a car and prompt questions and looks from her parents, force the explanations and announcements she did not want to make. She had stood on the bridge in a kind of satisfied ecstasy, the effect of his demonstration of love was complete and the casting was a gesture of bounty, of generosity: someone else might pick them up and the good fortune, the love, would be passed on. The woman, a Christian like herself, was full of hope and blessings. This was her donation to the cause of love, romantic or brotherly, a dollar in the poor box. Each sent a small ripple of feeling out into the world. The woman felt that she was beyond the need for tokens, that their love expanded beyond what a flower could express, yet they were lovely nonetheless.

Yet how much of this fullness, this sense of bounty and beauty, was the result of bounty and beauty, now, right now, at this very minute in her life? Was it possible to feel this expansiveness when the flowers did not come, when the words did not come? Smile and the world smiles too, but the sigh, the tears, are on a bridge, alone, on a Friday afternoon.

There it was again, that glide toward the solitary, the sadness. What in us always goes there?

The man is standing up and coming her way, walking deliberately on the grass rather than the sidewalk. He no longer seems familiar. His gait has a fixed but casual rhythm as if conscious of connoting ease. The book swings loosely in his hand, a gloomy novel no doubt. He is oddly handsome, probably an English major who likes the Beat poets, smokes marijuana, enjoys long rambling abstract conversations and writes poetry himself. He is the kind of man who sits in a corner at a party analyzing the snippets of conversation he overhears, who quotes lines to himself from poems, who dreams of having his name on a book, sees himself alone in a disinterested, even uninterested, universe and wants to know more about Buddhism. His party quips, lightly superior, protect an unsteady sense of self.

His curly, messy blond hair, wire-rimmed glasses, and that wrinkled shirt are probably a disguise. Perhaps his father owns a Ford dealership and has carlots in five cities, so the wrinkled shirt is a statement against excessive consumption, large houses, and extensive lawns and gardens that require too much water. Perhaps he sees himself as the man bringing his magic lantern into his father's carlot world? He is invention, inquiry, passion, and his lantern is hope, the lotus. But in a world full of technological marvels, what is the lantern-man but a fool to the carlot crowd, a quaint aberration, lawn-art?

The way he looked at her as he passed, his nod and smile, seemed sincere. She noticed that after their eyes met, his didn't go immediately or even surreptitiously to her breasts. He was cordial but airily abstract. Probably didn't even see the flowers in the water.

As he walks down the path, she watches the way his butt moves, his lean full strides, the triangle his back makes. She stands and looks at herself in the water, touches her blouse and wonders what is wrong with her breasts and why he seemed so arrogant.

II.

Matt sits in the grass outside the Language & Literature building, Pushkin in a new translation is upside-down in his lap, the distant ratchet of a sprinkler, the slow secretive slide of water at his feet. He is a Russian Studies major and has finished his classes for the day. Pushkin is something to nibble on during the stillness of a late afternoon amid the smell of cut grass and the shuffle of footsteps on the sidewalk leading to the library and its parkinglot. He sits in the sun, at the edge of the willow shade, because this is the first hot day of spring and the wind is not blowing. A pair of mallards feeding by the canal's edge repeatedly plunge their heads into the water and he can see their paddling orange feet, the ripple wedges they create. Sometimes they form an M, sometimes double inverted V's like a chevron. Silvio the marksman has just put a second hole in the painting of a "Swiss landscape," and Matt has stopped reading to think about the painting. Was it mountains and a lake, or a hilly pasture with cows and a rutted lane? Had Pushkin himself imagined that painting and erased it for the economy of the story or was it perhaps one his family owned at Boldino and thus required no imagination, only a touch of the familiar to keep the momentum of the story going?

Matt was in Ellensburg thinking about a Russian thinking about Switzerland when the first red rose floated by. It was a deep crimson like a ripe Bing cherry; perhaps it was the Count's cherries that made him associate the two, the ones he ate during the duel with Silvio. The flower had been cut with over a foot of stem, a few green leaves zagged up its stalk. It seemed early in the year for such long-stemmed and perfect roses, but he wasn't a gardener and didn't know if roses bloomed early or late in spring.

He thought the floating rose might be the product of a man's fanciful wish, a fellow student, a lover standing on a bridge donating a flower to a memory, an attachment to someone beyond his reach. Had she left school and town, had she merely chosen another? It was a kind of penny in a well, a sentence on a star. He watched the flower drift on the still water, riding the stream so effortlessly there was a fixed serenity riding with it. It seemed to be sitting on a window, the smallest margin held within the glass, the way a cyber rose can seem almost three dimensional. He had an urge to jump in, retrieve it, to do some honor to that dark impulse rather than have it float to the screen at the end of campus and be pitched into a refuse pile with willow branches, sticks, clumps of grass, textbooks, and dead fish.

He tried to see the student who threw it in. Is he thin and broody, unshaven, his hair tangled and needing a wash? Is his shirt wrinkled like his own, a thrift store necessity, as his was? He must also work evenings and weekends—a health food store, or Spot Janitorial vacuuming law offices? Did he favor Dostoevsky to Pushkin? Or Chekov? Yes, Chekov. Matt's mind had just shifted to the *Cherry Orchard* and that doomed aristocratic idleness that was too lazy to pick a cherry or prune an orchard when the second flowers floated by. A rose and a white chrysanthemum at the prime of its spiky bloom. They twist in a slow arc like slices of pie in a case.

A rose and a chrysanthemum. The man he imagined must now change because behind the chrysanthemum are three more flowers—two red roses, one white chrysanthemum. Anger threw them in, not an idle wishing. Perhaps he saw her get into a car with another man. He had just come from the florist's shop, the box in the backseat. She was the kind of woman who wore her hair up, put on glasses and a stern look when she went to class, asked trite questions with an earnest intensity, but whose pages were empty, her books scarcely opened. On Wednesday, Friday, and Saturday nights, the hair came down, the make-up on, along with the spaghetti-stringed tank top that revealed a small butterfly tattoo on her left shoulder, the tight low-rise jeans that showed the ring in her navel, the high-heeled sandals and polished toenails. It was their first month anniversary, and the bouquet was for after dinner. She had kissed the driver lightly on the cheek, reached over to shut the door, and scooted in next to him. The flowers, which had been a joy a few minutes before, were now poisoned, a chorus of grim laughing heads in a box.

Matt hears the rhythmic thudding of the leather against concrete before he sees the athlete who is wearing blue sweatpants, black tennis shoes, a blue and white sweatshirt. Perhaps the man who threw the flowers was just such a man. After hours of agonized judging and weighing and calculation, he had decided to buy them for the girl at the 18th Street Deli who served him slices of pizza. She was talkative and easy around him, touched his shoulder once when she delivered his order, letting her hand rest there. He's ashamed of flowers and what they say against the power in his legs, the height of his leaping. The flowers were a claim, a little flag plunged into all his unclaimed and undiscovered territory.

A short while later, after a carload of his teammates passed, whistling and laughing, and angered by the invasion and revelation of his privacy, he tossed them. Angry at himself, at the waitress for putting him in this situation, at that weakness the flowers caused.

But did that explain, really, the last rose riding at least a full minute behind the group of three? The athlete's impulsive disgust wouldn't allow sentimental stragglers. What happened? Did one fall to the grass and need to be re-thrown? But the ditch is wide and he is an athlete, his aim would have been true.

Tired finally of his own speculation, Matt turns back to the Pushkin in his lap, that world of intricate classes that the Table of Ranks delineated in 1722, Peter's scheme to get the nobles competing for civic duties, defining fourteen divisions, the eighth of which allowed one to be called a noble. Even in a deliberately classless society there were invisible layers and levels. As he sat in the grass and the ducks bobbed and their orange feet paddled the moving surface and the water slipped by, his heart secretly goes out to the man of his imagination standing on the bridge casting flower after flower into that reflection of his future that stared back at him like the powerful words of a writer from the past. He finishes the story that left Silvio, the great marksman and lonely traveler, dead in the Battle of Skulyani, the Count sitting comfortably in his library with his loving wife. He shut the book, suddenly hungry.

Walking towards the bridge, he sees a woman sitting on a wooden bench, a book in her hands. She is wearing green Capris and a white blouse. Her brown hair is held back with a tortoise-shell clip on each side. Her right breast sways in an ample arc as she straightens her back and looks at him. They exchange glances. He nods as he passes. He can't see what kind of textbook it is but thinks she looks like a music major: disciplined, private, slightly eccentric.

She is so preoccupied with notes, measures and counter-measures, syncopated alliances that the world as it is—its water and light, its ducks and willows, its people—is but a backdrop, the lined paper on which the notes are transcribed. Yet her eyes had a soft charity about them as did her greeting. Perhaps her smile was designed to meet his wrinkled shirt and his thin face. He wonders what tune, what performance he might, now, be a passing part of.

A week ago he had participated in the "Take Back The Night" rally to protest sexual assault which made him acutely aware of how his own eyes traveled when he encountered any new woman. It was a habit he wished to break, so when her breast wobbled inside her white blouse, he felt a pang of shame and looked away. Yet there was something in her face he found suddenly and warmly attractive, contradicted by the boldness of her eye-contact, held a little too intently beyond the casualness of two people passing on an otherwise deserted walkway. Was she judging his wrinkled shirt, the length of his hair, Pushkin? What did she know about art? She probably wasn't a musician but a business major who saw the way he dressed as failure, a lack of drive and ambition. What arrogance. She probably thought he had been sailing the flowers toward her.

MISSING PERSONS

This is a story about an English department at any small university in America at the end of the 20th century. I am its narrator who, in our post-modern times, cannot be trusted, or at least cannot be trusted any more than you would trust some acquaintance, a friend even, for how well does anyone really know another? Where might the lines of trust be drawn? If the tragedies and disappointments of our era have proven anything, we know there is nothing beyond the last shadow of a doubt, that all things are gathering momentum for their final plunge into a nameless obscurity. Moments of trust are but precursors, perhaps even gauges, of how deep the abyss into which we fall is. How can we trust something that does not exist? Some would say that a narrator is a figment, some *ignus fatuus*, some chimera, projected by an author's mood, an ambience from his or her past, a feeble optimistic wish that encodes a future world, an ambitious hormone that bends an ear like a scout listening for the far-off herd. And you, the reader, are a little glass jar through which the light temporarily passes.

I thought that if I came forward and admitted that I'm unreliable, that my long acquaintance with academe has obliterated all objectivity, that my interests are tainted with a retaliatory vanity, I know you might view this as just another ruse, a dishonest honesty with designs on your sympathies. This would make you even more suspicious because you are used to feeling superior to most people, including all narrators. They sit like flies in amber as you twist the story, twist it this way and that, turn it before the loupe of your educated eye. Yes, that is what we've come to at the graceless end of the 20th century. You have been trained not to trust anything and for very good reasons.

But I would like to state at the outset that you *are* superior because you can change your mind. These words are footprints in cement, drying instantly behind me. A word dries as fast as you can read. As soon as someone enters the room, I must exit. I dry and harden like a sidewalk. I suspect that the self-pity bell has just been given a tinkle inside your brain, but let me continue. I am not the author's alter-ego, nor any part easy to identify except a certain *fin-de-siècle* world-weariness, a curious onlooker.

For years now, you have been sitting still for all kinds of foolishness. Gregor Sampsa with an apple stuck to his back, his sister's declining attentions; archie typing his little poems at night by leaping on the typewriter keys; Calvino and Borges slipping behind paper doors, slipping again, and again. So when I tell you I am just a bit of conscious-ness—just a trifle, like most people—you will not be surprised because very little surprises you any more. I know that an overlong preamble is tiresome and likely to cause you to quit even before you've begun, so let us begin.

This story is most ostensibly about a missing person, or perhaps missing persons, in the sense that each individual is composed of a variety of people rather than mere traits and behaviors. Given another arrangement of years and circum-stances the same characters may disport themselves in divergent and perhaps even wholly contrary ways. People have a style of being that lies beyond what psychologists might call a personality. But let me introduce Royce

Dickerson. He is a fiction writer who received a phone call and walked out of his office and has not returned. He has since become the object of much conversation, from empathetic to spiteful. He published a novel, *Grass Widows*, and put together a collection of stories. His style is minimalist with occasional flurries into psychological analysis that seemed a bit, shall we say, adorned. The protagonists are street people, hardware store clerks, a janitor for a company that made party paraphernalia, a man who fed mink, a man who put the rubber bands on the claws of lobsters, you get the idea. "Salt of the earth sorts," as he liked to say.

Royce has a wife and two children. He came to town three years prior to the sudden influx of retirees and computer-mobile yuppies that inflated housing prices and consigned subsequent professors to tract housing and apartments. He has a substantial Victorian house in the country. This fortunate timing made his departure all the more curious. Why would a man who seemed to have his life neatly shaped, who had had some success in the attainment of his dreams, who had labored for over a decade in the ivory halls of judgment just to get here, who had an attractive artistic wife and a loving teenage son and daughter, who had been regularly promoted and given merit raises, who was popular with the English majors, who had one of the largest offices with a panoramic view of the mountains, why would that man walk out the door, without so much as a word to anyone, and never come back?

Royce has a full head of black wavy hair which always seems windblown. He often wore jeans and a workshirt with four or five pens and pencils in the left breast pocket. His eyes are quiet and reflective, but his eyebrows animated them the way a grin works a mouth. They found a humor in what he saw and softened what might have been misconstrued as a harsh fixity of purpose. The Renaissance man, Dexter Cox, thought Royce's grades were too high which belied a native softness in both his acumen and his heart. He was a man unable to chew the stale truth and thus preferred artificial sweeteners. Royce, though, believed in rewarding potential and effort rather than strictly adhering to a standard of competence that was itself imaginary and arbitrary, suggesting an anal preoccupation with perfection, precision, order. He thought lapses of intensity and clarity, small errors in the forms of grammar, were integral parts of the mental landscape to be read. They signified something important about the way the student viewed his or her world and language's capacity to convey that world. In fact, Royce's grade averages were not much higher than Dexter's, perhaps two-tenths of a percent, but in Dexter's mind that was the difference between the Grand Canyon and Snoqualmie Falls.

Royce believes that we are often what we read. His favorite writers are Sherwood Anderson, Anton Chekov, and Eudora Welty. He thinks there is a humorlessness in much modern fiction which suggests that writers take themselves and their craft too seriously. Almost as proof of this perception, he photocopies stories from the newspaper such as "Endangered Antelopes of Indian Region Killed for Highly Prized Shawls," "Skagit Man, Trapped By Flood, Watched Logs Dash By," "Man On Motorcycle Killed By Searching Wife." He underlined passages like "a shahtoosh shawl is a royal wrap and the warmest natural fiber in the world" and "one of the things that made me maddest was to see them fool chickens hopping on a log and just floating away." He also photocopied political images like the one of an American soldier in full camouflage regalia, including little sprays of plastic leaves around his helmet, having his shoes shined by an old Panamanian man; the caption read "The Luster of Colonialism."

▲ ▶ ▼ ◀ ▶ ▼ ◀ ▲

Maxine Sothby hadn't much cared for Royce because he seemed to appeal to the counter-culture element amongst the majors who gave her the most trouble. She thought he left for the same reason she wanted to—the tedious, numbing obligation of reading the juvenile ponderings of the mentally delinquent. Concerned about developing lesions on her brain from reading 7,500 words of their crippled prose per week, she felt keenly the irony of one's love for literature and the endless reading of mangled sentences. In case she needed counseling, she saved specimens like these: (1) "The youth of today should not give thought to the idea of being intimate with a perfect stranger or even consider sexual relations with an extended partner without disease prevention devices." (2) "Surviving one's death is extremely painful but can be done." (3) "I didn't know eagles were extinct until I went to Alaska and saw them flying around." (4) "Genitally, I eased the window toward the sky." (5) "Tom in the *Glass Menagerie* works in a wherehouse, and Jim will drudge up Laura's fear of rejection." She herself had fantasized about leaving but knew in the subterranean recesses of her soul that this was her role in life, the place where she most belonged.

Maxine's specialization was women of the Romantic era. The univeristy has a small library, and the books she needs are somewhat difficult to find. She spends an ample quantity of time at the copy machine, usually early in the morning or late at night when there is no one around to keep track of how many copies she makes. For someone whose studied charm and wary repartee absolutely scintillate during the peak communal hours (10 to 2), she is a bit mean-spirited and bleak in the dark. She curses and actually kicks and slams. She is thin and gaunt-looking with hair neatly curled and set upon her head like a hat. She wears flowered dresses with plain-colored belts, a finely knitted shawl that is tied in the front. Her cheeks are heavily rouged, and she has tiny lips so that she looks somewhat like those late 18th century women who painted fake lips inside their real ones. Occasionally, small mother-of-pearl combs on each side of her head put parentheses around her face. She usually wears a filigreed locket with pictures inside. She showed them once to her colleague, Rita Oversby, who could not guess who they were. "Emily Brontë and Mary Shelley," Maxine said with an airy hauteur, a slightly withering disdain which was all the more searing because of its slightness. Her mock surprise said that they were actually President and Vice President of their century and she was intellectually mortified by Oversby's oversight. The pictures were miniature portraits from the writers' youths, and Rita's one comment was "Oh, they look so young, just like our students!"

Maxine has been working on Shelley's poems and is dedicated to proving that Mary's editorial decisions were better, more appropriate, more deeply understanding of her husband's work, and that the two succeeding *(unsucceeding,* as she likes to say) centuries of male marginalia obtusely and widely miss the mark. Male English scholars who specialize in the Romantic poets are testosterone-impaired and subliminally compete with Percy and delight in the posthumous power of manipulating his work; they are so set on judging it that they do not see it as it should be seen. Maxine has particular spite for William Rossetti who had the unmitigated temerity to fix uncouth rhymes, misspellings, metrical lapses, and punctuation. She felt that Miss Mathilde Blind was well-named, George Woodberry was a soured curmudgeon, and that Buxton Forman was an industrious little superintendent.

She felt that the work must be treated as a child newly born, slick with the wetness of birth, needy and dependent. Percy was an unspoiled genius, and she agrees with Mary that every line he wrote was "instinct with peculiar beauty." She has written all this to her friend at another university and shamefully admitted loathing this birth metaphor and all its trappings of domesticity and maternalism. She went on to describe the need to *conceive* of new metaphors (*there we go again*!!!, she noted), and that when she wrote her paper she would find them. Her kinship with Mary was divinely intuitive; she felt that she may actually be her, reincarnated. As fantastic as this may sound, something deep inside her wanted very much to believe it. She had underlined this passage from Mary: "Anyone, once attached to Shelley, must feel all other affections, however true and fond, as wasted on barren soil in comparison. It is our best consolation to know that such a pure-minded and exalted being was once among us." She had drawn a colossal exclamation mark in the margin, for she felt that barrenness in her own life, the poor earth-bound knuckle-dragging louts of her acquaintance were a tribulation devoutly to be missed. She had married her high-school sweetheart but divorced him because he was an embarrassment at faculty parties and cared not a jot for the poetry she admired most. He was a physical therapist; she so liked his long hours that she made them permanent. When she received $8,000 from her school, the Women's Resource Center, and the Whiting Foundation to fly to Oxford and examine the actual copies of Mary's and Percy's notes and manuscripts in the Bodleian Library, she was thrilled. It was like leaving earth and finding Hesperides, the Isles of the Blest. She was able to spend almost a month—July 3 to August 1, 1998.

Since her return, she has been a different woman. Her curses and kicks at the copy machine have subsided somewhat. She's been preoccupied and a bit dreamy. It is as if she were hiding something, and this change in character was an act of concealment. She had put on a habit like a nun so that her outward appearance protected her innerness; she had bowdlerized herself to move more independently and smoothly through the traps and locutions of social life in an English department. Today, when the Shakespearean scholar—a kind of Bowdler himself (academically speaking)—asked if she were "quite through making copies," she said, "Why yes, yes I am" and left. In the past, she would never have let a "quite" creep around like that. She would have built a doghouse out of it and put him in it. She would have said something like "O, brave new world" and let her look fill in the rest of the quotation.

▲ ► ▼ ◄ ► ▼ ◄ ▲

Yet it was an innocent "quite." Dexter Cox was a large man given to quaint affectations. It was his mission to pronounce every syllable in every word and scorn the malfeasant cretins who wallowed their way through everyday life dropping suffixes, eliding syllables, or misusing a word altogether. He said "bastion" with three very pronounced and distinct syllables and the first seemed to languish in the sun of his erudite attention; he eschewed the Philistines who put the accent on the second syllable of "harassment"; he excoriated the bumpkins who might pronounce "family" as if it had only two syllables. So his "quite" was merely a way of adding some air to his sentence; it would be rather pedestrian to ask simply, "Are you finished?" Maxine's retort would have surprised him the way the telephone can interrupt an afternoon snooze.

Dexter thought Royce's sudden departure was perfectly understandable. One can lead a fraudulent life only so long. Royce had been raised a Catholic and the guilt surrounding the sham of his professorial performance—the pitiful body of work that he had produced which to Dexter was over-bearingly romantic and solipsistic, his vulgar imitation of a working stiff, his peripheral contributions to academic committees, and the stunning ignorance of his own literary antecedents— ("Why he thinks Lovelace is a porno queen!")—merely made the obvious more apparent: he should clear out and leave the pond to the swans.

Albeit fussy in his diction and elocution, Dexter did not apply the same scrutiny to his physical hygiene. He was slightly near-sighted, and when he leaned close his breath could shrivel paper. He also had the habit of picking his nose in a distant scholarly way, especially when there was no one in the office, but never used the clean handkerchief folded snugly in his old Harris tweed jacket pocket, preferring the paper in the wastecan. There would be little dribbles of milk on his vee-necked sweaters or white curly hairs from his mustache. Or bits of his lunch.

▲ ► ▼ ◄ ► ▼ ◄ ▲

Rita would watch him bend over, the seat of his wool trousers glossy from long periods of sitting and grading papers. One eyebrow would raise slightly, almost imperceptibly. She was an English Education specialist and often photocopied cartoons of children at their desks making satirical remarks about their teachers. She was very athletic and told Maxine that she runs every morning at 6:00 just to have a good think. She worked out her day's plans and emotional ways of approaching things while her feet slapped the tarmac. She took Yoga classes two nights per week and worked diligently on centering, balancing, letting her opposite desires and impulses achieve harmony. This run also allowed her to register the weather and see if the masculine-sun-light mood dominated or if the moon-shade-feminine did. For her a person's butt was the symbol of his or her personality, the way the twin halves curved out and rejoined, the way they moved separately yet simultaneously like a perfect marriage. She saw the shoulders the same way, but they were always concealed by clothing. The butt, with its gluteal lift and sway, its pendulous pondering, was nearly as visible as words on a page or that frontispiece drawing in old books sheathed by a thin protective covering. Dexter was a man who was out of sync, right lobe dominant, more yang than yin.

Rita thought that Royce had left because he was also unbalanced. Not in the same way that Dexter was, however. Royce had full, even hemispheres. There was gluteal harmony, an enviable syncopation. Each hearkened after the other in symbiotic dependence yet retaining a rigid independence. They were like Donne's couple in "A Valediction: Forbidding Mourning" where the firmness of one made the other just; where if one roamed the other leaned but remained centered and fixed. The irony for her was that he seemed so outwardly dissatisfied: there was an inner agitation that needed to be resolved to fully achieve the harmony he already possessed. His leaving was merely the long-expected synthesis of body and soul, hand and heart, male and female, sun and shade. She knew with the surety of Cassandra that he had found a higher and better place.

Rita had to be careful with this passion of hers, this habit of butt-reading, for she feared it may be misconstrued. As in fact it was, for Dexter often made adjustments he didn't have to make. He would displace his perfect alignment just to be able to do it again. Human circumambulation as a response to having to wait for the Xerox machine is a curious thing. Intelligent people who have a clear sense of their mission in life are the worst. They shift their weight restlessly, shuffle their papers as if they were written in disappearing ink and may vanish soon. They maliciously eye the back of the one controlling the machine as if to generate enough heat to atomize and disperse the interloper. They tap the erasure end of a pencil, click their pens, doodle, make the smallest talk seem large in an easy off-hand way like a tennis player swatting aces while conversing with his partner. The young poet is especially bad, Seymour Renquist. This little dalliance in his day seems to cut into his productivity, and he grimly resents it. The more resentful and grim he gets the more intense and pushy his small talk.

Rita admires Seymour's butt immeasurably. He's well balanced. The sun and the shade complement each other. The male and female principles are conjoined amicably. She senses his impatience and often asks him to go ahead of her. She watches his busy ministrations astutely, musedly. He is athletic too, and spirit and body rhyme, passion and compassion, power and amour. He has a clean freshly-shaven look, a heavy dark beard that contrasts singularly with his pale skin. His hair is black and Byronic; though she has not read Byron, she does know he was a sexy rich English poet. She would be surprised to know he had a clubfoot. When Seymour leaned over the glass, she leaned too like a heliotrope. He wore jeans, bright shirts without ties, and sport coats. Sometimes he wore a necklace of beads that clinked when he adjusted his margins. He tried to cultivate the image of a free spirit, and occasionally he leaned toward the side of shabby as if to show how deliberately insouciant, how bohemian he could be.

When an art professor was charged with sexual harassment, Rita pontificated loudly about liaisons between faculty members and students, between faculty members, between faculty and administrators. Any violator should be immediately fired, few questions asked. She said this loudly and with gusto because Seymour was in the adjoining coffee room and needed to hear her opinion. It was also a kind of safeguard against herself. This was in the days before Maxine's "Bodleian experience," as a number of the faculty have begun to call this pivot in her personality.

"Just whack their dicks off," Rita said under her breath to Maxine who was in line behind her. They giggled and Maxine wriggled her right pinkie in the air which sent Rita into a paroxysm of stifled snuffles.

"Around here there isn't much to wack," Maxine said, keeping the snorting going.

"What's so funny?" Seymour asked, carrying his full cup toward the door.

"We were just talking about Kafka," Maxine, said smiling deviously.

Seymour felt the dismissive tone, the patronizing politeness. "The 'Metamorphosis'?" he asked trying to shift the tone, the atmospheric imbalance. He sipped his coffee knowingly.

"No, 'In the Penal Colony'," she said coolly.

Rita's poorly suppressed snort sent flecks of spittle over the glass of the copy machine, and Seymour forced a complicitous smile and watched his cup leave the room.

▲ ▶ ▼ ◀ ▶ ▼ ◀ ▲

Seymour is particularly fond of the Byzantine era. He took Yeats seriously about returning to Byzantium and joining "the sages standing in God's Holy fire," about creating a pure art devoid of artifice. Yet what he had discovered among the Byzantines was a savage autocracy where innocents were blinded, castrated, tortured, exiled, sent to the nunnery for political purposes or because of the emperor's ego, ambition, sexual pleasure, spite. The daily business of the empire was run by eunuchs and slaves. This realignment of his perspective resulted in his desire to write a book of poems about the real Byzantium. He has composed poems about the 30,000 people put to death at the end of the hippodrome revolt in the 6th century; the way Michael IV embraced the diseased and bathed and waited on them, how he built a refuge for prostitutes who had renounced their profession; the ineffable Zoe with her trenchant wit, sexual appetites, and work for the church (he made much in the poem of the mushroom miracle); the audacious Theodora who accepted the reins of the empire and ran a short but brilliant race; and Arslan the sultan who refused to flog Emperor Romanus to death after he had been captured because unlike Romanus he was impressed by the Christian virtues of forgiveness, humility, and grace. Seymour's poem portraits were composed in blank verse, but he had such difficulty publishing them that he began to doubt the wisdom of the project and his dedication to an art that was reviled by almost everyone in America, including his colleagues.

Seymour photocopied articles in newspapers about Brodsky's American Poetry and Literacy Project where Brodsky advocated putting poetry in motel rooms next to the Bible, in supermarkets, at factory gates, and in phone books. Seymour copied articles about the poet traveling around the country handing out 100,000 free poetry books during National Poetry Month. He photocopied all things relating to the Byzantine empire and seemed to have a special ire reserved for editorials that slandered English professors, perhaps because as a poet he felt like an outsider, some colorful facsimile. He would underline sentences like "John Thompson and education-minded coaches like him are more responsible for their kids' well-being than, say, English professors are for English majors. It's full-time mentoring, not a class or two a week, a test, and see you around." He would scribble in the margin "Guess what bench warmer got a D in composition!" He deeply resented the way athletes' characters were deified by sycophantic sports writers, parents, and coaches when a majority of his student athletes plagiarized, cut classes, had the intellectual curiosity of a doorknob, and sneered at poetry as if reading it were like standing in front of class swaddled in only a jockstrap. He had a Haitian proverb at the top of all his syllabi: "Ignorance won't kill you but will make you sweat a lot."

Seymour felt that Royce had abdicated because the

remuneration for his labor in the vineyard of sour grapes was but a pittance to what he could earn as a successful novelist. As a full professor he made $37,000, and he could get that as an advance on a well-timed book. Furthermore, he would not have to suffer the daily indignities proffered by illiterate students, corrupt administrators who held an unchecked and Byzantine power over the purse strings and worked assiduously at preserving their own jobs rather than representing the needs of students or faculty, and sniveling scholars who may understand Latin syntax but dismiss all writing in the twentieth century as the solipsistic outpourings of charlatans. Royce had quit to save himself—his writing career, his sanity, his dignity. Seymour envied that option because it was not available to a poet. He must valiantly withstand the tittering jibes tossed out by the likes of Maxine and Rita.

▲ ► ▼ ◄ ► ▼ ◄ ▲

Shelton is a burly man who rolls his long-sleeved Pendletons above the elbow, and the hair from his chest curls over the tops of his white tee-shirts. Maxine thinks he combs it so that it droops neatly, a calculated negligence across the top of his shirt. He has full lips and shaggy eyebrows. His beard is rarely trimmed. He has the ruddy appearance of having just chopped a cord of firewood.

Shelton put his manuscript in the tray, pressed the button to start, and flipped idly through the garbage to see what others had been doing—what knuckleheaded tests they had constructed, what bits of flotsam they'd retrieved from the literary sea, what samples of student inanity they'd chosen to congratulate or condemn. He farted luxuriously as he pitched it all back into the recycle bin. He was a Hemingway devotee and had done his dissertation on the African stories and had even hiked Kilamanjaro to get a sense of place, a feel for the prose. He wanted to sniff the scat of a leopard, to see the pink dust of the wildebeest, to hear the grim laughter of the hyena. He talked with the preternatural fatalism of Harry in "The Snows of Kilamanjaro" whose broken leg was slowly killing him. Impending death was a license to verbally flog his rich bitch wife for being rich and ruining his immense potential by making it too easy for him. Shelton regarded writing as the supreme craft: it required one's rapt attention, a giving over of one's complete inner resources—and all those pampered dough-belly bastards who wrote for the *New Yorker* could use a night staked to the flank of The Mountain. The logo on his course descriptions was *montani semper liberi* which (aside from his being from West Virginia whose motto it is) means mountaineers are always free men. Shelton was a world class traveler, a hunter, had whored and drank, had seen the blood of Viet Nam. Yet here he was serving the offspring, the mewling whelps, the drunken children begat by Microsoft millionaires who knew nothing of creative genius. He had been to the House of God, what the Masai called the mountain, and made it back with the golden tablets of his experience, yet all his students wanted to know was why they got a C- and not a C. They had the lethargic passion and single-minded self-interest of mating Galapagos tortoises. Last week one followed him into the Xerox room with a paper in her hands. She was nearly crying. Her angry frustration was subdued by an official regard for politeness and the hope of a better grade. She said, "But I don't understand how I can get a C when I did *exactly* what you told me to do. . ." Her finger pointed to the grade as if it were from an alphabet she didn't understand, and her paper trembled slightly.

"My policy is not to discuss it until you've had time to think about it. See me during my office hours tomorrow," he said, his back to her while he photocopied the paper of a student he suspected of plagiarism.

"But you don't understand, I need to talk to you *now.*" Her chin was tense, but her voice was severe and resolute as if she were demanding her rights in a court of law yet knowing the power and weight of the institution were against her. She thought, too, that if she played the role of a beleaguered feminist, if she asserted her rights in the face of a patrimonial dismissal, he would have to listen to her. It would be his duty.

"No, I believe it is *you* who doesn't understand. If you had bothered to read the course description I handed out at the beginning of class, you would know what the policies are. I'll see you tomorrow." He had turned toward her and used the fullness of his size and voice to make her wither and turn away. She flipped her ponytail indignantly and marched out of the office, her finger still pointing to that C.

"The little bitch needs a good fuck *exactly* the way she's read about it," he whispered to Harrold Driggers who had come in and was going through the tapes in the cassette cabinet. Harrold had a PhD in Applied Linguistics. His dissertation was on the metrics of Robert Hayden, but he was now working on Hemingway. He was counting the adjectives, adverbs, and nouns in every sentence of *The Sun Also Rises* and was plotting graphs about Hemingway's subordination, where in a sentence an adjective was most likely to appear, and his system of predication. He was dedicated, often the last to leave the building. He had developed a system by which to keep tallies without losing his place when he was interrupted. He thought about publishing it but decided to keep it to himself, perhaps to reveal later. Shelton felt that Harrold was something of a dilettante; he needed a little passion in his life, some verve and vim. He liked making crude comments to him privately, just to "shake him up a little." Harrold needed a good fuck too, which was Shelton's solution for many of life's problems, and was perhaps the solution for his own. He suspected that Harrold's interest in Hemingway was a sublimation, or perhaps a compensation. He thought Harrold secretly admired virility, yet he deliberately approached Hemingway like a surgeon sneaking up to cut off his balls. He was Peter Abelard's Fulbert. He wanted to emasculate dominant white male culture, to turn it into numbers and graphs, to siphon the passion out of it and see it as a twisted, flaccid thing.

▲ ▶ ▼ ◀ ▶ ▼ ◀ ▲

Harrold is a black homosexual who has a facility with languages, and has turned that skill into a career. He has precise diction and enclosed mannerisms. He often stands with his arms crossed, or walks with his hands in his hip pockets. Piqued, he would remonstrate against a cyclist who had sped through the breezeway that separated the wings of his building, "Young man, young man," he said with his righteous finger in the air, "do not ride your bicycle at such speeds through here, it's dangerous. You're going to hurt someone." He used "young woman" in the same way.

Shelton felt that Royce had left because of the sexual

harassment rules at the college. Sexual politics had so undermined common human interaction that living this sterile hypocrisy was intolerable. Sexual abuse was defined as any unwanted touch regardless of intention. If one's elbow brushed a nipple on its way to retrieve the OED, or cutting through the xerox line to retrieve a folder, then a citation could follow. A look could be perceived as harassing, regardless of the fact that women wore necklaces whose little jewel ended in their cleavage. He felt that Rita's spirited ogling of posteriors proved the obvious and sexist contradictions in the ways these rules were managed. To him, Royce had put his middle finger in the air, had strapped it to his ship's mast like the lumberjack in *Sometimes A Great Notion*, and sailed right out of this tweed-choked Sargasso sea.

Harrold, on the other hand, sees Royce's departure differently. Royce was merely responding to a latency in his character. Perhaps he had seen it in the eyes of others. Perhaps it was the recognition of an unaccountable strangeness when he tallied the events of any given day. The slow accretion of dailiness—the class preparation, the grading, the conferences, the writing of assignments, the committee meetings, the assessments of assessments—was a suffocation, a slow compaction of the rind around him. He felt squeezed into a smaller and smaller self until he finally exploded. He metamorphosed, shook out his wings and flew off. Harrold had felt the same way. He was required to wear his race and sexual orientation like a shirt and a pair of trousers, and in his daily representation, he had defiled both his race and himself, he had perjured them, had turned them into a kind of commodity, a common oddity. Royce had stopped representing himself and had finally decided to be himself.

▲ ► ▼ ◄ ► ▼ ◄ ▲

    Representation is one of the great critical conundrums of our time. Some artists think of it in the way creationists view secularists: those who do not subscribe are incomplete, spiritual homunculi, glib pedants. Abstractionists are the truly enlightened, the chosen, because they know form is an illusion, that any image dissolves into a thousand color-dots; any composition has a next frame which interprets, contradicts, befuddles the one on view; any choice is one of a world of choices and therefore selection is arbitrary, facile, egocentric; all things are aleatory, a dice-game of minutes and hours, now in the flux of the now; relationships are random collisions in a world of contingencies, butterfly wings toppling towers, scattering pollen, shuddering shutters; and our highest hope is to feel "in harmony with the disharmony of others" as one of Calvino's narrators (I met him at an illusionist's party) so aptly puts it. There are few rules of engagement because each image, scene, gesture is endowed with an inner volition that stumbles simultaneously toward and away from the reader, sometimes playfully like a rock kicked by a fellow traveler, sometimes painfully, sometimes plaintively like a head bowed into a rosary. A wilted rose, a three-legged dog, a shiny green apple, a loveletter in the gutter. All things happen at once, and the invention of our moods and perfect tenses only takes us farther and farther from the world. We are metaphysical aliens, and when a narrator faces the "immensity of the non-written," makes a gesture toward form, fixity, fact, he or she is pleading, demanding time of the universe, renewal of a minute, an hour, a day? Most crimes and achievements are just such pleadings. I, as your narrator, have a quaint, antique regard for the truth which, of course, is only another manifestly prejudiced focus on one issue rather than another. And isn't all reading a prodigal luxury?

However, having come this far, we must get on with it. I know you are thinking that this story so far seems but an outline, some sketch for a bigger, roomier house. The characters' names are a trifle too much, that one alone in a story would be okay, but for these names to congregate so brazenly pushes the boundaries of good taste; there should be more action, they should *do* something, shake the little pennants of themselves into the faces of other characters, punch some lights out, flirt, pitch a spotted metaphorical pig into the ebony tower, mate, scream, something!

I would like to say this is my story and you are just eavesdropping, but as we all know by now, without you I wouldn't exist, nor would any of these characters waiting for an ending so they can get out of the straight-jackets imposed by me and the whole left-to-right paradigm; the inevitable ontology licking its lips at the smell of phylology; the left/right brain alignment. So in my defense, I must say that these characters are borderline stereotypes, like some schizophrenics, and action carries with it risks, fearsome consequences; it is like a wind to a house of cards. Inertness is a prerequisite to preservation. So I appeal to your readerly expectations and assure you there is an end, a point, a denoument, a climax; this crude orthodoxy stems from my long association with the writer's Catholic childhood, but that, of course, is another story, or perhaps several.

▲ ► ▼ ◄ ► ▼ ◄ ▲

Two days ago, Shelton discovered Maxine's secret. She is in the habit of photocopying her journals for fear of fire. She keeps one copy at school and one at home. She saw this journal as an updated version of the commonplace books kept by schoolboys of the 17th Century. Hers was somewhere just left of Bacon's and right of Milton's. She was not so interested in a miscellany of elegancies, the "juggleries of words," by which one accouters the "palace of the mind"; no, her journal had three parts: the spontaneous spots of wisdom that would suddenly appear like jewels in a swine's snout, out of the muck and bother of her daily existence; the flippant and often caustic sexism of literary men, those little jibes that exposed so handsomely their fears and weaknesses; and her own literary travelogues. The loss of all her *in situ* observation and reflection—at the Bodleian ("what a wobbling house of bards"), Biscombe Manor, Keats's house, wandering the hills of the Lake District, the reconstruction of the rubble that is Tinturn Abbey ("the English! Such feckless and mercenary antiquarians with a peculiar relish of the absurd"), a lonely wind-tossed daffodil—would be the death-knell of her career and all her professional joy. She meticulously dates the entries in the upper right corner of the pages and keeps them in a black manuscript binder to perhaps connote to some janitorial posterity—should an untimely fatality occur—that this work is original. She has tried on various titles over the years: *Feminist field Notes* (inspired by a sense of scientific industry and meticulousness, the attractive image of a female Livingston bushwacking her way into history), *Max's Aide-Memoir* (she thought the odd alliance of culture and the commonplace fittingly described her, not to mention the subconscious connection to Max Gate, a place she had also visited), but she had finally settled on *Wanderings Unbound* (she liked the hint of Shelley, the little joke, the intimation that these jottings were the witty cerebrations of a wanderlust). Her name and address are typed at the bottom of the title page with a lavishly florid signature above; its jaunty and intricate vigor seems to share something with that mawkish 18th Century confidence in the inherent order of the world, in the potentiality and dignity of human endeavor.

Maxine no longer wore her coveted locket with the callow images of Mary Shelley and Emily Brontë face to face inside it. She now wore a tiny stoppered vial made of silver with an ornate Ottoman design: peacocks, leaves, and flowers daintily etched in a tightly woven mesh of images much like the panels separating the narthex from the nave in Greek Orthodox churches. One night after she had finished photocopying parts of her journal, she unstoppered the vial and dumped its contents into the palm of her hand. She held it up to the light, then placed it delicately on her tongue as if it were a host and briefly closed her eyes. When she took it out of her mouth, she held it up to the light again. The spittle made it shine.

She had gone to Keats House in Hampstead one rainy morning. Tremendous showers were followed by streaks of sunlight that suffused the sidewalks and crumbling edifices with an antique light, a Turneresque feeling of immanence touched by the glorious. She felt that something large and consequential was going to happen to her. Her heart was pounding, blocks before Keats House swung into view. She felt as if her body and spirit had disengaged, and her spirit floated slightly above her body, looking down. She could hardly feel her legs, and she was sure that if someone had suddenly snapped a photograph, her aura might be observed, an ethereal nimbus like the halos of the lesser saints in Medieval paintings. She felt radiant, and this realization produced a shiver of portentousness.

When she gained admission to Keats House that morning, there was only one person there. He was a student, thin-bearded and pale, dressed in jeans and a purple Guatemalan shirt. His coat, backpack, and ashplant leaned against a chairleg. She wryly noted his jejune glances, his furtive but determined perusal whose intention was merely to imbibe the original mind of the Odes, to perhaps access its aura, its bountiful milieu. She saw her own youth reflected back, and she gave him a liberal berth. Yet it was his presence that resulted in her discovery. In circumventing his privacy, she had herself been granted a serendipitous felicity. For in that instant of turning away, she had turned toward *The Cenci*, and she felt "like some watcher of the skies/ when a new planet swims into her ken." She presented her credentials to the docent and explained that she had come 2,000 miles to look at a few books here. The docent nodded understandingly, fetched it for her, and showed her how she was to use the book and turn its pages. Tucked deeply into the interstices of Act IV, scene iv, near where the voices cry "Murder, Murder, Murder," she found it. As she noted in her journal, *"it was slightly ragged on the left edge but cut clean on the right. Its curvature seemed to match the left hand. I held it to mine and determined it to be from the third finger, the ring finger. It has a faint nacreous opalescence when held to the light. It is yellowed but retains the pristine softness and native indulgence of an idle aristocrat. It was most probably a nail severed while Shelley was casually proofing the edition he wished to send his sympathetic friend."* In later entries she acknowledged that the fingernail could indeed have been Keats's, but she trusted that deep upwelling of passionate surety she felt in the presence of its discovery. To her, intuition had its own truth. It might be a slanted truth, but it was as much a resource as the truths of mathematics, physics, machines, and economics. And sometimes the power of the spirit, its unequivocal rightness, the way it seemed to click into place like a Tyrolean music box and emit a sensation decidedly close to music, was irrefutable and could not be fettered by facts.

While photocopying her journals, the machine heaved to a halt, and Maxine was forced to extract several sheets with dry ink congealed along their margins. She crumpled them with the angry delicacy of someone still aware of her dress and hands.

Rita has asked about the Ottoman vial, and Maxine merely replied that she found it in a flea market in Dorset. Harrold had also commented on it—he felt free to make such comments because he was somewhat exempt from harassment charges from women—but she had told him the same thing and would neither elaborate nor reveal its contents. While photocopying late one evening, Shelton had retrieved Maxine's soot encrusted page and read it. Like that famous Doylean sleuth, he surmised that Maxine had investigated the possibilities of cloning a Shelley to fill her empty nest at home and amend the patriclinous depravity that so troubled the world. If a gut can actually be busted, Shelton's would have positively detonated.

▲ ► ▼ ◄ ► ▼ ◄ ▲

The news of this secret as well as the enigma of Royce's disappearance achieved a kind of conclusion at the retirement party of Ethel McCarthy. Ethel had spent thirty-five years at this university, had raised two children, remained successfully married, had written three books (one on the mysticism of Richard Crashaw called "The Diversities of Chatt'ring Strings," one on the work of John Fletcher called "A Wife for a Month & Other Comedies," and one called "Grooms of the Bedchamber" about the two Thomas Killigrews). Her specialty was the 17th century, but she read willingly and amply in other areas.

She has not shared her opinion about Royce's leaving. In fact, she is not given to colleague-gossip and is more likely to expose a foible rather bluntly in front of the offender himself. Her tongue is rather like a hatpin amid the various tumescences that pretensions create.

She is a stout woman who has recently employed the use of a cane to aid her determined transport through the world. She wears navy blue frequently and her silvery hair has its retinue of mutinous malcontents which stand out as if they had been buffed by a balloon. Yet she doesn't seem to mind, and occasionally pats them as if to reassure herself that they haven't sailed off altogether. She speaks very directly and doesn't abide any "puling nonsense" (that is what she said to Rita when asked if she thought Shakespeare's work had really been written by a woman, Shakespeare's sister). She received her degrees the hard way and feels the new race of women scholars is pampered, self-indulgent, and angry with little to be angry about. They faint at the sight of a codpiece, castigate their fathers, and laud the small-minded drivel of some women writers who just happened to have had the luxury of taking up a pen in their idle hours, regardless of their talent. They choose these writers because they can contain them without seriously impeding their private lives.

She emits an imperious *psssht* when she wishes to dismiss a point or extract herself from a conversation. Ethel is a heavy smoker and still smokes in her office with a mechanical ventilator despite state regulations about smoking in public buildings. No one has dared to report her, not even the janitor. Almost everyone is glad that she is retiring.

The chair has decided to have the retirement party in the main office which is adjoined by the only carpeted classroom in the building and houses all the video and sound equipment. Typically, retirement parties are held in the Chair's home, but she lives in a neighboring town and did not want to make everyone drive that far on a night when they might have been drinking. No one volunteered to have it at his or her house either.

The English Department supplied the napkins, cups, plates, utensils, soda, and hor d'oerves which came from the university's catering service. Some of the women brought plates of vegetables and snacks, and most of the men brought wine, brandy, liquors, ice, and mixers. Harrold and Seymour brought little triangular sandwiches, baguette-sized slices of bread, sliced salami, pickles, olives, and hot peppers. Rita brought non-fat wafers, tofu spread, and 94% fat-free potato chips.

The first to arrive were the graduate students and some of the part-time instructors. They felt that if they timed it right, this would be dinner. Both had such miserable contracts that they shopped at second-hand stores and gravitated towards functions where food was free. They felt it was owed to them and planned their evenings with considerable calculation: art openings, dedications for new wings or buildings, the hoopla following interviews of administrative candidates, the Celebration of Cultures put on by the International Programs Office, the city welcoming students back, Arbor Day. One graduate student has compiled a list of such events and photocopied them for distribution amongst his fellows. A Mendelssohn violin concerto played in the next room; its somber elegance, its plaintive but determined pulse seemed to encourage their appetites. The women gathered at one side of the room and the men at the other.

Ethel arrived at 8:15 with her husband holding one arm and her cane hooked over the other. She wore a navy blue skirt and matching jacket, a white silk blouse, with a string of grey Majorcan pearls around her neck. Her hair was neatly tucked into a bun at the back of her head, and she seemed pleased with the number of people already in attendance, the cheerful mood, and the secretary's desk covered with bottles of alcohol. She made her way to the desk where her husband fixed her a double scotch. After pouring his own drink, Ethel's husband walked toward the group of young women, and Ethel toward the group of men.

Aaron Aker, a graduate student, had unwittingly left a cup of wine sitting precariously on the copy machine; he and his friend, Clinton Davis, had come hot from fencing in their office and hastily circumnavigated the room to apprehend the choicest hor d'oerves off each plate. One was a fine poet, the other a linguist who loved phrasal verbs and snakes; their fencing was a blaze of activity both meteoric and metaphoric, for they relished the clashing of words and worlds. The wine on the copy machine was alternately a duplicitous Hippocrene, an ode to forgetfulness, an inelegant homophone, and a splash of the wine-dark sea. Harrold retrieved the cup before it was spilled. The gap he created by this move was filled by Ethel herself. She was surrounded by Shelton, Seymour, Dexter, and a young part-time instructor named Kent.

Leaning conspiratorially toward Ethel, Shelton asked if she had heard the latest.

"What's that?" she asked after taking another sip of scotch, her loud voice did not in the least bit share his sense of conspiracy.

"Maxine thinks she's solved all her problems."

"How?"

"Remember when she spent that month in London? She went to Keats House and found *The Cenci* that Shelley had given Keats. In it was a fingernail she thinks is Shelley's, and she's trying to use it to clone him." His festive whispering was just loud enough for those around him to hear.

"*Psssht*," she hissed, nearly gagging on an ice cube. "What poppycock! *Clone* him? God-a-mercy!"

"Just what is a poppycock, Ethel?" Kent asked who had a nose for etymologies and wished to engage the lady of honor.

"Stamens," retorted Shelton.

"Dutch subliminal father-envy," said Dexter carefully, as if to mock the nerd in the back row and deliver a fine riposte in the process.

"What do you mean, Ethel? Why is it 'poppycock'?" asked Seymour, who half wished to honor Maxine's regard for a poet.

"Poppycock, Kent, is soft shit. It's poppycock because Shelley never sent that book to Keats. He was in Italy, and Ollier, his publisher, sent it. Furthermore, Keats willed his books to his friends. That one went to Benjamin Bailey. The nail's probably his or Charles Brown's, his first biographer. Or any host of delinquents since. The idea's preposterous." She retrieved a cigarette from her handbag and lit it. She exhaled a long sensuous, contemptuous stream of smoke as if to provide visual proof that all was a shabby smokescreen.

"My God, Ethel, how would you know something like that?" asked Kent whose respect for the arcane bordered the boundless.

"When this old warhorse goes down, honey, a damn fine library shuts its doors."

It was at this moment that Royce Dickerson walked into the office dressed in jeans and a plaid workshirt, with a crudely wrapped package under his left arm. He had leather boots and rolled up cuffs. His black hair was wavy and wild as if he had shaken it after he showered and let it dry. He set the package beside the desk of booze, walked up to Ethel, and gave her a huge, rollicking hug. Ethel's feet left the ground and swung around like pigtails. When he set her down, he kissed her loudly and unapologetically on the right cheek. He stood chatting with Ethel, one arm around her neck.

▲ ► ▼ ◄ ► ▼ ◄ ▲

Allow what Royce told his colleagues about his sudden departure to stand as a fragmentary truth, for the reasons always change. Yesterday, Royce may have left because of the absolute lethargy that influenced the student mind which is so often coupled with an astonishing arrogance; tomorrow it will be a moral choice about the integrity of his soul, a hearkening after God's voice; a month from now, it will be a belief in independence, self-reliance, making things with one's own hands, having something to point to and say, "I made that," as every laborer in the fields and factories needs a thing to point to, a worthy product. Nothing is reliable beyond the truth of the moment. When Monsieur Boileau wrote that *"Rien n'est beau le vrai; le vrai seul est aimable,"* he was speaking of those sweet and innocent days of palms and sunny lakes and butterflies and bright birds which existed before our present century. Any return to that far-off time when endings could be tidy, when people had straight-forward, simple reasons for doing things, must now require an archaeologist's purpose, a mask, a shovel, and a little brush. With this warning and apology, let us continue.

The women and Mr. McCarthy—Mike, as he liked to be called—had come over to see more closely Ethel's feet paddling the air. The entire department seemed to encircle them as in a small primitive theater. Maxine folded her arms protectively across her chest, a plastic glass was poised elegantly in her right hand. She wore a nearly floor-length brocade dress with a batik shawl made in Greece. Her hair was curled and tortoise-shell combs were placed on the sides of her head as if her ears had eyebrows. A pinched scowl hyphenated her face. Rita was wearing tight jeans, a green cotton blouse, low heels, and a necklace made of malachite beads. She wore red lipstick, blue eye-shadow, and her vibrantly healthy body seemed imprisoned, but poised on the verge of action. She held a carrot stick like a piece of chalk before a blackboard. She assessed Royce's spiritual character as he swung Ethel around. Dexter smiled as he distantly approved of this carnal ruffianism. His tan sweater, brown coat, brown pants and socks, and brown shirt were all glazed with wear but clean. Seymour had a restrained gladness on his face, and he really wanted to join in. He held several olive pits in his hand and was considering how best to dispose of them without losing his front-row position. He wore a black Hawaiian shirt with pink flamingoes on it, white slacks, and Birkenstocks with black socks. His glass was empty, but he held it neatly with a napkin still wrapped around it. Shelton had his thumb hooked over his belt buckle and rattled his glass of icecubes like a dice cup. He looked as if he had pulled his rifle up on a lion and his guide had told him it had been stuffed to catch poachers. Harrold stood with his legs crossed holding the elbow that held his drink. He enjoyed this. The graduate students chewed their sandwiches methodically, satisfied and contemplative. Kent was distracted as if he were still working on *poppycock*. For a brief, encapsulated moment, time seemed to stand still as if people were waiting for a snapshot to be taken.

"Well, it's about time, Ethel. Thirty-five years! Thir-tee-five years of beating your head against the same brick walls and you look great. You deserve the Congressional Medal of Honor, but all I've got is that package over there." He released her and retrieved the package.

People started milling about, and the Chair went to get the department's present for Ethel. Seymour picked up her cane which had dropped to the floor during the twirling and gave it back to her. Mr. McCarthy had walked up and straightened her jacket which had slipped a bit over her right shoulder. Rita busily consumed her carrot. Shelton went to get more bourbon. Dexter moved over near Maxine to engage in some small talk.

Perhaps it is possible to ascribe our need for neat and orderly endings to the mechanical aspects of our nature. A flash of light should produce an image. The image should be produced faithfully, accurately, with a high resolution. A margin shift should reduce or enlarge the margins. The depressed collating button should nonetheless collate dutifully. It is built into us the way day-dreaming is. Pre-programmed, as it were. In any event, they had assembled not for contentious demonstrations of mental agility, nor for the innumerable qualifications that any proposition could sponsor, nor for the age-old wrangle about administrative malfeasance and parsimoniousness, but for the quiet passing on of one of their stalwart cohorts whose blunt directness had always been a kind of anchor for this wind-tossed vessel they called an English Department. Their sense of relaxed constraints, or dogged determination to at least erect an edifice of good-will and congratulations, created a mood of uncharacteristic affability. Their closed-door conspiracies to launch new chairs, to grant or deny tenure, to construct prioritized merit lists, to capsize or sail forth promotions, were at least temporarily forgotten. Although it must be admitted that the diminishing rows of bottles had pried the locks and refocused the lights a bit.

Royce gave Ethel a large wooden box whose lid was inlaid with a scene he called "The Garden of Earthly Delights." The box was meticulously constructed out of many woods: cherry, ebony, mahogany, sycamore, koa, rose, and oak. He said it was for her paint brushes, charcoal pencils, and erasers, for he knew that she intended to take up drawing as soon as she graded her last paper. He had made it himself, and they all found out that the phone call he received over a year ago was from Woodworld, a custom woodshop that specialized in personal designs. He had submitted some of his work, and he was enthusiastically hired. There were no Chairs or Deans or students to write surly evaluations of him. He was judged merely on the work itself and the satisfaction of the person who ordered it. He loved this simplicity, this untainted cause and effect.

Perhaps it is for this reason that he suddenly jumped up on the metal secretary's desk and emitted a loud ear-numbing, show-stopping whistle. In the silence that immediately followed, he invited everyone over to his house, for this was not the proper place for the retirement of such a gifted teacher, scholar, and trusted friend. He did not pause for retaliatory arguments, but launched into a sequence of instructions: Maxine and Rita could put the remaining hor d'oerves onto a platter and bring them along; Dexter and Shelton could collect and assimilate the bottles; Seymour and Harrold could gather the napkins, olives, pickles, and vegetables; and Mike could begin the caravan to his place and take Kent and the few adjuncts who were still there; and he would draw and photocopy a map for everyone in case they should happen to lose their way. Ethel was the only one who had been to Royce's house which may seem odd for colleagues of such long-standing association, but there has been a rather strict, though perhaps unconscious, division between their professional and social lives. It wasn't so much a well-guarded privacy that caused this aloofness, as weariness with the official code of conduct, the hot-house decorum and perfunctory civilities, that whole wobbling super-structure that seemed to guide every action and reaction. It was safer to have two doors, two hats, because the genii of genius could only be bottled so many hours per day before he popped out: naked, singing off-key, hungry for junk food, randy.

Ethel and Mike gathered their coats and led their troop of followers out the door and over to the elevator. Everyone else began packing, tidying, and assembling things. No one balked, felt the division of labor was sexist, or made excuses to go home. A curiously cooperative spell had been cast by Royce's presence, the drinks, or the simple curiosity about Royce's house which had been the subject of much internecine discussion. Or perhaps it was a simple need to continue.

After all, it was only 10:30, the end of spring term was a short week away, and it had been an unseasonably warm day and a particularly lovely night.

Royce lived in a large Victorian house that was once owned by a successful banker. It had been well-maintained, and was but two miles from the university. The red maples that lined the driveway obscured the house and yard. Every other tree had a light nailed about half way into the leaves; the green and golden glow was warm and mysterious, flickering with soft shadows. The porchlight over the door was also on, so it was clear that Royce's wife was expecting company.

When the guests arrived, Anne greeted them, hung coats in the hall closet, told them to take a look around, make themselves comfortable. She explained that their girls were spending the night with cousins, so noise and the hour were inconsequential. There was a bar in the living room, and they were welcome to anything they could find to drink. A hot-tub and deck were out the back door for a clear view of the stars. The bathroom was down the hall and to the left.

Anne was a tall woman with long brown hair and a narrow nose. She was dressed in jeans and a yellow silk blouse with grey piping around the collar and hems on the sleeves. She had strong arms and a trim confidence, a pleasant and immediately sincere affability. She had hugged Ethel and Mike, warmly shook the hands of Rita, Maxine, Kent, and Denise and Robert, the two adjuncts that had come with Ethel. Anne told them to explore the house and furniture, for Royce had made most of it. Each piece seemed to defy expectations of space. The top of the desk in the library was shaped like a painter's pallet or a lily pad; the sides bulged out and curved to the floor. A large rolled-up drawer was on one side, and a line of drawers with knobs shaped like large buttons was on the other. The light on the wall above it seemed embedded in leaves made out of a creamy white wood, casting a web of shadows up the wall. In the living room was a loveseat whose back was in the shape of an open pair of scissors; the seats curved like light fabric being cut. In one corner stood a sinuous wood sculpture that looked like a centrifuged archaeopteryx that had swallowed a glass shaped like an old ship's lantern. The visitors went from piece to piece touching, rubbing, opening drawers, marveling.

Maxine accompanied Ethel to the study, and Rita and Mike took their drinks to the back deck. Maxine took off her shawl and settled into the rocker beside the recliner that Ethel had chosen.

"Hand me that ashtray, would you, dear?" Ethel said, pointing to the table beside Maxine.

"Sure."

Ethel lit her cigarette. "So, tell me about this cloning business."

"What do you mean?" Maxine asked, leaning forward in her rocking chair, a measured caution filled each syllable.

"Shelton said something about Shelley and a fingernail you found in the *Cenci*. Is that true or not?"

Her face flushed. "How would he know?"

"I didn't ask. Is it true?" A languid swirl of smoke curled out her nose.

"Yes. I found a fingernail that I believe to be Shelley's," she answered uneasily.

"Well," said Ethel putting her elbow on the arm of the recliner and letting the smoke drift off into the dark, "let me tell you a little story. I was engaged to the love-of-my-life before the war broke out. I was eighteen. I wanted to marry him before he left, but he thought we should wait, in case something happened and I would be burdened, a teenage widow. A silly gallantry more than a compassionate foresight. For a year I felt my heart listened 'to the tuning-fork that had been struck upon a star,' as Fitzgerald put it. Have you ever noticed that the world's great literary lovers are children? Paolo & Francesca, Tristram & Iseult, Romeo & Juliet. And we can't imagine them at forty, with bags of groceries, tying their kids' shoes, cleaning vomit off the bathroom floor. They have to die because the blazing meteor of their love always falls into the sea. I followed my own vapor trails for years. My fiancé came home from the war missing a leg and half his heart. He was so set on not accepting pity, he couldn't accept love either. So sorry for himself no one else had a right to be. He was stubborn, prideful, touchingly quaint. I soon realized how much the beauty of his character—his valiant honesty, a bottomless kindness in his eyes—was connected to the astonishing beauty of his body. When he lost that, he lost the other."

"If it's not one flaw, it's another," Maxine said airily.

"And you think we're different? What I'm trying to say is that tuning-fork isn't music to live by."

"I've never really been in love, except with literature," Maxine said quietly. "I married early, to prove my parents wrong, but not for love. I knew walking down the aisle he couldn't ever be what I wanted, he hadn't the talent for it, or the heart."

"No one ever does. Books are no safe harbor, no substitute for life and neither is writing them. They're like those little mirrors the British put on roadsides to anticipate the corners ahead. They can help us avoid collisions, to see the world condensed in this beautiful, funny way. They help us put our two feet back on the ground, or make peace with the magnitude of our own minds and feelings. . . Oh, hell, I'm not saying it well, but perhaps love, romantic love I mean, is the work of those mirrors. They make us want what's impossible. In our profession, we all know that, yet we hold on to this silvery hope and it goes deep. We half-believe some saving radiance will suddenly walk through the door. But it's all artificial light until we learn to move in the darkness, touch what we know, and know what we touch."

Ethel ground out the glowing coal at the stub end of her cigarette and stood up, "Well, here come the muscled wayfarers now."

"With wax in their ears and music on their minds," Maxine added, wearily allowing the old woman's last bit of wholesome pedantry to drift away with her smoke. She collected her shawl from the back of the chair.

The loud rustle of voices in the kitchen, the thumping and cracking of ice trays, the trilling but polite laughter, had suddenly made them feel isolated, caught in some eddy while the river of the night flowed steadily on.

When they came out of the study, Harrold and Seymour were in the library, each with a drink. Harrold's left hand was unself-consciously resting on Seymour's right shoulder as they examined an antique wooden viewer and a few of its images. In the soft lighting, the pink flamingoes on Seymour's shirt seemed to strut curiously out of the dark. His white pants glowed like a field of snow in moonlight. Harrold's gold necklace and ear-ring were also touched with light.

"Sounds like the host has arrived," Ethel said as she passed them.

"Watch out for the drinks," Harrold warned, "they're x-rated."

"I've been to this waterhole before, and the lion and lambs have at least heard of the peaceable kingdom," Ethel said, deliberately changing the metaphor. Maxine smiled vaguely as they entered the kitchen.

The kitchen was commodious and full of activity. Anne was laying out platters of coldcuts, cheese spreads, chutneys, and bowls of nuts. Royce was making drinks, Shelton and Dexter were deep in an argument about Hemingway and the Lost Generation, and Rita and Mike were seated at the table discussing the benefits of yoga for the aged.

"Here's to the lady of honor," Anne said cheerily, picking up her wine glass.

A straggling chorus of cheers accompanied the wine glasses, beer bottles, and mixed drinks hoisted into the air.

Royce put five discs into his CD player—Mose Allison, Bessie Smith, John Lee Hooker, Billie Holiday, and Muddy Waters—and turned up the volume. As the night progressed, they began to fill their glasses fuller, walk with a slow drumbeat strut, letting the rhythms and phrases of the music get inside their nodding heads so they all seemed to be having interviews with the blind. Their shoulders swayed, their eyes closed mid-sentence to let a chord's echo echo again. They were caught by the irresistibly plaintive and insistent outbursts of the electric guitar, the melancholy truth waiting to get back in, a dialogue between a desolate spirit and its slim pleasures, between oppression's soul-sorrow and the wild, temporary excursions into forgetfulness, between an arrogant and easy male latency and its destructiveness, the woman's honey and the bee's sting, the fire and the ice. This swirl of direct emotional consequence, its rising temperature of tribulation, created a certain sympathetic receptivity in them. Could they lay down their effete burdens, their historical divisions, and turf-wars, their disappointments, in the face of such tragedy? One can't think of his wallet during a grand eulogy.

At about 2:00 in the morning, Shelton stripped from his clothes and welcomed the remaining guests into the hot-tub. Maxine, Ethel, and Mike, and Kent had managed to duck out gracefully a little after midnight. With his broad shoulders, wavy black hair and beard, and the black map of hair on his chest which tapered down to his navel like Florida to Key West, he was Adonis striding towards Aphrodite's bath. His welcome was more of a challenge, and Seymour whose maleness was most in question because of his name and his dedication to writing poetry, was the next to fling his clothes into a heap and make his way to the tub. Rita's gluteal speculations were given immediate and graphic gratification. He was as harmonious as the spring equinox. In Rita's mind one of Billie Holiday's lines kept involuntarily repeating itself: *Oh, what a little moonlight can do to you.* Seymour had not been circumcised, and outside a Greek vase this was the first time Rita had seen one. Dexter crossed his legs, took another drink, and adjusted his glasses.

After Harrold took his unabashed and sprightly plunge, Shelton began working on Anne and Rita, enticing them into the water. He told them they needed to scale the mountain of their own fears, to hearken to the call of the wild, to bare their white soles. Amidst his woolly hyperbole was a self-mockery that none of them had heard before as if he knew full well that the wind in his sails was purely literary and not meant to push a real boat.

Royce came back from changing the CD's carrying a bottle of Courvoisier and a tray of seven small snifters. He set them on the table next to his wife and sat down heavily, putting his arm around her. The gentle gurgling of the tub's water mixed with the slower cadences of the music. The stars rolled out across the heavens in their various shapes of human effort and providential intercession, their tragedies and triumphs. The moon was a vague glow through the maple leaves. The night was full and warm. Frogs and crickets seemed to take turns casting their voices, their loud urgencies, through the gaps in the music.

I don't want to be no slave, to work all day. . . Muddy Waters sang into the frog chorus.

"I never knew we had so many frogs around here. I thought they were endangered or something," Rita said swishing her feet in the water, having some difficulty making her mouth work properly.

"Only the bullfrogs, the cowfrogs have nothing to worry about," Shelton said, booming like a frog himself, "Come on in, the water's fine."

"I never could trust three men in a tub. Besides, I still have my modesty. I'm not that drunk," Rita said, fruitily.

"Immodesty's best in the observance than in the breeches," said Dexter whose drunken elocution was slow but deliberately, painfully accurate. He had slipped out of his shoes, but his collar was still buttoned down tight.

"Whose?" asked Anne, warily, "we're a little outnumbered here."

Hear my phone ringin, sound like a long distant call. . . "Dexter, that's the funniest thing I've ever heard you say," said Royce, laughing so hard tears streaked his cheeks.

"I think I smell a shift of wit," Shelton said, curiously nosing the air.

. . .another mule's kickin' in your stall. . . "Why do you look at the black man when somebody says something like that?" asked Harrold with mock indignation.

"It's your jewels, honey," Seymour replied, flicking his gold ear-ring.

…One of these days I'm going to show you just how nice a man can be… Harrold sang with Muddy in playful harmony.

The music finally ended at 3:30 in the morning when the neighbor's rooster began crowing. Anne drove Rita and Dexter to their homes which weren't far away. Seymour and Harrold insisted on sharing a taxi. Sheldon called his wife and slept on the Dickerson's couch. Royce managed to make it upstairs to his bed. He didn't remember his wife taking anyone home, nor her taking off his shoes and socks and pants.

▲ ► ▼ ◄ ► ▼ ◄ ▲

There were several interesting effects of this party. Rita and Seymour agreed to a jog on Saturday morning on a trail near the river; they were beginning to feel a certain harmony of the spheres. Shelton and Harrold decided to exchange manuscripts. Maxine replaced the Ottoman vial with the old locket. Dexter asked Shelton if he could get the names of the CDs, not, of course, to supplant his madrigals and chamber music but to supplement them. Kent was allowed to move into Ethel's office since she was retiring.

The department had given Ethel a leather daybook with empty calendar pages and little leather pen holders. It had a calculator and a coupon for a cellular phone. Her name was stencilled sternly in gold leaf across the lower right corner, and represented quite a discovery for the graduate student who found it two months later at St. Vincent de Paul's among the answering machines and tape recorders.

One night in the video room where the graduate students often gathered to watch movies and eat popcorn, they laughed bitterly at the piquancy of Ethel's snub, its rich ironies, this whole tiny inwrought, capsized world whose halls couldn't wait for their silky radiance, the many gifts their reading brought.

Yet we are all readers here, all passengers of light—whether green or gold or blue or black and white—all aspiring to neon, all haunting the dark that will make us shine. And reading has become part of the mystery of who we are, part of us, both vessel and sea, and the waves coming in and going out like lines of script define what's there and what's missing until, in the end, they are indistinguishable. We are all missing persons and home is never where we've lost or found it. The word is only a wave of light arching and sparking from eye to eye, the glow, and then the darkness. In the video room the light of Houston's version of *The Dead* quietly strung the graduate students together like beads of a rosary until the screen whitened and the lights came on. They sat for a second or two as the story's prayer disappeared inside them. Then they all got up and settled in different parts of town, different precincts and neighborhoods, streets and avenues, taking a bit of the glow with them.

They were sure that they would pass on the golden tablets. They would write their odes and paeons and elegies; they would sit in their offices and elaborately dispense their wisdom to the warm-hearted thanks and adoration of their students. They would be Mr. Chips, John Keating, somebody's Socrates. They would accept their awards and rewards with a magnanimous and witty grace.

Fond Desire

"As fruit once ripe then falls to ground
As flies that seek for flames are brought
To cinders by the flames they sought:
So fond desire, when it attains,
The life expires, the woe remains."
—SIR WALTER RALEGH

SWIMMING

One of the first things that surprised Elin after her arrival in Corfu was the man on a motorcycle with a gun strapped to its side. He wore a black beret, a silver-gray mustache, and hunched into a green coat that fluttered behind him as he drove the winding roads to Paleokastritsa. The gun looked as though it had been through several wars. Attached by leather straps, it jostled as their van passed him on a curve.

"What does he have that gun for?" she asked Spiro.

"Hunting season started this week."

"What's he hunting here?"

"Pheasants, larks, things like that. You like this American music? I love American movies. Sylvester Stallone. Rambo. And Bill Clinton. Many Greeks don't like him, but I do, he's had lots of women. When I was a waiter I had lots of friends and people liked me. Now, I'm successful, have my own hotel and car rentals, and people don't like me. It's the way it is."

Elin watched the olive trees pass, their silvery, twisted forms. A man stood at the edge of the road beside a small table lined with jars of honey and bottles of wine. His hair and mustache were almost white, and under his straw hat he smiled and looked into her face, a silent greeting which seemed honest, direct, but reserved too. He wore a pale blue-and-white plaid shirt and green pants that bunched at his boots. As they passed, he held out a Dixie-cup of wine like a toast.

"How long, Mum, before we're there?" Mary asked from the backseat, a hand resting on her father's knee.

"Ten minutes, that's all" Spiro answered with a shrug of

his shoulders, his right palm up and open, suggesting that time here was easy, inconsequential, inappropriate even.

The hotel overlooked a small ravine of olive trees and stone walls. A wide path ran down the bottom of the ravine and curved toward the sea. The hotel was pink, and the shutters and windows were white. A few leaves floated in the pool's water; the umbrellas on the tables were closed. Puddles from the last rain dotted the cement around the pool. She noticed the red trumpets of hibiscus flowers beside the entrance.

Her brother-in-law, John, and Spiro helped Martin out of the van and into his wheelchair. She was pulling one of the suitcases out of the back when Spiro tapped her on the shoulder.

"No, no, dear lady. We will get that. Please go inside with the girls. We will be right in. No problem. The season is almost over and my son is in school. He usually carries the bags, but we will get them. Please." With his hand on her shoulder, he guided her a few steps toward the door. His expression was firm, unequivocal. She felt the lingering pressure of his hand as she walked, the charm of his earnest attention, his "dear lady."

Since her husband's accident over a year ago at Island Farm where a shell exploded during the excavation of Camp 198, she had not gotten out of Bridgend, not even so far as Cardiff. The morning mists and evening fogs, the dampness, had seemed to envelop her mind, to seep into her bones, her heart, so that she had no sense of what her life was beyond this obligation and the next, that fog and this mist. She was tired, worn out by the demands of Martin's injury: the special diet, the massages, the creams and ointments, and his constant presence in the house, his anger and tearful, frustrated reconciliations. It was like living in a fishbowl where some hand kept stirring the murk and gravel. Their church had helped to raise the money for this vacation, and she was grateful that John was willing to come along and help with the carrying and wheeling and dressing. She was ready for sunshine and the beaches, ready to let her hair down, and have someone serve her for a change. For three months, she had looked forward to this vacation—Martin's really, from the church's point of view—her vacation, too, perhaps foremost, now, in his condition. Her daughter was thirteen and had brought a classmate. They could entertain themselves; John and Martin would enjoy their time together. John, who drove large equipment—caterpillars and backhoes—for a construction company, looked forward to this vacation, too.

When she opened the windows in her new room to let the sunshine in, the air was thick with the smell of jasmine. Though they were on the first floor, the land sloped down and away from the hotel. A smoky haze curled over the ravine from the burning of the dead grass and fallen olive branches in preparation for laying the nets to catch the olives. In the car, Spiro had said he hated the damn olives, that they came at a time when he was worn out, and this harvest was more labor than it was worth. Yet he had set out his nets and would pick up the olives and haul them to the press like his father had done, generation after generation of hands harvesting, pressing, preserving. To Elin, this tradition, this ancient connection to the earth, was very appealing. She could smell the smoke within the thickness of the jasmine. All she could see of the water was a blue triangle where the ravine dipped toward the sea. In the late afternoon light, the birds were making a fine musical noise—robins, wagtails, sparrows, and warblers. Autumn birds in Bridgend seemed melancholy, all gulls and jackdaws.

Fresh towels were stacked neatly in the bathroom, extra blankets folded at the ends of the beds; the place was shiny, spotless, and she hadn't been the one to make it that way. There was a table and six chairs, a green sofa trimmed in gold, soft chairs and reading lights, French doors on both sides of the room—one to the hallway, one to the balcony. The balcony had a white table and plastic chairs, a twisted wrought-iron railing with leaves and bunches of iron grapes. Directly below them a group of olive trees was enclosed by a stone fence and under the trees orange nets were stitched together. She saw a few black olives on top of the nets. And in an open triangle between the trees was a patch of pink cyclamen. She breathed deep and smelled the smoke, something faintly sweet.

"Hey, not bad, can you see the water?" Her husband had just wheeled himself in, followed by Spiro and John with the luggage. The girls were still down by the pool, testing the water temperature and lounge chairs.

"Barely, but the view's nice."

That night they ate at the hotel. Only one other couple was dining. The choices for dinner were red mullet, lamb and potatoes, or pork and rice. There were Greek salads and omelets with fries and mushrooms if they wished, but because the hotel was closing next week, little was left on the menu. The cook was also the bartender and waiter, but he was jovial, handsome, charming, and gave them a free liter of his own wine, and for desert sliced apples sprinkled with a squeeze of orange juice and sugar. Their meals were delicious, and the wine strong. They toasted each other, Greece, the cook, Corfu, Martin, sunshine. And after the plates were cleared away, the cook brought out five aperitif glasses filled with a clear, sweet, lemon-flavored liqueur. The girls, thirteen and fourteen, were thrilled to be included in this ritual, and they giggled and smiled at each other, but couldn't manage more than a sip. John and Martin finished it for them.

"I'm going to take a walk. That all right with you, John?"

"Sure, got it all under control."

She walked out of the hotel toward the road that led to the beaches, shops, and restaurants. Paleokastritsa was not a village, but a town that had been created for tourists. The schools, churches, and civic buildings were in the village which was on top of the mountain that rose sharply from the sea. She had seen the sign for it on the way in, and Spiro said he was born there. The moon was a white disk in the sky, the ignited clouds were a pearly pink that dimmed toward gray. She looked for the lights of the village but couldn't see them. She passed a little store with barred doors, another hotel with a semi-circular drive, and on the pillars at the foot of the stairs were white pelicans with black-edged wings. After the drinks and the warmth of the kitchen, the air cooled her skin. Although the road was paved, it was patched and uneven, occasionally pitted and broken, so she had to watch her step, especially with her heels on. She came to a sidewalk which led to a view area with a bench. The water swept into a sandy cove and splashed along a basalt cliff. The moonlight fringed the restless waves with lace. The sea was quiet, rocking back and forth.

As she sat on the bench, she was seized by an up-welling

of excitement about this new place, the soft warm air, the moonlight like mother-of-pearl. It was as if she had stepped outside her life and looked at the world and found it strange like when she was a girl and dreamed about what love would be, a hope, opening out fragrantly, beautifully like a hibiscus flower. Yet the nameless anxiety in the love she had was not a flower, more like a weight, a pressure around her heart. What was it beyond the food and dishes, the laundry and shopping, the creams and ointments, the homework and ironing, the vacuum cleaning and mopping, that network of red scars and pleading looks? From this bench, she could see that the world in all its ample variety had not disappeared, that there was still something out there, that for so long she had squeezed herself into a smaller and smaller space until there was hardly anything left that was hers and hers alone. How sweet it would be to walk out onto the dock, climb into a boat and speed into another life. She was still lean and attractive; men looked at her as she walked by in her short skirts. How easy it would be.

"Mum, there you are. We've been looking for you. Can Kaitlin and me go swimming? Daddy says it's up to you."

"It's too cold, Mary. I don't want you getting sick on your vacation."

"Ah, Mum, we won't get sick…"

"Please, let's not argue."

She got up and put her arm around her daughter's shoulders, and they walked back to the hotel, sharing her light cotton shawl. When they returned, Martin and John were playing cribbage and drinking from a bottle of brandy they bought from the hotel bar. Kaitlin sat in a chair with her swimming suit and a towel in her lap. The door between the two rooms was open and a song sung by a Greek woman came from the TV, plaintive but resolute. Clothes from their dressing for dinner were in bunched piles on the floor and sofa, her hair dryer was coiled in a corner below the mirror.

Martin looked up from his cards. "Hi, Elin, do you want to play? Our game will be over in a minute."

"No thanks, I think I'll go to bed. We have a big day tomorrow."

"A big day of nothing, pure nothing," said John, grinning broadly.

Elin retrieved a sandal trapped under one of the rubber wheels of Martin's chair, rubbed his head, and retired to the other room.

The next morning she awoke to two loud pops. She got up and walked onto the balcony. The air was still hazy from the smoke. The sun was not yet to the first floor, though the geraniums on the balcony above her shone brightly. She saw below her a movement in the grass. It was a large bird running up the path along the ravine, dragging a wing which caught on a branch and the bird fell to its side and got up and ran again. It crawled into pile of unburned limbs and grass near a rock wall, not far from a small white shrine with a cross on the top and a glass window.

A young man with a gun walked slowly up the ravine. He examined the ground closely, pausing at a large bush. He walked around it, then continued on. When he reached the pile of branches, he looked in, and then raised his right foot and pressed down one edge. He bent over, withdrew the bird by the neck, and spun it around. The bird flapped its wings wildly, flew uselessly around his hand, kicking its feet, a few feathers spilling to the ground.

As he passed Elin, he held the pheasant by the feet and its loose feathers and wings swayed with each step. When he walked out from under the shade of the olive trees, he stopped, looked at her, raised the bird slightly, said "Kalimera," and resumed his hike. She nodded but couldn't bring herself to say good morning back. Something in the calm, open expression on his face, the casual flip of the bird frightened her. Upside down, the bird hung like a mop, not the bright, colorful thing it was just a few minutes ago.

She watched the man walk up the path. He was short, well-built, and the muscular casualness of his walk reminded her of Martin when they first met in Cardiff's Bute Park on a Saturday morning. He was training for a boat race and looked at her and smiled, prepared his boat, looked again, and fell getting in. Wet and dripping, his body was lean and rippled as he bent over and struggled with his shirt. He had an embarrassed, self-mocking grin that made his emotions as evident as skywriting. She fell in love with the little muscles along his ribs, the sweet heart-shaped patch of hairs on his chest. They were married within six months over the objections of her parents and his. Although they had had their difficulties, she was convinced it was the accident that had so changed things.

Because the men were still sleeping off their brandy, she took the girls down to breakfast. A woman in a light green dress was setting out bread and honey. An assortment of things to eat were already laid out: a basket of boiled brown eggs, pressed ham slices, wedges of sponge cake, a glass jar of cornflakes, yogurt, milk, coffee, and orange juice.

"No sausages this morning. We're out," the woman said, apologizing without a hint of apology in her voice, only in the obligatory shrug, the slight dip of her head.

"This will be fine, thank you," Elin said, smiling, but the woman did not smile back.

"Mum, can we go to the beach this morning. Spiro said it wasn't a long walk," Mary asked as she licked the honey from the edge of her bread.

"Yes, we'll all go down later."

"But I want to go this morning," Mary said, turning her face into a mask of disappointment.

Spiro walked into the breakfast room carrying a drill and an electric cord. He wore a red and white striped T-shirt, his hair was rumpled. His face looked tired as if he hadn't quite woken up.

"If you like, I take you in the van. I'm going soon, if you like," he smiled and nodded graciously.

"Oh, yes," Mary screamed and clapped her hands.

"When will you leave, Spiro?" Elin asked, trying to quiet her daughter's enthusiasm with a threatening but casual squint.

"Fifteen minutes, out in front," and he bowed ever so slightly and left.

"I'll leave Daddy a note," Mary said, and ran toward their room with Kaitlin not far behind.

It was a short drive to the beach, but it would be a long walk back and uphill. The beach was sandy, and portioned out by groups of white plastic lawnchairs. Two old women sat under an umbrella in an intense conversation, their hands and arms moving as they talked. One wore a flowered swimsuit and dug her toes in the sand; the other, a paisley housedress and tennis shoes. When the girls sat in the lawnchairs, the one in the swimsuit walked over with a cane, limping, taking her time.

"1500 drachmas, please," she said, her face was heavily wrinkled, her expression severe. She looked as if she had had enough of tourists and would rather be home.

"Excuse me?" Elin said, as brightly as she could.

"1500 drachmas" the woman said louder and more sternly.

"For what?"

The woman reached over and picked up the back of an empty lawnchair and shook it, the loose skin of her arm shaking, her face even more indignant. With her cane, she pointed to the other lawnchairs and then the little umbrella and table where the other woman stood.

"500 drachmas, for one, all day. Okay?"

Elin got out her purse and paid the woman, thinking that four pounds was a bit much for plastic seats in the sand. Tomorrow she would bring a blanket from the room. The cove itself was strikingly beautiful, shaped like an old keyhole. The craggy sides curved into a bowl, opening into a blue-green sea where rock islands dribbled into the horizon. The sand was soft but not so fine that it blew into their magazines, towels, and purses. On the west side of the inlet, a group of men had gathered to take the dock apart for the season. The young men had their shirts off and pants rolled. Some were drinking coffee, two empty frappé glasses with straws sat on a plank over the water. The men talked and laughed and shook their heads. One had light brown hair, but the others had dark hair and tanned skin.

As Elin sat in the lawnchair, her knees propping up a magazine, she looked over the top of her page and watched the trim, easy movements of their bodies, noted how the sun softened their skin and gave the young ones a buttery shine.

Fingering the skin at her throat, she thought how beautiful they were in their youth, in that fine ignorant moment of suppleness when dreams stretch to the stars and feet fall over shoelaces, yet they know nothing of how to lose and get up and go again. She had wanted to sing, and Martin wanted to row for the Edinburgh crew team because his favorite uncle had and his stories had fired his imagination, but after Mary was born, she stopped taking singing lessons, and Martin took the job at Farm Island. She wanted something in her life to keep that desire new, to feel the luxury of a dream, and this trip to Greece felt like a first tentative step.

When she had time enough to sit and think, she felt an uneasiness gather. What were these quiet transports which in lonely moments sent her spirit soaring—toward what? Regret, satisfaction, or yet another yearning, another dream? How like the waves her questions and feelings came and crashed against a shore and feathered out into foam.

As the girls swam and splashed, she could see them looking at the men too. The men were not in a hurry and seemed to be waiting for something. One was in the water and had retrieved the end of a cable. Another had a sledge hammer and was knocking boards off the front end of the dock. Another stacked the boards as they came off. Two stood with their arms folded, talking. Elin enjoyed this pace, watching the men's bodies in the sun, their confidence, familiarity, and ease. Although some of the bellies of the older men were beginning to bulge, the others were lean and their muscled movements glistened in the sun.

"Mum, come swim with us, the water's so warm," Mary said.

"Not just yet, I want to warm up first."

"Oh, Mum, you never do anything that's fun."

"The water's beautiful and it's easy to float, come swim with us," Kaitlin pleaded.

"Okay, okay, I will if you just give me some peace today."

She let the water splash over her toes and felt the sizzling swirl around her ankles. It was warm and the sand soft. She waded out to her knees and stood with her hands crossed over her chest. The hues of blue changed with the depth and growth on the sea floor. Open spaces were a deep turquoise like the wing of a teal, over the beds of seaweed it was dark green like back of a trout, and in the open sun it was like Windex. When she plunged in, the water was cool, but it soon felt warm. She swam out and rolled onto her back. The sun was warm on her face and her body floated without effort. She spread her arms and legs and drifted, letting the quiet undulations of the water seep into her. Her mind seemed to open up and drift like a kelp plant, its long spinal stem anchored to a rock, opening to light. When she came back to herself, it was like waking in a strange bed, and it took a few seconds to locate shore, the girls splashing there.

That afternoon they walked back to their hotel. During the two mile walk, the girls complained about the heat, they wished Spiro would come by, or one of the boys on the motorbikes would stop and give them a ride. They were hungry, then thirsty, and wanted to stop at one of the closed hotels and ask for water, but Elin pushed forward, told them they could have a snack and a swim when they got back to the hotel. As they neared the little store, she told the girls to go on and find out what John and Daddy were doing. They ran on ahead.

The store's shelves were almost empty. Cheese and milk were in the refrigerated section, boxes of cereal, tins of sardines, a row of goggles and masks and underwater cameras, a box of Kindereggs, bottles of soda, and a spinning case of warped postcards. All was coated with a fine dust from the road. The woman was reading a fashion magazine when Elin brought her juice, olives, and muesli to the counter.

"I would like some eggs and a loaf of bread, too, please."

"We do not have much left, we close next week," the woman said, turning her magazine over. "How many eggs?"

"Ten, please."

The woman cut off an end of the tray of eggs, put a top on it, and tied it up with string. She wrapped the bread in a thin paper sheet, and computed her bill on a corner of the paper. She wrote "2,235" and gave it to Elin who paid and said "Epharisto."

"Parakalo," the woman replied, without looking up or nodding.

The woman's deliberate coolness and the crisp page-flipping announced the interruption was over. The Greeks were tired of tourists, only Spiro retained his humor and kindness. Her feet were tired from the long walk in her high-heeled sandals and the heat was making her sweat. She walked into the hotel courtyard just in time to see John pick up the back of Martin's wheelchair and slide him, fully clothed, into the pool.

"John!" she screamed and ran as fast as she could to the pool's edge, "What are you doing? You fucking idiot."

She stood with her bag of groceries, looking into the water. Martin had slid in as limp as a corpse and sank slowly to the bottom. He lay face-down and arms outstretched, a thin stream of bubbles rising from his mouth. She set the groceries down and kicked off her sandals.

"Elin, he's okay, he wanted me to do it," John said, still holding the tipped chair.

"Mum, we asked Daddy to swim, he wants to do it," Mary said coming over to stand by her mother.

Still, Martin lay on the bottom of the pool, not moving. The seconds clicked by very slowly and seemed to amplify outwards. One minute. One minute fifteen seconds. One minute thirty. She dove in, grabbed him by the arm, and pushed off from the bottom. They rose and broke the surface simultaneously. Martin squirted a long arc of water and grinned at her, opening his eyes wide. He tried to put his arm around her waist, but she climbed out. Her wrap-around skirt sagged and exposed her panties, her hair stuck to her face and dripped. She put her arms on her hips.

"You bastards. You're real fucking funny." She turned and walked into the hotel, leaving her husband in the pool, her groceries sitting at its edge, and splotches of water behind her.

As she lay on the bed with the shutters drawn and the door locked, she let the anger ripple on. For a while it burned bright as a meteor, then blinked and smoked and smoldered. Then what rose up out of its ashes surprised her. What her mind could not release was a small thought that had risen in her mind while Martin lay at the bottom of the pool. It came like a thin, fanciful hope right in the middle of those widening seconds—that Martin would drown, that she would be absolved from the burdens of his care. Where had that little shark of a thought come from? There was the faintest shiver of gladness that rode with this thought, and now it was embarrassing, deeply embarrassing, and relit the anger and gave it a texture. Could anything be more despicable? If she were the one in that chair, would Martin come to feel this way about her? Martin and John and Mary had come to the door and knocked and pleaded, but they had no idea what had kept the door locked.

It was not until dinner time that Elin was persuaded to come out. She was dressed for dinner. They decided on a restaurant not far beyond the little grocery store, but on the other side of the road and among some pine trees. John wheeled Martin through the sparse gravel of the driveway and onto the road. Both girls had dressed up because at the ice-cream cart, they had met the boy who was the waiter at this hotel. Mary wore a blue dress and a pair of Elin's heels; the gap in back was a full inch so that her feet slid back and forth. Her lipstick was red and too wide at the corners of her mouth. Kaitlin was in a pink satin dress, white shoes, and wore a string of fake pearls. They each wore cotton wraps and carried cameras in their purses. For the entire walk, the girls argued about who got to ask him for a picture.

"I saw him first," Kaitlin said.

"But he said hello to me," Mary said.

"He said it to both of us."

"He was looking at me. I saw his eyes."

The dinner was a choice of octopus, mousaka, aubergine, roasted chicken with lemon and oregano, and pork in a tomato sauce. Greek salad and tzatziki were side dishes. The waiter was about seventeen years old with curly black hair that came down over his ears, bright dark eyes, and a grin that lit up his face like a candle in a rice-paper lantern. He was polite and charming, yet so aloof and independent and comfortable in his role he was more like a kindly host than a waiter. After he took their order, he put on a tape of Greek mountain music that filled the empty dining room. He moved some chairs and opened a space and invited them to dance, but they sat still. When the bartender came out with their drinks, he put down his tray and asked Kaitlin to dance. She laughed and went with him to the dance floor. Then John asked Mary.

While the music was at its most vigorous, Elin looked at Martin's face. He was absorbed in watching his daughter dance and John's version of the bouzouki. Even though he had gained weight after his injury and his inactivity, she could see the face of the man who looked at her from the edge of the boat. And she remembered the most touching moments during their relationship: after the death of Mary's dog, Martin was inconsolable, not for the dog but for his daugher's feelings; or when he stood up and clapped after Mary's fourth grade play, alone among all the parents and friends, oblivious and happy; or when after the accident he sold his handmade scull and bought her diamond earrings for her birthday. She wanted to reach out and touch his arm, but the residue of anger wouldn't allow it. As if aware of her gaze, he turned to her and smiled, the fingers of his right hand thrumming the tabletop in time with the music.

"So, why did you do that, Martin?"

"Do what?" he asked, stopping the movement of his hands.

"That little pool stunt."

"I was just playing with the girls. I thought it would be fun. I didn't even know you were there."

"I don't believe that."

"I'm sure you don't. You don't much care what I think."

"What do you mean by that?" she said, setting her drink on the table.

"Oh, like 'I'm going to take a walk, that all right with you, John' like I don't even exist. I may be stuck in this chair, but I can take care of my own daughter. Most of the time you treat me like I'm some kind of child. And I can still swim, for Christ's sake. You don't have to decide everything. We used to talk, Elin. We don't talk anymore."

"You think it's been easy for me?"

"Bugger off, Elin."

The raw scorn that passed across his face chilled her. She glimpsed a piece of him she had never seen. The depth of it made her wonder whether he had read her own thoughts at the pool. As the next song started, he unlocked the brake on his chair and wheeled rapidly onto the dancefloor. Mary came over and took him by the hand and pulled and turned him, trying to catch up to the music. Because the bartender went back to the kitchen, John danced with Kaitlin. The young waiter brought out a liter of wine and three glasses.

Not far beyond the turn toward Paleokastrisa from Corfu Town was a large ceramic shop, and Elin had asked Spiro to stop for a few minutes on their way from the laundromat because she wanted to get something for Martin's mother. Spiro had told her this was a good place, less expensive than the shops along the beach. She knew the pattern and the kind of plate she wanted, so this wouldn't take long. Spiro had an errand to run anyway.

Bells on the door announced her entrance, and she

went directly to the plates and pitchers. She favored the floral patterns set against a white background by artists from Skyros, but the more geometric patterns from a workshop in the Peloponnese were also very appealing. In an impulse of deliberate intuitive choice, she cast her decision between a Skyros plate which appeared to have two blue peacocks arced like hands around a bed of flowers and one from the peninsula of concentric blue acorn shapes with a circle and star at its center.

When she looked up, she almost gasped. Wearing gray dress pants and a cream colored short-sleeved shirt was the hunter. He seemed to recognize her, at least the knowing smile and nod suggested that he did. He had intense blue eyes that looked boldly into hers. She struggled to regain her composure.

"Can I help you?" his voice was but an extension of his eyes, the way a hand represents the body.

"How much is this plate?" she asked, the words sounding too quiet, her fingers pointing at the wrong plate.

"This one?"

"No, the blue one, there."

"It's very nice, a good choice, we sell many of these. It is made by an icon-painter in Nauplion. Let's see, 25,000 drachmas. We have the same design in smaller sizes."

She bought a smaller one and negotiated a better price, all the while watching the agile movements, the delicate loving way he handled the plates. As he leaned, his shirt stretched across his back, revealing a trim angularity. He was clean-shaven, had dark curly hair and heavy black eyebrows. His skin was a glossy tan with a tint of green against the creamy shirt. A healthy radiance imbued his skin and smile, the even white teeth, the pink of his mouth. Something deep inside her seemed to swell and break, a melting warmth ran through her arms, down her legs and settled in her knees. This ache was like the sensation of falling or feeling something precious and fragile slip from her hands and crash to the floor. She felt weak, loose and lifeless like that bird that hung so limply from his hand. A dread seemed to squat against the center of her chest, push out in waves, and then come back to a hard center.

"Will this be all?"

"Yes," she said, snapping her credit card onto the glass, and smiling firmly into his blue eyes.

The day before they were supposed to leave, Elin arranged with Spiro to take them all to the beach at 11:00 and pick them up at 3:00. Only the last section of the dock had been taken down. Spiro found a piece of plywood to put over the one stair, and they wheeled Martin down easily. The water was deep enough to dive off the dock, so the girls jumped in and swam and examined the barnacles and green anemones. They pleaded with John and Elin to join them, but they sat in the lawnchairs under a large umbrella, drinking beer and reading the *Athens News*. Elin rubbed a thick layer of sunblock on Martin, so the red scars were pink and blurry. An umbrella was tied to the chair and wedged into a crack between the boards.

When the shade disappeared from his newspaper, Martin looked up. Elin was folding the umbrella.

"What are you doing? I'm reading the paper. It's too bright."

"You'll see," she said.

She put the rolled umbrella on the planks behind her, unlocked the wheels of Martin's chair, and pushed him toward the end of the dock.

"Elin, what are you doing?"

"John, will you help me here?"

Against Martin's half-hearted protests, they lifted up the chair and dumped him into the sea. He sank in an envelope of bubbles and bobbed to the surface in a burst of air and laughter. With easy breaststrokes, he swam out beyond the dock. Resting on his back, using his hands as flippers, he tested his mobility and buoyancy.

Under their umbrellas, the girls were thumbing through magazines in lawnchairs, wondering how their pictures with the young waiter would turn out, and what their friends might say when they brought them to school.

Elin put on goggles, grabbed the other pair, and jumped in after Martin.

They swam out beyond the white fish taverna with a green corrugated roof and along the steep craggy walls of basalt where the waves broke in a thin fringe of foam. They would dive and resurface, each time going farther.

The strength in Martin's arms from pushing his wheelchair propelled him easily, and Elin had to swim hard to catch up. When they reached the cliffs, they stopped to watch the fish and the light-struck bubbles, the puddles of seagrass reflecting iridescent flecks of color. Pinkish hydroids gently swayed with the wash of the waves. When Martin scrubbed the nappy plantlife with his hand, fish came in to feed from the floating debris: peacock and Turkish wrasses, and the timid blue damsel fish. He pointed to the peacock wrasses—the Thalassoma Pavo, as they had learned from a book Mary bought on Mediterranean fish. He followed one with his finger to show Elin. He mimed his disbelief, letting bubbles escape like underwater smoke signals. His face was lit by a boyish delight. When a cuttlefish floated by on its brown rippling skirt, it seemed to move very slowly like a float in a parade, a fluttering, stately strangeness. It had a self-possessed dignity that rode above the frantic effort at propulsion. When Elin reached out to touch it, the cuttlefish squirted little clouds of ink and scuttled into a bed of seaweed.

They swam together back through the zones of blue, along the rocky ledges, with the waves. They swam strongly, easily, as if they were inventing space and color, testing degrees of bouyancy, as if the shore to which they traveled were getting closer.

BLOOD

Through one corner of one eye he could see the dark turning gray. David lay watching the shades on the window apportion light, listening to the scattered eruptions of robins in the trees around the house. His body was trying to hum his mind back to sleep, to a numb swirling sanctuary. Because it was Saturday, he eased back down into the blankets. He was nearly asleep when his wife threw back the covers, sat up, and ran to the bathroom. He heard the lock click. After an "Oh, Oh" that came from some inarticulate depth, some sorrow bigger than language, she started to moan and cry at the same time.

The moaning turned into irregular sobs. He sat, trying to gather some clue. In the white half-moon the thrown covers made, he saw one drop of blood; thick and glistening, it was no bigger than the head of a tack. Because his body was straight-forward about the issue of blood, he had only a few fears to rely on. He went to the door and knocked gently, timidly.

"Jean, what's the matter?"

"Ohhh, God," more sobbing.

"Are you sick? Can I get you something?"

"Noooo! I'm bleeding. . ."

He heard the toilet flush and out of the swirling gurgle came more sobs, a moan that sounded like a chant in some guttural foreign tongue. Resting his arm on the dresser near the door, he waited for her to emerge, yet his stance seemed absurdly inappropriate, like legs lounging at a funeral. So he stood there, foolishly, in his tee-shirt and shorts, staring at the door. He was regarding the pattern of the grain when the door opened and his wife came out, sobbing into his arms.

She was wearing a white flannel nightgown with pink pin-stripes and faint flowers around the collar. The pillow had flattened the left side of her hair and puffed up the right so that she looked lopsided, unbalanced. The streak of grey that rose from her forehead then scattered over the rest of her head, as well as the wrinkles around her eyes, suddenly made her look older than she had ever looked before. David held her tightly as she cried into his shoulder, the hot wetness soaking through his tee-shirt. He stroked her hair and rubbed her back until the tears stopped and the muscles under his hands relaxed.

"I'll call the doctor and see if I can get in."

"Don't you mean 'we'?"

"What difference does it make to you?"

"Why wouldn't I care?"

"You should be happy now."

"Happy?"

"What do you know about it? Oh, I don't want to talk about it. You never wanted it, what do you care anyway? I mean be honest about it, for once. No, don't say anything, I'll call the doctor."

He stood, listening to her bare feet pad down the wooden floor of the hallway. He felt he was trapped in a silence that was accusatory, bottomless. Anything he could say would be an excuse, a treachery.

The drive to the clinic took about twenty minutes. After a long silence, he tried again.

"What do you think happened? Why now?"

"I don't know. Maybe it was the test. I was sick the next day and the day following. It's only been a week. They said the procedure was safe, but new. That's why we had to sign consent forms... I knew I shouldn't have listened to you."

"Me? I didn't force you to do anything. I just wanted to know if there was anything wrong. There's more risk, you know that."

"I was willing to take it."

"Even if there was something wrong?"

"Yes."

"Well, I'm sorry, I wasn't, so it's my fault?"

"No. I didn't say that. I think men often just don't understand. To you it is like going to the store and picking up something that looks like you. It's abstract, an idea. It comes and goes like the dream of a boat or something. For us, our body and mind feel it at once, together, it's not abstract at all. We may not want it, or feel we can manage it, but it's not abstract. It's as real as blood, as a heart beating under your hand." Her face was pallid, distant.

David watched the storefronts and traffic lights and people along the streets pass in a blur like spectators at a race. He was thinking, now, about his father who ran his house with military order. The time his airplane, wound up with a rubberband, sailed into the mashed potatoes during one of those late after-work dinners caused a bloodless anger. As he sat in the dark closet to "think about it" he vowed never to have kids. He sat on large shoes and played with the tip of an umbrella. The hems of coats touched his head and the air smelled old, tinged with mothballs and wool and wood. As he drove along, he could still remember the smell.

His father was always disappointed that David was not more athletic, that he wasn't as popular with girls as he had been, that his regard for animals made him not want to hunt deer and elk, though he had done it. His father had come from a family of hunters, and they took pride in it perhaps because it was one of the few activities that excluded women—and they could revel in this privacy. He remembered the boyish play in the mornings as they prepared to go, the jokes full of bravado and whimsy, the shoulder slaps, the meticulous gathering and inspection of the guns, knives, and clothing. David loved it all except the one defining moment a split-second after the trigger was pulled: the paralyzed and bleeding struggle of the animal which a moment before was beautifully capable, alert to the faintest rustle of the dried balsam leaves, poised and charged with pure energy. When he was fifteen, he had killed a deer and an elk, yet each time the high-fives, beer salutes, and stories afterwards were not enough to outweigh that one moment, so he remained apart from them.

He remembered one incident as defining. He was in high school and had driven out to his grandfather's place where most of the hunting occurred. It was the afternoon of opening day, and everyone was back from the hunt. His grandfather, who was seventy-one, had shot a large four-point mule deer and was skinning it when he arrived. His father and uncles were there as well. His grandfather stood up, held the deer's scrotum and a fatty cord dangling on his knife-point, and said, "Anyone care for some oysters tonight?" His father pointed at David and said, "Give them to Dave, I think he's missing a set." David could still hear the laughter of his uncles, his father and grandfather. Perhaps it was only an attempt to draw him back into the fold, but it felt like a betrayal.

Women seemed to be able to achieve a kind of privacy

among men. By ironic insinuation, by eye-rolls and grins, by the occasional jab of open ridicule, they were able to carve out a place for themselves amidst family gatherings. Perhaps it came out of the work of meal preparations, the seasons and cycles of nurturing both the infants and the aged, the orders they could give men who preferred an ignorant idleness so they could watch football or baseball on television. The sanctuary of this shared power, the clear rightness of it, shielded them from whatever glib assaults the men might attempt. David knew he didn't understand the elements in this balance of power, but he felt their effects; he also felt a need for this camaraderie, this shared privacy, but for him it was never sustained over time. The friends from college that he felt most connected to had disappeared into their own lives, except for an occasional visit where good humored exuberance and affection were followed by another year or two of absence.

So, unsure of his allegiances, that promise to himself, made in the closet's darkness, had always stayed with him like a talisman he wore around his neck. He didn't exactly believe in it, but there was a superstitious reality about it that time had hardened. He knew it was silly, immature, but relinquishing it was almost like an admission that his father was right somehow, but he didn't know about what.

Yet for his wife he had relinquished it, consented to change his life dramatically, consented to change the look of every hour for the rest of his life. The decision wasn't entirely selfless, though. He was aware that having children was such an elemental part of life that to miss it was tantamount to evasion, to coddling his own preciousness, so that his vow seemed empty, merely vengeful. He also felt, deep down, that he could do it better, not only out of a sense of competition with his father, but as a measure of his generosity and patience.

When they got to the clinic, David put his arm around Jean as they walked up the steps. He opened the large glass doors that led into a carpeted waiting room with black and white pictures of farm scenes on the walls. Jean filled out the forms for the insurance, and they sat down near the window and water fountain. A jovial-looking man sat two seats down from them, his three year old was sitting on the floor scribbling in an animal coloring book. A young woman in the corner held a baby wrapped in a cotton blanket.

The boy on the floor looked up at David and Jean as they sat down. David watched the boy's hand move as it gripped a green crayon. It was erratic, wild at times, yet his intent reigned in the wildness, and the loops and shadings had a center like the illustration of an atom in motion. He thought about this wildness, how each of us uses and controls it, lets it control us occasionally, and most of the time our fists are locked around a crayon, an image as stylized as one of the animals in the boy's book. Then, a nurse with a clipboard walked smoothly into the waiting-room.

"Joyce Peterson?"

"Here" said the woman with the baby, and she began to gather her purse, diaper bag, and the pacifier that was upside down on the seat next to her.

The boy got up as the woman walked toward him. When she had passed, the boy looked at his father and said, "Daddy, my feet are sparkling."

"What do you mean?"

"My feet are sparkling."

"Oh, that's because you've been sitting on them. Just walk around a little and they'll be okay," the man said, as he reached down and rubbed the boy's leg.

David looked over at Jean who had a faint trace of a smile but her eyes were still dark and glistening. He touched her forearm but her arm lay limp on her lap, her fingers clenched. She looked away toward the wall with the picture of an antique hayrake half-buried in snow and sage. He crossed his arms and watched the clock's second hand make tiny spasmodic jumps around the clock-face.

"How are your feet now?" asked the man as his boy walked to him and crawled into his lap.

"Not pretty good," said the boy. His father put down his magazine, took off the boy's black tennis shoes, and rubbed his feet.

When at last Jean's name was called by another nurse with a clipboard, they followed her to the doctor's examination room. It had a poster with pictures of children pasted in concentric rings. David thought that they must be children the doctor delivered. There was a short counter of bottles, swabs, tongue depressors, a reflex hammer, a blood pressure kit, a vaginal speculum, scissors. On a door with a mirror was a little magazine rack with only one magazine, People, a month out of date. A snapshot of a blue columbine was taped to the ceiling above the examination table. Jean thumbed through the magazine, letting the images flash across her field of sight but not really focusing closely or reading. David thought about the picture of the columbine and wondered whether the nurse or the doctor had put it there. He decided it was the nurse.

When the doctor came in with Jean's chart, his white

coat open, a stethoscope dangling from his neck, he was cordial and wore a look of concern. He was nearly bald, had thick black-framed glasses, slightly crooked teeth, and a rotund middle-aged belly. He sat down, took off his stethoscope and put it on the counter.

"I see you've experienced some bleeding."

"Yes," she said, looking at the floor.

"There are several things that could have caused it. It could be intercourse related."

"No, it's not that."

"Have you taken any blood thinners?"

"No. I think it was the pregnancy test."

"Well, we really won't know until we take another ultrasound or examine the cervix for tissue." He then picked up his stethoscope and listened to her stomach. "I can't hear anything. Let's go have a look."

They all went to the small room that housed the ultrasound equipment. The woman who operated it before was not there, so the doctor opened a tube of gel and smeared it on Jean's stomach, then he operated the wand and looked at the screen.

"You know, Jean, that regardless of whether it was the test or not, usually a miscarriage is the body's way of correcting problems. Almost twenty percent of pregnancies end in a miscarriage. You shouldn't take it personally, it may have happened anyway. Probably would have, but we can't really know. When can you make it in for a D&C."

Through her tears, Jean managed, "Any time, really."

"Well, if you could come in tomorrow afternoon, at one, say, we could do it then."

"What's a DNC," asked David.

"Dilation and curettage, a procedure to clean the uterus and avoid infection. A curette is like a spoon which is used to scrape away dead tissue or growths from a body cavity."

David envied the doctor's easy voice that maneuvered through questions he must have answered hundreds of times. His answers were inflected with concern, calmly and gravely stated. His eyes, slightly magnified through his glasses, never wavered into self-consciousness even when addressing David with a sweeping look or gesture.

The doctor stood up, and Jean and David did too. Tears were streaming down Jean's face, and the doctor reached out his left hand and tucked the clipboard under his right arm. He gave Jean a rigid hug and the tears made a little wet smudge above the left pocket of his coat. David wondered whether the rigidness was caused by his presence. As they left, the hallway was too narrow for them to walk together, but when they got outside, he put his arm around Jean and she leaned her head against him as they walked slowly to their car. He asked if she'd like to go out for a late breakfast, but she said she wasn't hungry. They rode in silence back to their house.

It was evening before either of them felt like talking. After dinner, they sat for a while under the kitchen light as the other rooms darkened. It was quiet, and they could hear the hum of the refrigerator, the tick of the clock in the living room. Outside, a dog barked, a distant siren wailed. David rolled an olive seed back and forth on his plate with a fork.

"You know, I've been thinking about my Dad off and on all day. I don't want to be like him and the funny thing is the more we react against someone, the more we become them. So I have a toast. I have been dragging my feet for a long time and they're asleep and they should have been sparkling. So here's to sparkling feet."

"Okay," she said, "I'll drink to that," and they clinked their glasses.

Although she had said she didn't blame him, David thought she did. This blame was not apparent in anything she said, directly. It accumulated from gestures, sighs, sideways looks, a curt reply that ended a move toward love-making. He'd find tearspots on pillows. She'd get up in the middle of the night and read women's magazines about the psychology of men, the emotional needs of women, how to raise children, sex. She began to drink during these night-sessions. He'd wake to find her asleep on the couch and the new bourbon bottle half empty. Sometimes she would sit at her desk and stare out the window, and when the phone rang, she'd just let it ring even though there was a phone on her desk. Housework seemed a burden to her, so David did most of it. She might bake an elaborate dessert, but she would leave all the unused ingredients out, the dirty spoons and bowls and mixing equipment on the counters and in the sink. And often the desserts would go uneaten; they would dry in their pans and drop into the trash, hardened into disks.

She wouldn't talk to him about how she felt, but she talked to several of her friends, who told their husbands, and it would eventually come back to David. He didn't know if in this serial retelling things were exaggerated or down-played for his benefit. Every time he tried to open a conversation with her, she would get up, leave the room, and busy herself with some housework that at other times may have been left for weeks. A hard silence began to grow between them.

This rhythm of silent action, questions whose answers were yes or no, roast beef or chicken, this weekend or next, began to harden into habit. They would go months without making love and when they did it would be after a night of drinking and she would leave the bed crying when they were finished. They hadn't used any contraception since her miscarriage, yet she had not gotten pregnant again. The miscarriage had evolved into something exclusively "hers," as if David were merely a spectator.

Sometimes, at family gatherings or in a restaurant, she would watch a child who would have been their child's age. Her attention was detached and defeated; she would have to get up and make a bleary trip to the restroom. The silence that inevitably followed was as taut and cold as a skin of ice. She felt that she was not prepared for the emotions she was feeling. She had known few great disappointments in her life.

During her sophomore year of college, she wanted to be a painter. She had come to art through a love of paintings by the Impressionists: the fields of poppies by Monet and Renoir, Monet's haystacks and bridges and cathedrals, Renoir's hazy boaters, Degas's bathers and dancers which seemed to catch life in motion, to endow things and people with a fleeting beauty and intensity. In these paintings, the awkward, loud, sweaty edges had been rounded and modeled into a purity of sensation untainted by self-conscious and clumsy yearnings. This was what she wanted to paint, yet she never could. Her canvasses seemed garish, so removed from life her roommate who was an English major laughed at them, had told her they were "maudlin." When she looked the word up, she almost cried, but she

knew her roommate was cultivating harsh aesthetic judg-
ments under the guise of honesty and directness so that she
could appear wise and urbane. This realization, however,
was not a consolation. Although she defiantly kept on
painting, something inside her acknowledged the truth of
what her roommate had said, and the long all-night painting
vigils with other students before finals began to seem vain, a
game they played too seriously.

The lifelessness of her canvasses seemed to corre-
spond to her own emptiness. Besides her sister who had
chosen not to go to college, she had no real friends, no one
she could call at any hour just to talk, no one who cared
how she was feeling or what she was doing. The men she
knew looked at her as if she were a hatstand with breasts,
and their humor always seemed to have one agenda. Even
the art students, who were more clever and watchful than
the men who turned out for sports, seemed like frauds.
They talked about more interesting things, but the
impatient glaze that waited for her to finish talking so that
they could get back to themselves was the same, and their
eyes would rove to her breasts during some part of the
conversation, and back again.

Her mother had warned her repeatedly about men, but
she felt she could take care of herself. Her parents had a
small farm in Idaho near Pocatello. They raised goats, made
goat cheese and sold it, but few stores would carry it. She had
shown the goats in 4-H, and three out of four years she had
won grand champion. She had chosen goats because unlike
steers, lambs, and swine, they weren't sold and butchered
after the show. When she looked back on this time with her
parents and sister, she could still feel the confidence,

direction, and respect that accompanied those memories. The trips with her father across the state to livestock shows had about them a settled ease and safety she would give anything to feel again.

She disliked David's family, especially his father who had begun stopping by unexpectedly. He would pick up tools and fishing and hunting gear at yard sales and drop them off, whether they needed them or not. In recent weeks, he had begun talking about one last hunting trip with his boys. She hated hunting. She thought it was a ritual slaughter of innocents; it was violence tainted by a weird, almost sexual thrill. Their arguments about hunting intensified as David's father pushed for this last reunion and David seemed more and more willing to do it. He maintained that anybody who ate meat merely paid to have others do the killing and belittled the hard work they did; in order to truly appreciate the animal one should know its life intimately, see the blood on one's own hands. Each argument began and ended the same way, yet when David finally agreed to go on this trip, she felt that the argument had entered another level where words and actions were more closely and strictly aligned.

"So, you're going to go, then."

"Yes, it's what he wants and it's probably the last time."

"Oh, he'll probably live to be a hundred, as ornery as he his."

"Well, maybe. It's only three days in October, and I think I can manage it."

"Sounds like he's doing the managing."

Usually when this tone entered the conversation, he knew where it would end, so he got up and went out the door. He had bought a bow, some arrows, a bale of straw, and a target. He had decided that if he hunted he was going to do things on his own terms. His father and brothers had often criticized bow hunters as would-be Indians or people who wanted to manipulate hunting regulations, but David was interested in the interplay between hunter and prey, the unapologetic immediacy and directness of it. This became a kind of moral issue, a test which would prove he was neither a hypocrite nor a trigger-happy bum. To ready himself, he practiced shooting arrows almost every night after work. At first he had difficulty timing the pull, aim, and release, but in two months' time he could hit four out of five shots within the two innermost circles from seventy-five yards away.

As the days of the hunt approached, Jean seemed to get more sullen. In the evenings, she would sit with a cup of tea in her hands, a book in her lap, and stare out the window. Most conversations were complaints about her job in the City Manager's office. The manager was having an affair with one of the secretaries and the consequent shifts in relations among the office staff, the gossip, the amount of work piling up, upset her. Besides that, one of the women she disliked the most in the Light Department had announced that she was pregnant and due in March. Little ironies like this and David's hunting fueled an indefinable irritation.

The evening before the hunt, Jean watched David gather his gear: a camouflaged jacket, insulated boots, bow and arrows, candy bars. She found his absorption in this ritual, his unconscious ease and organization, grating. She watched him over her book, and suddenly felt a loathing she had never felt before. It came like the smell of rotted meat she might discover in the refrigerator. There was a queasy panic in the wake of this sensation that startled her. The words in her book seemed to melt and blur like a summer road-mirage, and she could not follow the story, but she sat under her lamp until David went to bed. She called her sister in Idaho and talked for over an hour.

David got up in the dark, and when he went out to load his car, it was cold. He held his breath to read the thermometer on the porch: twenty-six degrees. The grass was frosted, his windshield needed to be scraped, and the plastic hose was curled tight and hard as a snail. He made a thermos of coffee while his car was warming up.

He drove through a thin fog for an hour before reaching his brother's place in the foothills of the Cascades. Like his father, Deral was a lawyer and had bought their grandfather's place from his grandmother after he had died. He had torn down the old house and built a large modern one. David thought it belonged in a suburb, at the end of a cul-de-sac where it could compete with the other houses around it. Deral and his father often ridiculed him about his salary and told him that if he'd become anything but a history teacher he might have been able to make some money. When he and Deral were alone together, his brother was more candid and considerate. As David pulled into the driveway, he could tell that his father was already there. A single light shone from the kitchen.

"Why hello, little brother, I wasn't sure you were going to make it," he held the screen door open with one hand and the large scrolled oak door open with the other. He seemed to David like a bird taking him under its wing.

"I said I would," David replied, wiping his feet on the basket of daisies inscribed on the welcome mat.

"Come on in, Dad's already here, he spent the night."

Deral looked tired and hung-over, but his glossy manner

and host responsibilities seemed to revive and animate him. His father came out of the bathroom, zipping his fly, and mumbling to himself. His hands trembled and the zipper seemed stuck. finally he got it, looked up, and said, "Don't ever get old—you can't even put your own pecker away, and there's nobody left who might want to do it for you," his deliberate grin could not disguise his frustration.

They all sat down over a cup of coffee and plotted their strategy. Deral and their father would drive to the line-shack, climb the hill behind it, and sit beside the large ponderosa pine that faced the small meadow which stood at the intersection of two well-used deer trails. David would be dropped off on the way up, and he'd work the ridges and draws. They would meet for lunch.

At 9:30 David had been walking and climbing for nearly three hours, so he sat down to rest and have a Snickers bar. Just as he was about to start climbing again, he heard shale slide and scrape below him. He was on a knoll and didn't want to risk walking to its edge, so he strung an arrow and waited behind a fir tree. A two-point buck walked casually into view, browsing on tufts of wheatgrass. At about sixty-five yards, he stopped and scanned the opposite ridge as if he had detected some motion or scent. David pulled, aimed, exhaled slowly, and released the arrow. As it hit, the deer humped up like a doe that had to pee. It looked in David's direction, and in two jumps disappeared over the edge of the knoll. He ran after it, but when he got to the edge, he couldn't see it. Then, twenty yards away, the deer rose, looked at him and fell, its four legs spinning down the hill. David moved closer, and the deer got up again, blood running from its nose, its eyes glassy. It tried to move and again fell over and slid further down the slope through pine needles and a patch of snowberry bushes.

When David caught up to it, the buck's breathing was clogged with mucous and blood. Its neck pulsed with the effort to breathe. David grabbed a horn at the fork and twisted the head back, sliced his knife across the exposed throat. Although the knife was sharp, the hair and thickness of the skin prevented it from cutting deeply. He tried again, and the knife-stroke made a crude rasping sound as it nicked the windpipe. He cut again, wildly, digging deeper, until the blood gushed over his hand and drained to the ground. The hot odor of the deer's steam, wet hair, and blood surprised him. He had not remembered its pungent heaviness, like sage and sweat. Each time the rasping sound seemed to get louder, more brutal, and when he dropped its head, it hit solidly like rock on rock. He stood a minute, shaking, the wet blood cooling on his hand, then bent over and vomited. He sat down, his hand over his knee, the knife and his finger still dripping blood.

When the waves of sickness stopped, he got up to gut the deer. He rolled it over so the offal would slide out downhill. He pushed his knife through the skin near the anus and began to make a slit, but his knife had penetrated the colon and hot green pellets trickled out onto his hand and into the small cavity he had just made. He cursed, wiped his blade off on the deer's side, and began again. He sawed his blade past the penis and testicles—oysters. He thought it was strange that over twenty years had not erased the roil of embarrassment and anger he had felt then. It heated his arm and guided the knife smoothly to the breastbone. He laid the knife on the deer's side and reached in to pull out the paunch, intestines. The hot steam, sweat, membranes, the smell of composting grass, all seemed to invade his head and clothing. Although the offal had rolled out onto the grass, he had to reach back in with his knife in order to cut it loose from the backbone. In the process, he nicked the bladder which leaked urine over the pile of guts and his hands. Its smell was a mix of ammonia and wet sage. He held his breath and went in after the lungs and heart.

When he stood up, he looked like he had been shot himself. His shirt-sleeves were soaked even though he had rolled them up; his belly and thighs and pantlegs and boots were splattered and splashed with blood. He cut out the heart and liver, put them in a plastic bag he'd carried in his back pocket, and took out a red handkerchief to wipe his hands.

After he had rested a while, he tagged his deer, picked up his bow and arrows, and started to climb the mile or so back up towards his brother and father. As he climbed, the blood that had soiled his clothes hardened and darkened. His hands felt stiff and chalky. He rubbed them together but it did no good.

He wondered how many of his thoughts lacked the smells, tastes, textures, and sounds that qualified his strongest opinions. He wondered how many half-truths he had passed on in his classroom. He thought of Gettysburg. His lectures to seventeen year old boys. He had tried to explain what the Battle of Gettysburg was to the foot-soldier. He had read many accounts from historians, and the facts about it had solidified into a picture he illustrated again and again: he had described their thin, inappropriate uniforms, the caps that could not stop a bullet, their knapsacks, the rifled musket which replaced the Brown Bess with a deadly accuracy, Pickett's blind chivalrous cavalry charge up Cemetery Hill and the fierce slaughter, the smoke screen caused by the black powder of the artillery that made day dusk, the 51,000 casualties in three days, the chorus of cries they made in the moonlit night, the seventeen miles of wagons hauling away the Confederate dead, the pall of putrefaction that hung over the town of Gettysburg for three months. These facts were his own smoke screen. What did he know of the blood, the bayonets ripping into flesh and the rasping sound of metal through muscle, the screams and agony, the smells, the terrible fears and loneliness of these young boys for whom sex was as mysterious as death? What could he know of that? A man who puked at the death of a deer? Yet he had told them, had speculated grandly about what it was like. What did he know about the pangs of childbirth? The seeping dread of a miscarriage? Or children, what did he know? How else but by doing it yourself was it possible to know or judge others, even his father, or Deral?

After walking for nearly forty-five minutes over basalt scree, windfall, and through clumps of salal and thickets of pine, he decided to stop and have some coffee. The fog that had settled in the valleys had almost disappeared except for a thin line that still clung to the river. He could see patches of blue opening above him, and the sun and his walking made him unbutton his jacket, take off his camouflage stocking-cap. He sat in the duff beneath a ponderosa pine, breathing in the sweet fragrance of its needles and resins, its flakes of bark like thin puzzle pieces. He unscrewed the lid of his thermos and poured a cup. It was then that he realized with a sudden clarity his wife would not be home when he returned. He had seen the signs without actually seeing them, but now, suddenly, they came together. He felt a faint release like that second the key engages a stubborn doorlock, and opens. The blood on his hands had dried a deep red, making a crosshatch of creases and fissures. His skin was bright and white beneath this ruddy sheath. He sat, letting the warm coffee steam curl over his face.

FISH GROOMING

Seth used to pack his lunch and eat in his office, but since the separation from his wife he liked getting out. It felt invigorating in a way he didn't quite understand. He noticed now which stores had awnings, their colors, the pulleys and ratchets that held them to the edifice. He looked at the decorated windows and tried to guess the kind of woman who arranged the little stuffed animals so they watched a circling train, the man who spread out fishing gear and splayed the rods like pond reeds, the woman who painted a wedding cake and table on the glass so that the cake was on the verge of tipping into the street.

He was a large man—tall, bony-jointed, with a strong face whose blue eyes had a stubborn intensity. He had thick black eyebrows, high cheekbones, and a head full of curly silvery-black hair. His ears seemed pinned against his head or taped at the tops. His nose was thin and curved slightly at the end. When he stood up, he was like an antique piece of farming equipment lurching into life. His dark blue pants were a little too short, his white socks just visible below the cuff. He wore a broad leather belt with a rodeo buckle he had won years ago in a roping contest. His blue and black plaid cotton shirt was tucked in behind it. He always took off his hat when he went inside shops or offices, but kept it on in department stores.

Although it was nearly 1:30, he typically took his lunch late so his mechanics could take theirs at noon. Last month he had forgotten to renew his driver's license, and now the

Motor Vehicles Building was closed for a week for renovations, so he had to be cautious about where he drove. It seemed an odd twist of fate that he was kept from driving cars it was his job to put on the road. One of his mechanics was doing the test drives, a part of the work he liked. He prided himself on being able to hear what was wrong before opening the hoods of cars or trucks. It was as if they had voices and one merely had to know how to listen. Burnt points, crusted plugs, ticking radiators, whining u-joints, shuddering carburetors, each part had its specific complaint and wanted him to hear it. He could tell by the taste of leaking fluid what it was, where it came from, and what the repairs entailed.

As he sat at a corner café, waiting for his half sandwich and vegetable soup, he watched people walk by and wondered about the chaos they were stepping through at that moment. A man in khaki pants and a white knit sweater sat before a red and white checkered tablecloth, a red beret on his head, glasses strung around his neck, reading a book. He wondered if the book contributed to or diminished the man's personal chaos. Why a red beret? What was he saying with it? That he had traveled, that he walked under a separate sun, that the years swirled and washed against his feet differently? Was he deliberately trying to change his life? Was he having an affair? Affair. Such a quiet sleek noiseless word for the brassy cacophony which follows it. It seemed breezy and casual, perhaps even a little elegant, like aperitif. Yet it was rag and mop work, knives and bandages.

The old woman who had been looking for something in her purse now seemed to be interested in him. Perhaps he had been talking to himself? Her brown wig sat slightly askew so that her head seemed to be leaning forward. When he looked directly at her, she opened a gold compact and touched her cheeks with a rosy flesh-colored powder. Then she applied red lipstick, with a deliberate absorption as if it were more than habit, a moment of self-indulgence that was complete, entire, like that moment after a bowler releases the ball and his hand rests in air, hangs there poised. He thought of his wife's habits, those moments when she was most herself.

He had watched her once through the plate glass window of Werther's Department Store as she went through a table of discounted items. The sure abstract motion of her fingers, the settled intensity in her face, the little rhythmic swing of the purse on her arm, suggested a composure he rarely saw at home where schoolwork, meals, laundry, bills, and vacuuming bit holes in any vacant hour.

For over a month he had been suspicious of her schedule and the change in some of these habits. She worked at the Employment Security office part-time; she helped the unemployed register for benefits and clarify their job skills, working from 8-12 a.m. five days per week. She contacted potential employers, conducted seminars about resumes and the changing job market. Several nights in the past few months she had to go in to give evening seminars to people who could not come in during the day. If they were unemployed, why couldn't they come in during the day, he wanted to know. She would give him an exasperated, exhausted look and tell him that her agency also tried to help those who wanted to train for new jobs, better jobs.

When she got home at 10:30 or 11 at night, she locked herself in the bathroom, took a long shower, went into each of the kid's rooms and kissed them and went to bed. In the morning, she was always in a rush making the kids' lunches, putting out breakfast dishes, carrying armloads of laundry to the washer, sweeping the floor. Things she usually did in the evening. Most of their thorough housekeeping had been done on Saturdays and the house slowly filled with clutter from Monday to Friday. They each did small everyday things like taking out garbage, picking up clothes, loading and unloading the dishwasher. Her new rage for cleanliness was suspicious.

When she got off work at noon, she used to come to the garage several times a week. They ate sack lunches together, talked about school activities their kids were involved in, worked out the schedules for picking them up from soccer practice and piano lessons. About two months ago she had taken on the responsibility for the children's schedules almost exclusively, without any discussion. And she had stopped having lunch at his garage.

"Would you like more crackers with your soup, sir?" the young waitress asked, smiling as if crackers was a word that was odd and strange on her tongue.

"Yes, please," he said, nodding his head, picking up a soup spoon. His hat sat across from him and he suddenly noticed how peculiar it seemed, as if he were having lunch with it or advertising his garage to himself. He hung it on the back of his chair. The waitress's youth, her aura of awkward self-awareness, the carelessness in her walk made him sit up straighter, conscious of the spoon rising and aiming for his mouth. He watched her sure movements, the slide of her dress across her butt, the sway of her breasts as she leaned to set tables. Her blonde hair was pulled up and pinned but some escaped to fringe her face like the frayed cuff on a pair of jeans. Her eyes were dark brown, her lips a little pouty as if this job were only an amusement, a plaything, until her life assumed its greater, fuller shape. He suddenly saw her naked, stepping out of the shower, the smoothness of her flesh which had not yet begun to dimple or pucker or flatten. He thought of his hand brushing her breasts, sweeping down across her belly, on into the soft tufted tangled mesh between her thighs.

"Coffee, sir?" said some voice behind him. It was another waitress, young but tired, as if she had children at home and was driven by a schedule she neither desired nor remembered choosing. There was a residue of contempt in her "sir."

He nodded, the spoon still in his mouth. It was not a silver spoon, and for many years he had been proud of that. He had his life in his own hands without obligation to anyone. His father had worked for a John Deere dealership most of his life, and his mother was a teacher in a small Christian school. They never made much money, but it was enough. They could afford the few things they wanted most, yet had enough to give something to the church every Sunday. Seth had worked hard all his life, too. His garage had four bays, and he hired three mechanics full-time and one part-time. It wasn't that he made a lot of money, but it was his, nobody was telling him what to clean up or put away, how to hang the wrenches, how many greaserags to use. Yet he wondered how long it would be his.

He thought of the pained, impossible, stricken look that flashed across his wife's face on the last day that they had shared the same house, and it gave him no pleasure. For her

birthday, he was going to have a blue sapphire set in gold.
They had bought the stone at a gem show, but she had kept it
in her jewelry box for three years. He was going to surprise her
and show that he had not forgotten. Yet what he found under
the felt compartment of earrings and buried beneath the
necklaces was a packet of condoms. After their last child was
born, she wanted him to get a vasectomy, and he did, willingly.
He had thought it was an unequal bargain, given the rigors of
childbirth. He stood there holding the little packet in his hands
as all the odd wayward questions were suddenly answered.

He had let it go on for two more weeks. At first, he felt
enraged, then eviscerated, stupid. Where was the center of
his anger? Was it the violation of their vows, the trust
implicit in their intimacy? Was it the violation of ownership,
possession, like people who come home to find objects
stolen, a window broken, their things pawed through? Was it
embarrassment, being the chump, the fool, the cuckold? Was
it sorrow, sorry for himself, the weight of their time together,
their children's changing lives? Was it jealousy, another man
inside his wife's body, her moving on so finally and completely without him? Was it failure, to satisfy, to love well?
Was it this acquiescence that made him seem paltry, weak?
Was it the sheer and utter boredom in fifteen years together?
He knew well the lewd daydreams, the lusty visions that rose
unbidden from the hormonal murk within him, but he had
never once acted upon them, had never uttered an encourag-
ing word to another woman—only because he felt so much
regard for the easy peace of trust, the suspicionless assump-
tions and liberties of that trust.

Why did his mind always come back to their nakedness,
the gleeful secrecy, the heightened rush of the illicit? The

more he thought about it, the more the question seemed like a tank of orange feeder fish. All the answers swam in and out of the shadowy cloud of themselves, over and under each other so that he never knew which was which. When he looked at one in isolation, it was bright and orange and true. Yet all were imprisoned, for sale, on show, and the one struggling flopping thing he'd netted began to look like all the others. For two weeks, he listened to the tractable confidence of her lies, watching the patterns of her deceit: the long showers, the housework, the good-night kisses for the children, her averted eyes. There was a power in this knowledge which began to feel like a kind of revenge. finally, there was the confrontation, the shouting match, tears, slammed doors, his bitter accusations, her leaving.

The man in the red beret had closed his book and exhaled loudly, almost a sigh. Seth watched him stand, straighten his unseasonable sweater, and walk to the counter with a slight limp as if in sitting too long a muscle had tightened. He tucked his book under his arm, then got out his wallet and paid his bill. The old woman sat under her wig, sipping tea. The blonde waitress seemed to have disappeared, and when he paid the bill, the tired waitress who a had pencil stuck behind her ear said, "that'll be $4.89" as if she were calling the next bingo number in some endless, all-night game.

Their first irresolvable arguments had centered on how best to raise their son. Colin did not sleep well and each night ended with him in their bed. Often, he started out there just to save having to get up. Their bed wasn't big enough for all of them, so each had a cramped, fitful night of sleep. He thought his son should be forced to stay in his own bed. She began to think of him as hard-hearted and selfish. He began to think of her as pampering and using the child to avoid intimacy. He saw himself as being slowly replaced by his children; he was there to plop down his paycheck and keep quiet. She thought he was using the issue of money to remind her of his power, her dependency; he thought she needed some independence, some sense of accomplishment that was hers and hers alone.

Slowly, they had entered patterns of opposition. They communicated, but neither acted on that communication. She found fulfillment in shopping at thrift stores. At first, this seemed wonderful. She brought home beautiful dishes and pots, knives and glasses, vases and furniture, and clothes. Most of their things they had gotten out of need at second-hand stores anyway, and this was a way of replacing the shabby and worn-out. She had brought home surprising items like a hand-painted plate from Greece, a clay fish-shaped platter, Irish crystal, Cole Haan loafers without detectable wear, Harris tweed, Versace and Vuitton clothes.

Then, after all the shabby things in their house had been replaced, their storage began to fill up with leather purses, boxes of shoes, wooden tripods for cameras and survey lenses, silverware, wineglasses. The closets filled with coats and jackets and dresses, most of which were never worn more than once. The garage was filled with plastic storage boxes full of clothes. There were pictures and picture frames stacked behind the sofa, storage boxes of videos under the bed; they bought extra bookcases for the children's rooms for all the books, and still they were stacked in heaps on the floor; the utility room was full of clothes and boxes, it was almost impossible to do laundry without restacking things. The lid to the dryer couldn't open without removing a basket of hand-woven throw rugs. The house was getting harder and harder to clean because of the stacks of things, and no place to put them. When he complained, she recoiled and argued that this was her one joy, her one happiness, and he was denying it.

He was bullying, it was her house too. She started taking Prozac. There would be whole days of silence, a month would go by without their having sex; she would read stacks of books about women and spirituality. finally, she started seeing a counselor, then he did. They talked about their complaints, talked about them, but always the same patterns came slowly back.

The counselor's waiting room was small, airless, and sparsely decorated like most of the fringe professionals in a small town—the massage therapist, the credit counselor, the lawyer with a fishing habit. The plants rose on spindly stalks, the magazines were old and looked like they had been collected from the library's free bin because the subscriber's name had been torn off, a few dusty western prints hung on the walls, papers were piled on an empty desk, messages stuck to a cork board above the phone. As Seth waited, he could overhear the loud voice of Bob Severin because the door wasn't closed. He had been required to have counseling after two DWIs and a charge of domestic violence. He was a large man with a larger voice; he filled a room just by walking into it. He was the head mechanic at Valley Ford, and Seth had worked with him a number of years ago.

"Okay, I'm a man. I like being a man. So what's wrong with that? I'm not saying I like being with men, in that sense, the sexual sense. But yes I prefer men. We can talk and do something at the same time. We can lie on our backs, with a light hooked to a tie rod, open up a gear box, check out the wheels, the collar, the dogteeth, and carry on a perfectly simple conversation about the Yakima River and what's hitting. Or the Mariners without Griffey. Or a play. I mean the art kind, or a movie. I said that for you because you probably don't think I've ever been to a goddamn play in my life. I watch pieces of them go by everyday, like clockwork. Just because you got your nose in grease every day doesn't mean it's never been anywhere else. The grease doesn't hurt either."

"I never implied it did," the counselor said, shifting in his seat.

"You didn't need to. Now you take your average woman. They fall all over themselves trying to be nice to each other, high moral standards, no dirt under the nails, hair curlered to match some princess hairdo. Little flowers embroidered on the lapel. That sort of shit. They spray on some French perfume like it wasn't made from the ass of a cat. They try to make a house the same way. Ruffled curtains, little scenes laid out in angelhair on a windowsill, plates on the wall instead of the cupboard, bookshelves lined with photos of vacations which were designed as just another decoration. It's all a play, invisible actors, the director's on a lunch-run."

"What do you think this bitterness, in any way, goes back to?"

"That's about all you guys can think of. Can I smoke in here?"

"No, but you may step outside that door over there and take a break if you wish."

"I'll smoke on my own time. The way I see it Freud left you a gold mine. My mother put her shoulders to the harness and pulled straight and narrow all day long. She didn't have time for princess hairdos. People today lift a finger, turn around, and look for applause. Hell, I can't get a mechanic to stay more than a year, and they got a thousand excuses for not showing up."

"Let's get back to your problem with women."

"Is that what this is? If that's it then there's no point in me being here. If that's the extent of it. I thought you were supposed to be some kind of objective voice."

"I was merely describing what you've been talking about, it's not a clinical diagnosis. How do you and your wife get along, usually?"

"Well, probably like most men and women. Our bodies are about as different as night and day. A botched design. Why in the hell does a man get an erection at 4:30 in the morning every goddamn morning of his life? Ever seen a woman awake at that hour? It's all a dumbshow."

"Why do you think so?"

"A male body is like a firecracker with a fuse that gets a bit longer as you get older. It burns quietly for a couple of days, getting hotter as it goes. It's like that fruit-waste dumped in pits. It heats up in a slow smokeless burn. That fire smolders there, quietly heating up, until a little heat pocket raises the voice, slams doors, or kicks dogs. You have sex and you're in love again, the fire's put out, the steam rises. You want to help little old ladies across the goddamned street. It's the fountain of youth. Then the next day the fuse is lit again. The heat heats up slowly. A piss-poor design."

"And women are different?"

"You married or you just earnin' the boat here?"

"I'm only trying to help you. Although you are required to be here because of your DWI's, Mr. Severin, I recommend that you co-operate, that you try to turn this into a positive experience, one that will help you with the problems you've been having. It is time for you to go now, but I hope we can have a better conversation next week."

As Bob left, he saw Seth in the waiting room, said, "Numbnuts is all yours."

Bob Severin was a very prepossessing kind of man—to men. Although his size had something to do with it, it was his easy maleness, his comfort with all the rights and privileges apportioned to men. He never paused two seconds over his "role." It was a man's duty to chase women and they expected it. He was merely fulfilling a social obligation; other men were closet daydreamers, chumps. He had a quick wit and loved nothing more than being surrounded by four or five men, drinking, throwing out more barbs than a boatload of fishermen. He thrilled to the attack and used hyperbole as efficiently as understatement. This was the first time Seth had heard Bob try to be serious, yet that greed for control could not be disguised. Seth had chosen counseling because he felt he didn't understand Claudia's depression, her swings of mood. He had been surprised to find out that the junk-store buying was an addiction, and that each purchase was accompanied by a tiny rush of endorphins like runners get. And that it was a kind of antidote to the depression which was generally unsponsored, a veil suddenly dropped over the brain. A cigarette or a purchase was a lifting of a corner of the veil, a peek at feeling good about herself. Yet the Severin view of the world had an attractive, palliative effortlessness and simplicity. Wouldn't it be better to cross the bridge instead of always being eternally and ineffectually standing in the middle? To cross over into his life, a male life, that was clear and predictable? Yet one morning on National Public Radio, Seth had heard a man describe his depression, the fights he picked to stop the downward plunge, the swoon over the pit, the sadness that welled up and up and had no top or bottom, the death-dance over the heads of his loved ones. Depression was not prejudiced.

"Daddy, will you button this? I can't do it." Jennifer's twelve year old fingers held the top of her dress together, her black hair flowing over her hands.

"Sure, honey, is your brother about ready?"

"He's in the shower with the dog, again. I told him to hurry up and he'd have to dry Penelope before we go. Uncle Don doesn't want a wet dog to take care of."

"It will be okay, I'll go help him."

Since Claudia left two months ago, Jennifer has taken over the job of fretting about the particulars of everyday life. Seth felt it pressing on her like sauna heat. Colin had the opposite reaction. He took longer, thought of ways to postpone action—a shower, brushing his teeth, changing his clothes, changing his mind. The dog showered almost as often as he did.

Three days ago, Claudia called, and through thick sobs told him her mother had died of a heart attack. She was leaving to be with her father, to help him out. He was "incapable of making decisions." He was "paralyzed." And wouldn't he bring the kids on Saturday, the funeral was at

2:30 in her parents' church? She was going to fly.

"Of course, and if there's anything I can do…"

"No…no," she had said as if answering some other question.

Claudia's mother was the most selfless woman Seth had ever met. Perhaps it wasn't selflessness so much as a generous, curious surety that allowed people to be themselves around her. She was a librarian, not by training or even necessity, but by a calling she discovered after the kids had grown and moved out. She lived in a small town in Idaho, knew everyone who came through the door and what kinds of books they might like, and handled each book as if it had been written by her favorite dead grandmother. She liked repairing their small damages—erasing, taping, or mending the dog-eared corners where someone had left off but aimed to return. She made her own bookmarks. They were made of pastel cardstock and laminated. Pressed, dried flowers—pansies and petunias mainly—were laminated onto the cards with quotations under them like "Thinking is but the intrepid effort of the soul to keep the open independence of her sea" —Herman Melville, or "I am fretting, scratching. What a heavy oar the pen is, and what a strong current ideas are to row in" —Gustav Flaubert; or "There is no frigate like a book/ to take us lands away…" Emily Dickinson. For someone who was landlocked, this attraction to ship imagery seemed strange, yet she gave them out to other landlocked book-borrowers, especially the ones whose pages came back a little bent and crippled.

Seth thought she was too indulgent with her grandchildren. She allowed them to do almost anything. They could pull out every pot and pan and spoon in her cupboards and make the biggest racket they could invent; they could go around the house flinging salt from the saltshaker ("Oh, it vacuums up, it's okay, don't worry"); they could bake any concoction they dreamed up and she would merely suggest the few ingredients that would actually make the mess edible ("Leave them alone, they're just having fun"); they could dress up in her clothes, use her make-up, or drown themselves in her perfume. She even let them pound on her piano, her most prized possession on which she had given each of her children lessons. She never talked to her grandchildren as if they were children. They had the wildest, weirdest conversations with the dead-pan seriousness of a farmer and his wife over morning coffee ("What if the dog told the Giant he had to play the tuba?").

Whenever people were in her house, she hovered like a waitress. She seemed to try to account for everyone's pleasure. Delivering coffee, setting up a puzzle or board game, adjusting blinds so the light didn't make streaks across the TV, picking up shoes, wiping off counters, cooking. It was exhausting if he paid attention to it. But Claudia was completely devoted to her, her dependable goodwill was an anchor against the daily shocks, the inconsiderate gestures, the remarks with hooks in them, the looks that scratched your heart, or the simple inattentions that made you think you didn't exist at all. Claudia had a need to be noticed, perhaps because of the whole-souled and devoted noticing her mother had given her for forty-three years. She felt each dismissal personally, and though she knew the wayward habits of the heart and how they bent and fractured the most amiable and trusting attentions, she would feel, despite herself, a pang of neglect when a waiter looked away while talking, when a salesclerk recited inappropriate compliments, when a driver honked as he passed.

Seth had watched these icy moments move through her. Her face stiffened. Her walk became more determined or her grip on the steering wheel. But there was nothing he could say that wouldn't be taken wrong—it would either be an insensitive defense of beleaguered duty or patronizing in some way, and he had learned to let the small storm pass without comment. Yet when Claudia was around her mother, the world was at peace, the waters calm. No one's insult—real or supposed—could penetrate the insulation her mother's surety provided. Although the targets of their merriment were often the predictable foibles of men, they laughed with an indulgent abandon that did not seem personal to Seth, but earthy, an acceptance of the frailty at the center of human relations. Their small touches were so natural that it made him wish that that was what a marriage was.

What preoccupied Seth most in his drive to the funeral was how Claudia could possibly weather this one. Colin liked reading signs to show his skills and to get praised for tackling the hard words. All the way out of town he had read billboards and the boldest advertisements. The last signs identified crops as they passed through farms. A potato field was marked "Tater-Tots"; a cornfield, "Tortillas"; a wheatfield, "Bread." He asked about the meaning of "tater" and how to pronounce "tortilla," but now was sunk in his gameboy with the volume turned off, and Jennifer was reading a Harry Potter book. This left miles of empty air-space.

It was a sunny day full of clear, rain-washed fall light. Along the river, cottonwoods fluttered a few yellow leaves like votive flames along a plume of green. Most of the fields had been harvested and had a clean, shorn look as if order had been randomly imposed by some futile but fastidious hand. The heavy, dusty green of the hawthorns and poplars fissured the gold of the grain fields. The few clouds were high, still, fluffy puffs like scattered swans in some Caribbean Sea. It seemed like a good day to be buried. What might the soul do on such a day.

They arrived at Claudia's parents' house about two hours before the service. Claudia was slicing meats for the small gathering afterwards. Her eyes were swollen, red-edged. She hugged Jennifer and Colin with that lingering, rocking, desperate energy that death inspires. As if she were embracing them before they were cast into the sea and they too would be gone forever. It was a hug that tried to rip the heart out of advancing time. When she stood up, her face dissolved into tears. She sobbed into Seth's shoulders. Her moan was reckless, deep, animal-like, as if all the burdens of the world had pressed at her throat and some escaped and flew out into broad daylight. It was beyond sorrow, judgment, forgiveness.

Claudia's father came in putting the final wrap on his blue tie, looking deliberately controlled, stoical. He was clean-shaven, his white hair parted and oiled into submission. He hugged the children too, but with a dry, formal detachment and shook Seth's hand, without vigor, without heat.

The service took place in a new church that Claudia's parents had contributed to. The chapel was a large open room with folding chairs. The walls were made of evenly milled logs decorated with banners the women had sewn: of white doves descending through a chasm of blue space, three golden kings kneeling before a child in a crib on a green

225

background, a profile of Christ praying in the garden against a blood-red sky. There was a small oak pulpit and a remote-controlled screen that illustrated the words of the songs as they were sung. Tall candles on brass pedestals stood around the altar, sprays of roses and chrysanthemums and baby's breath, colored lights flickering from two side panels of stained glass. The preacher said that he had known Ruth and Bill for eight years, felt that he had been allowed into their house and hearts generously and sincerely. He spoke about Ruth's service at the library, at the nursing home, at the Senior Center. Her good heart, her many friends, the support of the church, the happiness with which God would embrace her soul. They played and sang "The Old Rugged Cross" and then a recording of Ruth's favorite pieces: the aria at the end of part one in Handel's Messiah, "He shall feed his flock"; Ravel's left-handed concerto for Paul Wittgenstein, a concert pianist who had lost his right hand in WWI—not so much for the music as the friendship it conveyed; and one of the Tenebrae psalms by Francois Couperin. These were listed and described in the obituary notes, for they had been chosen and the tape made by Ruth herself. She had arranged for the music, flowers, casket, plot, and biblical passages to be read.

Seth heard an old woman dressed in a black wool suit lean to her husband and say "It's so like her." He wasn't sure what she was referring to, but felt that the organizational thoroughness was indeed "like her." It wasn't a regard for control that prompted her completeness, but an unwillingness for anyone to have to make a fuss over her, to have to agonize over details in the midst of emotional turmoil. She had been in good health and this foresight seemed uncanny.

After the preacher's eulogy, Claudia's brother said a

few words, as did one of Ruth's friends from the library. And then Claudia got up, her papers and voice shaking, a lock of grey hair falling over her forehead, her hand pushing it back as she read:

"I've been thinking about my mother for days, a month now, as it seems. I don't think we deal with grief, it deals with us.

"I know that for years I will encounter something that sends me down vistas of time, down blind alleys, tunnels with no visible ends or escapes. It could be a bookmark in the half-read book that she will never finish; one tied shoe in the closet and its untied mate; the bulbs that she planted but never saw bloom; a favorite hairbrush; her photos; just a thousand and one things bringing me back, stopping me.

"One of the saddest sights of my life was going into a room where Daddy had laid out some of Mother's things and wanted me to choose from necklaces, rings, blouses, shoes, gloves, and embroidered hankies. Much of which had been presents from us over the years. Now what to do with it all? And Daddy having to lay it out in the empty house, one item at a time. A life laid out in stacks and rows on the guest bed. It seemed so futile and stark. Yet I was to go in and choose something, something I wanted to remember her by. I looked, but there was nothing I wanted. Nothing but her.

"I see us all, like I was, surrounded by a thousand memories—both good and bad. And the bad ones trail with them a little quiet, a little anger, that can now only go one way—back into us. Yet I cannot, I simply cannot, now, refer to her in the past tense. 'Was' is a verb that stops us cold. Mom 'is' because all her things are here, her voice is in my head, on the answering machine. How do we one day put 43 years of daily presentness in the past tense? It defies who we are, any meaning we've put on human relations.

"The truth is, I don't have many consolations to recommend. Grief doesn't respect any religion: same tears, same night-terrors. You knew her, you know what I mean.

"Yet the ship must sail on and we ultimately have to sail with it. We watch the waters churn behind us, the wake go out, the shore recede, the world get smaller and smaller. Before it disappears entirely, we must love one another the way we wish to be loved. With forgiveness and joy, humility and humor, the way my mother encountered each and every day."

At the gravesite, Claudia, her two brothers, and Bill were seated in velvety green high-backed chairs like movie seats. A white canopy with scalloped edges was set up over the grave and artificial turf covered the piles of dirt at one end. About fifty people in suits and dresses, western shirts and slacks, some in jeans, stood around among the blue spruce and birches. As the minister began to read from his black Bible, someone coughed, another blew her nose, and Jennifer walked over and crawled into her mother's lap. Claudia leaned her cheek into Jennifer's hair, patted her face. A group of goldfinches flew into one of the birch trees, then out again, twittering in their hilly flight. A robin lit on the top of a Celtic cross with a grasshopper in its mouth. A bull bellowed across the pasture bordering the cemetery. It was a fine, warm day.

As they walked back toward their cars, Seth led Colin through the maze of stones. One had a bouquet of roses and a balloon swaying languidly in the breeze, Tweetie-Bird floating in its silvery mirror on a red banner that said "I Love You."

"Who's that?" Colin asked, watching the motions of the balloon.

"Susanne Wilcox, she was 16 when she died."

"How'd she die?"

"I don't know, maybe a car wreck." Seth felt a gloved hand slipping into his. He had never seen her with dress gloves; they must have been her mother's. Claudia stood beside him, her other arm around Jennifer, the balloon casting little spots of light in the trees around them. They stood in this silence for a while until Jennifer and Colin walked over to a glossy stone of black marble, shaped like a broken obelisk.

Claudia withdrew her hand. She folded her arms across her chest.

"He had all the right words, but none of them meant anything. Despite what you think, I never wanted to hurt you. I was only unhappy, I felt cornered, somehow. You don't know what the bottom looks like, that long black skid. But it's over, now. I never stopped loving you, I can't even tell you why it happened. But I'm sorry I hurt you, very, very sorry. I'd like another chance, for us to try again." She was looking away across the pasture, tears dribbling down her cheeks, her arms tightly crossed.

"We'll see," he said, touching her shoulder, looking out into the same green beyond the fence, the way the sky came down to meet it unevenly.

"Hey," Jennifer said as she and Colin ran back, "this man's birthday was the same as mine, July 23rd."

When the service and reception were over, Claudia, Seth, Bill, and the kids were left to clean up the dishes and take out the trash. After the dishwasher was loaded, Claudia washed the platters, bowls, and pans while Seth dried. Jennifer was repackaging the leftover toothpicks that had been spilled on the counter, and Colin had settled into an armchair with Louise, the cat. Bill leaned against the doorway with a double scotch in his hand, stirring the ice with his finger.

"Daddy, Seth wants me to drive back with him and the kids, are you going to be okay?"

"Sure, honey. Dave sent me a ticket to see him in Boston, and after I get things taken care of here, I'm going to go for a couple of weeks."

"Why wasn't he at the funeral?"

"He just had his prostate removed and he didn't think he could travel."

"You didn't tell me he had cancer."

"I guess they got it all."

"Well, I'd be glad to stay with you a few more days if you want me to."

"It's not necessary. You have your own family to look out for."

Claudia had not told her parents about their separation, and the innocence of this appeal to their private family life cast them in a thick silence.

"Where shall I put this?" Seth finally said holding up a large yellow earthenware platter with both hands.

"Here, I'll take it," Claudia said, wiping her hands on an apron. When she took the platter from him, her finger overlapped one corner of his towel. The platter slipped to the side, wobbled in the air, and they both lunged to catch it. They stood for a moment facing each other with their hands entwined around the towel, platter, and themselves. Jennifer jumped in and put her hands underneath them both, so the extrication of parts was as slow and careful as the end of a game of Twister.

"That was close," Jennifer said, her eyes wide with the drama of it.

"Your mother hated that platter," Bill said, chuckling, "you should have just let it drop."

Each of them still held an edge of the platter and looked at each other, Jennifer at her mother, her mother at Seth, Seth at Jennifer, and then they let it drop. As they did, each sprang back, but the platter hit the floor, bounced once, and sat there, shivering but intact. They stood around the ugly unbreakable dish, laughing.

"What happened?" Colin asked, running into the room, the old cat dangling by its neck and one front leg.

"Let the cat breathe, honey," Claudia said, trying to rescue Louise who seemed as imperturbable as the dish.

As they were leaving town, Seth told Claudia that he liked what she had said at Ruth's funeral, that he had felt like that when his father died. She patted his shoulder, her eyes reflecting the buildings passing her window. They allowed a silence to settle between them; it was like the on-coming dusk, a transition, some shade their minds and hearts moved toward, merged with, like the flow of traffic. Colin saw a sign on a large cement wall at the end of a mall facing the freeway:

**Supplies
Fish Grooming**

"Daddy, what's 'fish grooming'?" he asked, his finger bumping against the glass.

"It is what you do to fish that have grown shaggy, when their fins have grown too long from swimming around in that tiny bowl and have to be trimmed," Seth said, the words coming softly and seriously in the cadence of Claudia's mother. "It takes a swift and delicate hand, is usually performed under water. People practice by trimming their own hair in the mirror. It's hard to get the tiny scissors to move the way your hand wants them to. You have to retrain it. It's a very delicate art. Some people go to school to learn it, others just learn on their own. It takes some imagination. You have to think like a fish to get it right. You have to know how it moves in response to your move."

"Is that right, mom?" Colin asked, with a skeptical sigh.

"Yes, honey, it's true," she said, settling back for the long drive home, but for now the valley was soaked in a mellow light. Cottonwood trees glowed like Chinese lanterns, blonde grass lit up the fields, and the powerlines and poles stretched like a river of light, a thick line of music, up and over the darkening hills.

PEBBLES
& EGRETS

"It's their kids I feel sorry for," I said, as we talked through our pickup windows, the exhaust spilling into the cold like October ground fog. "They have to play in the mud and the junk with those dogs swarming around."

"That's how mud people learn muddin'," Larry said, unwrapping another pack of Camels, "can't tell molehills from dogshit, if yer raised right." He grinned and lit himself another. The smoke curled around his squinted eye and out the window. He wore a coyote skin cap with flaps on four sides. The breeze waved the long guard hairs in front as he spoke. It was lined, the insulating layer of cloth carefully stitched and pleated. A friend had bought it in Alaska for him. He once had me try it on just to feel how well made it was.

Although he liked to laugh and usually seemed close to it, his temper often overcame him while talking of people or actions he disliked. The transitions between these moods were oily, quixotic. He sometimes seemed to hate himself for being so harsh and could step back and look at himself with disgust. Yet he seemed helpless to correct it.

"You want to meet tomorrow and figure out what to do with this so's it don't wash again?" he said, gesturing toward the washout. "I already called Lyle, and he don't think he can make it. I guess it's you and me again, champ."

"What time?"

"Oh, ten o'clock. Tennish," the -ish lingering farcically.

"That'll be fine, I'll just walk down."

"See ya tomorrow then," Larry waved his cigarette hand and drove off.

Three families shared our driveway and each had adjoining property. I was the latest arrival and came here twelve years ago. Without a written road agreement, there had been an ongoing squabble for almost twenty years. Larry Monson operated large equipment and did excavation work, put in septic systems, dug trenches for electric lines. He was mainly an independent; a few contractors used him, but he always felt good about refusing a job. He ran his business out of his wallet. A year ago I asked him to clean a ditch and doze out a willow stump. I never got a bill, and finally, at the mailboxes one day, I asked him for it. He pulled out a four-inch thick wallet, and started going through scraps of folded paper; some were thin, frayed at the edges, discolored. He had a little pile of them in his lap like punchcard tabs. finally, he produced mine. On the flap of an envelope, written in pencil, he had his time, price per hour, the tax and a total: $158.73. The bill smelled like cigarette smoke, and I put it on my dash. This was like all the bills he had given me over the years for road maintenance. The price may have been on the high side of fair, but the work was good, convenient, and he'd make deals to cut tax costs or even to subvert minimal environmental regulations. He plowed our snow in the winter, repaired the washout damage in spring, put shalerock down occasionally. He charged $75 an hour, and as near as I could tell, roadwork and water were the chronic problems he had with the mud people.

The mud people had the property next to ours on the west. Jack Cobb had given it to his son Lyle. He lived in a trailer house that his father had left abandoned for several years. Jack was a truck driver, rancher, and repairman in his spare time. He was the first of the mud men. Both families have the rat instinct. There were old batteries, dead coffee makers and radios and electric fence boxes, bedsprings, blue plastic barrels, a refrigerator, a dryer, two collapsed horse trailers, a shed that had been brought in for lumber that now slumped into a heap, a string of burn barrels (some full and spilling on the ground), two dog kennels, galvanized water troughs filled with wire, a rusted swingset, toys, and plastic tarps that snapped and popped and shredded in the wind. Larry lived on the east side of this property and received even more trash than I did because the wind blew his way.

For ten years, I've been throwing wire, kids' clothes, hats, tires, boards, plastic toys, cardboard, and pieces of roofing back onto their side of the fence. His son has continued the junk tradition. The only noticeable up-grade in the transition from father to son was a septic tank and well. Jack had used an outhouse and had gotten water from public faucets in town.

Larry and Jack feuded about the outhouse as well as the water. This was one time Larry approved of environmental laws. He was afraid the outhouse would pollute his drinking water, but Jack said he had no running water and couldn't do without the privy. The county gave him a year, but that stretched into ten and nothing was done until Lyle and his wife and kids moved in.

One of my friends asked if I ever heard squealin' going on up there in Mud Holler. I tried to explain the difference between mud people and the *Deliverance* boys. First, they haven't had time to get successively in-bred, so they don't have that scratchy, window-peeking sunken look. There was no sense of responsibility, only a right endowed. Second, they grinned at the world. They didn't peep behind windowshades or sulk in the woods. They weren't skinheads, didn't give a lick about politics. They once ordered the local paper, but no one ever picked it up. The papers yellowed right there in the box, then dribbled onto the ground. Third, they lacked a playful imagination. Keats might say that "if a sparrow comes before my window, I take part in its existence and pick about in the gravel," but the Cobbs would pop it with a well-aimed BB.

When Lyle arrived we did have a glint of hope. Once after we had run one of his cows back in, Lyle told Larry and me that he was not his father and that he would clean things up. He said he used to live near the Mukilteo reservation and didn't want to look like that. Two months later a lowboy was hauled in and parked alongside their driveway. It slowly filled with metal debris and was finally in such a heap that he wired it down. It took three years for this junk to disperse again and for the lowboy to become part of the smothered landscape.

Why had Lyle felt obliged to apologize for his father? Was it a temporary appeasement? Or was his sense of difference, in the catacombs of his identity, only a fleeting shadow, a light-flicker in an otherwise subterranean place? Was it a mud-move, a gesture toward being neighborly, like a bone thrown out to his dogs? I wanted it to be genuine, so I gnawed on it for a couple of years.

Gail, Lyle's wife, once asked Larry to plow them out with his Cat because the snow was so deep they couldn't get up the hill to their trailer. They had used a ditcher to try to plow the snow but that had only made it worse, and they got the tractor stuck. Larry told me he couldn't plow much of a turn-around because of the grinding and snarling of litter under his blade. This small turn-around annoyed the Cobbs because they didn't think they had gotten their money's worth. They only paid part of the bill and told Larry in a note that when he finished the job they'd pay him the rest. Larry never went back, and the next time it snowed he plowed their driveway shut. When Lyle called to complain that he was the only one whose driveway was plowed shut, Larry told him that when he paid something on the last fifteen years of road bills (which were still in his wallet), he'd talk to him. And every winter since he has plowed their lane shut.

We have long wet springs, and the arrival of meadowlarks and snipe is accompanied by the whine and roar from the trucks and the van of the mud people. One year the Dodge van sunk to its axles and stayed for two months where it had veered off their driveway and slid down a slope toward my place. This too is something of a tradition. Before Lyle arrived, Jack drove an old green Cadillac half way up the hill and got it stuck. The next weekend, he brought in a sputtering 1952 International one-ton, backed it up to the Cadillac, and they both sprayed mud in a greasy cloud of blue smoke. The truck was parked in the driveway for two years and the Cadillac was there for three. It would cost about $1200 to haul in enough shale rock to solve all their mud problems, but in their twenty years of ownership they haven't done it. Horse deals, old tractors, or a new used boat always got in the way.

Larry is a short man with bushy blond eyebrows, a lean face, a boyish grin, and a prankster's eyes. He usually wears brown insulated coveralls over jeans and a plaid cotton shirt. In the winter he wears his coyote cap and in the summer a black baseball cap. Brown rubber boots match the coveralls. The track of his cat stands higher than his waist. He often invites me over to have a drink—coffee and whiskey in the morning, whiskey on the rocks at night. The kitchen is functional. Jen, his wife, serves us from the kitchen which is slightly recessed from the dining area. Jen and Larry both smoke so there is a haze in the air, a film on walls and windows and curtains. It is an old farm kitchen: ancient linoleum with metal molding, grimy stairs leading to a basement and root cellar, painted wood cupboards that have been slammed and leaned on for so long they hang open like the lips of an old horse. We talk about the weather, the road, environmental regulations, but eventually work our way back to the mud people. He told me the feud started when he cleaned a ditch so that he could catch the runoff water after Cobb irrigated his pasture. Jack thought he had dug too deep and caused an erosion problem, so he diverted the runoff so Larry couldn't get any water at all.

"Them cows was so confused they didn't know where home was," Larry said one day, sipping from his favorite blue plastic cup whose interior was as brown as a Brazil nut.

"When they got out on my place, I called Lyle and it took three days for him to come get them."

"I bet he never paid for no pasture either."

"No. The next time they got out, I ran them back through the fence."

"He starves them to death in the winter anyhow. Shit, he don't take care of em. I called the Humane Society one year. He left those cows up there in the snow and no water. Didn't feed em for two weeks. I had to slip em a few bales of my own. Then when he did come, he gave them that rained-on moldy shit that's been out there for over a year and gave me hell for feedin em. It's a crime. Criminal's what it is."

"What did the Humane Society do?"

"Same as everybody else does. Nuthin. They're afraid to come out here. He packs a gun, ya know. That's why I got a .30/30 in my pickup. He starts to shoot at me and I'll drop the sonofabitch and I ain't jokin." He said this dryly, matter-of-factly, and I believed him.

When the gun talk came out, that's when I usually had somewhere to go. But, it's true, the man had more cows than he had grass for and that's why they always got out. Last summer one of his cows died. It probably ate a coil of wire from a washing machine. Lyle got on his tractor and dragged the animal to a little depression beside the creek, just west of my house. He threw some old cottonwood branches over it, the closest thing to fence-building I'd seen him do. A week later my house was full of fat flies. It was August, the month of little wind and plenty of heat. The smell could've poached eggs. The heat made shutting the windows impossible. Even our clothes smelled like a sulphur springs. We called the Department of Ecology because the carcass was beside the creek. Lyle drove in four days later, sprinkled lime over it, and left. It putrefied all fall. With my face wrapped in a red bandana, I finally went to see how much more we had to endure. Its whole body was a writhing mass of maggots that simmered and glistened in the afternoon sun. Fumes of putrescence thickened the air like heat vapor on a highway. Green-glistered flies roamed in and out of the eyes, into the stomach cavity and over the bleached organs; they clustered around the anus and vulva. The bumbling hum of their good fortune, their egg-laying frenzy, was almost deafening. Even with my nose and mouth clamped shut, the gorge rose in my throat and I had to run. I must admit, though, that lime helped. In the winter, my dog brought bone after bone into my yard until I rendered it piecemeal into my garbage cans.

Larry hated to let them win, yet they always seemed to. For Larry, honor and his word were palpable things. They were like a flag you bore through the world representing your mother country. Contractual agreements were a modern nuisance; they showed a lack of character, of upbringing, or in Larry's language, balls. Yet honor has a shadow, a dark underside that rides with it. I thought maybe Larry had stepped on the shadow, had tasted the lust in honor and found a certain sweetness there. Larry once took the Cobbs to court for failure to pay their share of the road repairs. It cost Larry $2,500, and all he got for his effort and money was the judge's recommendation that the Cobbs pay something, that it was the decent thing to do, as if the Cobbs cared about decency.

Another spring when the road was washed out, Lyle put his Chevy in four wheel drive and drove through my place to get to his. I had bought the house and property next to mine which had another bridge across the creek, but there isn't a road that connects the two places, so Lyle created mud trenches that three years later look like remnants of the Oregon Trail. When I told him he couldn't drive across this muddy field but was welcome to park in the barnyard—as I was doing—and walk to his house, he said it was too damn far to walk and hung up. He called the Sheriff so that when his kids got off the bus, someone would be there to pick them up. He told the Sheriff we refused to let him drive across our land and he was stranded—that his was a flooding disaster and he needed emergency aid. Lyle's call was not an admission of dependency, of neediness. It wasn't even an actual need because Gail works at a pizza parlor during the weekends and helps out some evenings when they call her. She was free to walk her kids the extra half mile. This was merely opportunity. They could make the sheriff, the law, the county, this country, do something for them. It was leverage against a chickenshit world. We were just the rock that allowed this lever to work. In their private affairs, they were not particularly competitive or communicative, yet there was this need to flex, to demonstrate a right.

Both men, Jack and Lyle, although very different in outward temperament—the one dour and surly, the other soft-spoken and a bit dreamy—carried a burden as if something weighed them down, pulled at them. There was a slow seethe inside them trained like rifle sights at any power that might oppose them, real or imagined.

Jack was also a short man, but with a broad muscular frame, thick rough hands, a grizzled face with a scar in his forehead where he had been kicked by a bull during his rodeo days. He had a bow-legged strut as if he were galled, or his jeans were too tight. We could all hear him yelling at his wife whenever he had to load a trailer, chase cows or horses, or rotate a piece of junk that happened to be in the way. This was a trait that Lyle had not inherited. He was a quiet slow-moving man, and pushed his way through the world behind a huge belly as if it were a shopping cart. He folded his hands and rested them on it while he talked or he scratched it absently like the head of one of his children. His wife, Gail, however, had the voice of a meat cleaver. Their children were 2, 6, 8, and 10 years old, and she would ride her horse around the muddy dilapidated arena, yelling orders at each of them so loud any neighbor could add the punctuation. She rode in a black felt English riding helmet, her long black hair bouncing behind. If dinner was ready she would hang her head out the windowless and screenless aluminum door and scream them home. Once I saw her beat the head of the six year old because the two year old had been left at the bottom of their driveway, playing in the mud at the edge of a pond. I was out fixing a fence, and the child had played by herself for over an hour.

Gail was something of a horse-expert, and yelled at Lyle whenever she thought he was making a mistake with one of her mares. Of course, the time she was gone and he chased one of them with his four-wheeler around and around and around the pasture because it wouldn't allow itself to be caught even with a bucket of grain in his hand didn't exactly plead his case. He had run it so hard its tongue hung out, it was lathered from nose to tail, and it stood blowing and wheezing in the fence corner. When she came home and saw it, even the field mice hunted cover. He kept saying, "It's better to have a dead horse than one you can't catch." He seemed particularly fond of these maxims. The bumper stickers on his jacked-up Chevy pickup with flotation tires and rust spots the size of grapefruit displayed them proudly: "Honk Again, I'm Reloading," and "For Truckers Every Day Is Hump Day" and "Have You Hugged Your Gun Today?"

I've thought about the mud people off and on for years now. Jack owns three places that he tries to support by trucking whenever and wherever he can. His hands are as rough and hard as burlap, yet when he shakes hands, his is like a warm potholder—there's no reciprocal vigor, no will. It is as if he were afraid of this formality. It seems an enigmatic politeness whose motives he couldn't quite fathom. In social situations, he sometimes seemed like an outlaw who had just ducked into church to escape, yet when he turned and saw the service, there was a kind of paralysis, a stunned inkling of expectation that he didn't know how to meet.

With his cattle, his irrigation and trucking and maintenance, he doesn't have time to take two breaths in the shade. Larry says he's like a pig on ice. Yet work is his central ethic, his sense of being. From the outside he seems to be trying to stockpile sand in a windstorm. His cows die, his irrigation ditches wash out because the water is left too long on one set, his roof leaks, siding flaps in the wind. Roping horses are his one passion, yet he has no time for them, so they become pasture ornaments, hay burners, and wild as mustangs because they aren't worked enough to be decent saddle horses. He never has a vehicle whose parts were made for each other. He pops and sputters and clangs into and out of our driveway. He's always late either because he was on a long haul and just arrived or his car or pickup broke down. He means well, he wants to get his cows out of my pasture or remove the dam so I can get water, but mine is just one of the hundreds of demands he meets or tries to on any given day. He always seems to need a haircut, his teeth haven't seen a dentist in years, his nose and ear hairs sprout wildly and nod while he talks. He is so focused on work, the accomplishment of this chore and the next, that he has never taken the time to prioritize, to reflect on a system of choices, to even know what might make him happier, or more efficient, his life easier.

His wife, Mae, is a quiet, burden-bearing woman whose motherly devotion yields only randomly to streaks of determined self-approval and self-satisfaction. On these occasions she likes to read celebrity gossip magazines, inspirational poetry about love and flowers and nature, or to dress up and go out. When she found out I taught English at the high school, she asked if she could read one of the poetry books I used in class because she wrote poems herself and maybe that would help get hers published.

I knew this was not a good idea. I had used Bruce Weigl's *Song of Napalm* in a section on literature that came out of the Viet Nam War. We read *The Things They Carried* by O'Brien, "Break On Through" from Thom Jones's *The Pugilist At Rest*. A few other poems and stories. I knew that her reading of Weigl's book would be like watching a mouse in a belljar. But I gave it to her anyway.

Mae gave it back the next week and said she liked the little stories in some of them, but for the most part they weren't what she considered poems. There was a fleeting sternness on her face as if she had had to practice this emotion to be able to say the words. She didn't want her poetry devalued by this experience; she didn't want bugs on any of her roses and dusting them with these words helped. She said my carnations were lovely for this time of year.

On her night out with a girlfriend she dressed in a black cotton skirt and blouse, a belt of silver flowers chained together and studded with lumps of turquoise. She wore earrings, matching bracelets on both arms, and a silver necklace. I saw her once at the Best Western which had a dance floor the size of three tables put together. She wore a snazzy red lipstick and swept her greying hair back. She looked like Dale Evans, refusing to believe she was in her sixties. She had threatened several times to divorce Jack, and during the three years the trailer was abandoned before Lyle came, she spent a couple of weeks in it each year to prove a point. It was during one of these visits that she borrowed Weigl's book of poems. She joked then about how a few of her friends had been able to use the trailer as a halfway house between marriages.

It is hard for me to imagine Jack having to take the time to re-court his wife, to coax her back into the mud and squalor they had made of their lives together. I see him in a bolo tie with a silver dollar at his neck, a clean cowboy shirt, clean blue jeans, a little Old Spice splashed on his neck. His thumb stroking her cheek must feel like a farrier's rasp.

I was convinced that it wasn't just a cussed meanness that made them live the way they do, but a lack of vision. It was the habit of work and the bane of laziness that drove them on. It was their definition of work: sweat, busyness, the sense of running from one end of the day to the next as if it were time itself they raced. Jack's father had beat laziness and forgetfulness out of him. I know because Jack grew up next to my grandfather, and my grandfather told me. If Jack broke a broom handle, his father broke it again, on him, or tried to. If he didn't finish off a cow's udder, he could kiss his dinner goodbye. If he didn't finish his dinner, it was tomorrow's breakfast. If he complained about the heat and said he was tired during the hay-hauling, they skipped lunch and kept on going to dinner. His mother often made Jack put a small stone in his shoe so he would remember God all day and praise Him. When he got home, the first thing she wanted to see was that stone. "He ain't walked straight since" my grandfather said. This was pioneer grit passed down and perverted through successive generations. *Waste Not Want Not* was burnt into a piece of cedar and hung above the broken fireplace, and it too had been handed down as if it were a law Moses missed.

At 10:00 the morning Larry and I were to meet, I watched the blackbirds scrabble with the finches over the few seeds that remained in the feeder. I finished my coffee and pulled on my black knee-high irrigation boots. It was a cold spring day and the wind was just coming up. With my yellow lab, I walked down the lane to where I was to meet Larry. I was glad I had put on a stockingcap and down-lined jacket. The thin layer of ice on the puddles tinkled and cracked as I walked through them. Larry had piled enough rock into the washout so that we could drive over it with a pickup, but we wanted to find a less bumpy and perhaps more permanent solution to the problem. I don't know grades of rock or the costs of construction work, so I felt like I was merely a weathervane for his brainstorming. Soon I could hear the rumbling rhythm of his Caterpillar coming down the lane.

When he shut off the deafening engine and jumped to the ground, he removed his cigarette and let the smoke leak out of his mouth. He spit a flake of tobacco and pitched his butt into the muddy snow.

"I'm glad it got cold last night. Slow down this floodin a bit. I don't know what to do with this. We ain't got any tailins left. It's all been washed away. I used to have some shale stockpiled here, but Lyle's been stealing it for his goddamn fenceposts, not that he'd actually use it." He gathered a long measuring stick and a surveyor's scope on a tripod.

"There's a mound of small stuff against that bank that the water piled up, will that work?"

"Ain't big enough, you need rock about this size here," he said, measuring with his hands after he had set up the tripod.

"Well, you can't order any because there isn't any way to dump it where you need it."

"Couldn't get it anyhow. With this floodin there's a run on that rock."

This sentence was interrupted by a honking behind the Cat. Gail was sitting in the Chevy, so we walked around to her window.

"Would you pleeese move that thing, I gotta get to work." Her voice and tone put needles in each word. She smiled with a taut politeness.

"Well, you're going to have to wait a few minutes because we got some measurin to do," Larry said, a hardness in his voice as if he were talking to a petulant child.

"Well, I gotta go. I gotta be at work in ten minutes," she said as her eyes narrowed and the wired smile disappeared altogether.

"If you people ever paid for a goddamned thing in your lives, I'd be more concerned about gettin' out of your way." Larry spit onto the ground as a kind of exclamation point and slowly walked to a point across the washout and instructed me to give him a reading. We took our measurements, and Larry walked slowly back to his cat, put his measuring stick and tripod and scope away, climbed up, and moved the cat out of her way. She tromped on the gas and hit the gap, spraying gravel in all directions.

"Hell's bells, she knew what time we was meetin' down here. Goddamn people anyway."

Two days later at the mailbox, Larry told me he got his ass

chewed out by Lyle for giving his wife hell. He shook his head disgustedly as if he had made a mistake and was sorry for it. Larry's honor and irritation often battled over the Cobbs. He was usually a straight shooter; you could count on him to be fair. He called me after my father died and said he was damn sorry to hear it, damn sorry, and if there was anything he could do like feed the animals or anything he'd be glad to do it. Glad to.

One hot summer day when I was walking down the lane and Larry and his son drove in, he stopped and introduced him in a plain, proud, unassuming way. He leaned back in his seat and gave an open-palmed introductory gesture. His son had a willowy, sickly pallor, bleached blond hair that was rumpled and snarly and fell over his shoulders. He didn't have a shirt on, and a large red tattoo of an otter ran down his back and the tail slipped around his hip and onto his firm, well-muscled stomach. A leather band wound around his throat with a large silver ring in front. His left ear had a row of similar but tiny rings. His teeth were as yellow as the otter's, and he had a drugged, far-away look. He took a heavy drag on his cigarette, let the smoke ease out of his nose and mouth, and nodded to me without a word. Larry and I chatted amiably. They both gave a one-finger wave as Larry drove away. I assumed that Larry's drop-the-sonofabitch attitude permeated other aspects of his character, that his moral resolve had thresholds clearly marked like some kind of pissing cougar. I saw him as a gun-patting red-neck who understood the everyday world of earth-moving and engines, but this solemn pride in his son implied to me that he bore his disappointments with a kind of grace, that he had successfully revised expectations when moral challenges occurred, that he could take a red otter smack in the face and still stand up. I had patronized him and wondered how long he knew it. There was pride in that leaning gesture, but also a little message.

The nights got warmer and the creek did rise again. It washed out the makeshift patch and dented the culvert, but the bridge and rip-rap held. Larry had to fix it again when the water subsided. We had more rain and the driveways were puddled and gluey with mud. Mornings and nights, the mud people spun their tires and fishtailed and roared up and down their hill. One evening after the water cleared up and slowed down, I was in the creek with my hipboots cleaning out the debris in front of the culvert when I saw Jack stop in the driveway. His grandson and dog were in the back of his pickup. The boy was wearing a tattered green jacket, no gloves, and was pulling at the dog's collar. The dog was a red heeler with a bobbed tail. Jack walked over to the mailboxes, stopped and leafed through Lyle's letters, then folded them into a large auction notice. When he tried to start his pickup, the motor whined but didn't turn over. Jack got out and opened the hood. The dog jumped over the side and stood beside him. There was no tailgate on the back of the pickup, and the boy climbed down and stood in the gravel. He pitched pieces of it at passing cars and trucks. When a car honked and swerved and honked again in a long angry blast, Jack looked up and marched after the boy. He cuffed him on both sides of the head, picked him up and slammed his butt onto the bed of the pickup. He bounced a finger in the boy's face. He pulled off one of the boy's boots and put a pebble in it. He picked him up again, set him on the ground, turned the boy's shoulders toward the house, and gave his butt a hot little boost towards it. The boy was howling and sniffling, tears streaking down his cheeks.

Jack seemed to go through life this way, from one broken-down moment to another. This odd and contrary dance with Larry, with his wife, his grandchild and probably everyone else he let under his skin, this twisted helix of act and counter-act, balance and imbalance, had determined the force and direction of his life. The teacher in me always wanted to find the generative seed, the human flower that could be nourished in the right way towards blossoming, but I knew I was as guilty as Jack's wife of hot-house fantasies. There was a stone in Jack's boot that could never be removed, and he walked on it every day of his life.

It occurred to me, too, that sometimes intelligence could be a stone of the same hue and hardness that we use to build a wall around us, a platform to stand a little taller than the rest, to sit like Zeus in his airy chamber looking down at the earth and all its mud-squishing mortals.

I walked through a stand of willows and pine trees, paused near an ant pile where a killdeer had died and the ants crawled over its white belly and into its eye cavities. It must have been shot by Lyle's ten year old boy; there was no reason for it to die here. I thought of a poem by Weigl in the book I loaned to Mae where a boy accidentally killed an egret. His father beat him often, so when the neighbor heard the boy crying in his yard, he went out to investigate. The boy stroked the egret and cried, saying he only meant to scare it, to watch it fly, but the shot spread out too far. The neighbor was a man given to Viet Nam flashbacks, visions of bodies, of friends ripped apart, trembling terrors, cries and nightfire filling and falling on every corner of his world. And set against this was one crumpled white thing of beauty lying in the grass at their feet, one eye pressed to the earth. Its other filmy and half-closed and filled with starlight, the wings spread in useless flight, the twiggy black legs like balloon sticks, the dribble of red from the corner of its mouth staining the cheek. The white, downy feathers were so light they moved when the shovel moved, almost seeming to hover an inch or two above the grass itself, a palpable vision of loss, of the beating his father would give him if he found out. The boy crying for the lost bright thing in himself. The neighbor standing there yet falling down through layers of blood and tears, screams, shudders, and finding that fragment of egret still left him, returned to him on that night like a coin recovered from his past. And they stood out in the moonlight and buried the bird together, each holding a wing as they eased it into the hole, and the boy shoveling, shoveling at his dense shame in the moonlight. I saw that boy, my mind working the edges of the pebble.

I slipped into the creek, noticed how the mud on my boots dissolved into the water, a chocolate smoke. I walked back toward my house and wife and daughter, my tracks washing away downstream. Willow branches pulled at my hat, and I could smell the deep musty odor of wet cotton-wood like syrup on a hot radiator. The leafless clumps of rosebushes were maroon and grey, yet still thorned and the sun glinted off them. They seemed to be sheathed in an orange light. I thought then about molehills and mud, and a slim red otter swimming down-stream, allowed to ride a current of its own no matter how poorly it did it.

Jack's pickup sat at the edge of the driveway for two days until I called Lyle, and we pulled it into town. Yesterday, I gave a dozen eggs to Corey, the pebble kid. The school bus had dropped him off and he was walking home. They were green and blue from our araucanas. He thought I dyed them. I told him we had green and blue chickens and he should come see them. He looked like he was wearing the jeans and plaid shirt his brother used to wear, a cowlick made a swirl of black hair stand up on his head, and the extra length of his black leather belt curled to the middle of his thigh. There was a blue patch on one knee. He half-closed his left eye and said, "No way." He stood for a few minutes, holding a box of blue and green light, squinting.

"Well," I said, "you'll just have to see for yourself.

THE HALF-WAY HOUSE

"It's just radicalus. If'n it's me, I'd a dozed it and burnt it years ago. Goddamn reservation anyway." Jack stood on the other side of the fence holding the top strand of the barbed wire, soft, like someone holding cards. I had come up the hill to catch my horse, the halter and rope were draped over my arm.

"I can't see the use of all this stuff, myself."

"He's handy, gotta give em that, but this here…" His thumbs are now petting the barbs like somebody thumbing the sights of his gun, waiting. When we shook hands, his dry callused fingers were like grabbing a fistful of straw.

In a gray coat dangling off the end of his arms, his grandson comes toward us, hopping the piles of junk or jumping from one piece to another, riding that idle inside, hoping to spring off a bouncy one or almost fall. This is the first clear day in a week. There is snow all along the mountains to the north. The knee-high grass on my side of the fence is bleached blond so the horses and black calves in their new winter coats are as bright as shoe polish in a tin.

"You gotta come, Grandpa, if we're gonna start the fire." The kid looks sideways towards the next pile to jump to. His hair sticks straight up like a baby bird's.

"I'll get there when I get there. You go on, now." He never looks over his shoulder, knows where he is well enough.

"Come Tuesday, all this will be settled. We're sellin Lyle

this here'n. Sold all the cows a year ago and put the money in a pot at the bank for decidin expenses. We agreed to say where ever dime went, a course she's been spendin it and won't say where. That's been the biggest holdup. Three years we been doin this. We ain't got nothin but land. Had to pass up two good places in Montana because of no money to put down. And she wants this damn yeller trailer, and most of the tack. The land was all we ever had and now that's... " a little pop of air and a flutter of his lips finishes the sentence.

I hadn't seen him in over a year and never saw him look worse. Fifteen years ago when I moved here and he was living with Mae, he was lean and feisty, as strong as a bull. They lived with no well, no toilet. They had electricity and an outhouse. Everything was patched in a loose and wild way—their yellow trailer, the corral, the fence between our property. One hole was stitched closed with bedsprings, another with a rusted hay elevator; the corral was patched with tin roofing and the sides of a horsetrailer. The wooden gates were hung up and locked with blue bailing twine. There were blue plastic barrels, wood whose stack could almost be imagined under the tumbled outline. A metal wheel-less shopping cart leaned against the shed, a bathtub watering trough poked half way into the stud's enclosure. The divorce was news to me. I thought a woman who'd live eleven years without running water was in for the long haul.

Mae sure had a tight-lipped fix on things. Never looked up if she could help it, even if I was riding the fenceline. The dogs barking their goddamn heads off, all nine of them, the commotion enough to raise the tarpaper off the roof, and she just went on carrying the bucket of water or brushing down the horse. Even in the wind she didn't wear a scarf or a cap, letting her hair dance like electricity was pumping through it. She yelled at her kids all day long but patted the horses, talking to them like they were dead relatives. If the stud horse was all out, she'd stroke his dick and say what a good boy he was, never mind who was standing around. I only saw her twice in anything but jeans. When her dad died, she went from the saddle to his funeral, shit on her boots, her pickup truck looking like it was in some strange collision and emerged with more parts than it went in with. It was a bitty funeral anyway on account of his being a drunk, but he could have been King Tut, and it wouldn't a changed a thing she did. The only reason I went was I took my dad, he was alive then, who knew her dad way back when.

That yellow trailer house was empty for almost six years after they bought their other place and before Lyle and his kids moved in. She called it The Half-Way House, and some of her woman friends would move in after they moved out of their own homes. Without water and a good toilet, these gals didn't stay long. When Lyle moved in, he dug a well, put in a septic tank, and rolled a red trailer behind the yellow one.

What I was thinking as Jack thumbed that barbed wire was that me and him was the same now and I didn't really relish the idea. It may look to some like my wife left me, but it was more you choose your end of the planet and I'll choose mine. There's two thousand blessed miles between us. But we stood there, two bachelors sharing a fence line, and I had rather liked the pity they'd throw my way, it put a few strands on the fence. But here he was in pink glasses, his workshirt torn off at the sleeves and frayed, a new tattoo on his right arm, the shirt over his big belly black with motor oil and grease. A stockingcap perched on top of his head like an orange cowpie. He still wore his wedding ring, not out of habit. It was just so embedded it would have to be popped off with bolt cutters. Jesus, pink glasses and a tattoo on a fat sixty year old man who had long since lost his toothbrush was like an old whore in feathers.

"Gran-pa! We gotta start that fire, Daddy says so." The kid has come back but he's dawdling and looking the other way, messenger being better than woodpiler by a long shot.

"I'm a-comin. I ain't so sure I'll see ya anytime soon, but I'll be damned glad to get outa this place. It's 'bout over-grown." He turns and follows his grandson through the junk and on towards the smoke just lifting above the roof of the red trailer. He walks without purpose, his arms at his side, hands curled like he's carrying invisible buckets.

When we talked, he looked out over the fields and the road in the distance, his thick thumb stroking the barb. His eyes were dead tired and through that pink lens he looked beat. His skin was pale and saggy and his face stubbly with grey whiskers. He could have died and not given a good goddamn, right there, I swear. When his grandson raised his voice at him, I saw a little flicker of light run across his eyes, a muscle in his face twitch and die.

His hands were powerful, and I hated his handshakes. He wasn't trying to squeeze hard, and it was done with a distracted ease like opening a jar lid, but my bones tingled afterward. Like me, he was nobody any woman'd ever think twice about. The years of driving trucks through winter after winter, of chasing cattle and mending fences when you got back home, of irrigating till dark, and putting up hay, trying to keep that old shit we drive on the road, piecing together rag-tag equipment, then walking into the house and catching it there too, had finally piled up on him, had chipped so much away that all he could think of was the next thing to do and the thing after that and the thing after that. It was an endless list because he believed in the land, that if he gathered enough in, it would save him. Yet he stood at the fence like a man on a train platform several stops beyond where he aimed to get off. The land had failed him, his wife had failed him, his son had failed him, he had failed himself. The list of failures was like the list of things to do, deep and endless. I know because I got off that same train in some new place I couldn't recognize either.

I caught my horse, then, and walked back to the barn. The horse was always glad to see me because he knew grain was not too far away. His enthusiasm and little eager noises were an illusion I liked. I wanted to take his shoes off before winter fully set in. I cut off the crimped ends of the nails and pried them out one by one, not having nippers for shoe-pulling, only the ones for trimming their feet. A farrier could do it in about ten minutes, but it took me a good forty-five. When I stood up, my back felt like I'd been swatting my way out of a den of snakes with a short stick. When I turned my horse back into the pasture, the smoke was rising in a thick roiling column and trailing off toward the east. The calves had come in thinking they'd get something to eat, the chickens ran in to catch whatever bugs the calves might stir up, and my dog barked at a cat under the barn.

I hadn't even heard that other sound until the shouting

started. For some reason words from their place to mine travel on air better than on the telephone. I don't know if it works the other way, not having been up there and down here at the same time. I can hear every word of their kid-screaming, if I want to. But now there's a whole swarm of them—the kids, Lyle, and Gail—all yelling their fool heads off, but Jack's on that caterpillar, little black puffs calmly rising like smoke signals, and he's pushin that yellow trailer in the direction of the fire. The end of the house near the blade has crumpled like a stomped beer can, but the front end just begins sliding along, floating forwards. Its front end has no idea what its hind end is doing, but it's out there doin' it like it's the most natural thing in the world. Which reminded me of the last time I saw Mae in something besides jeans. She was at the Iron Horse, a long turquoise dress on, with black velvety calf-high boots, lipstick pinker than a chimp's ass. That image she pushed forward couldn't quite ignore the bulldozer of her past, or what I saw of her past, in my own mind. She was actually dancing, not with Jack, he wasn't anywhere in sight. I got a kick out of it at the time, but that feller she was dancing with couldn't see the dozer and was dancing right back.

It was when Jack turned the corner that the front end of The Half-Way House, which really was half a house now, caught on something and started to crumple, to fold up on itself. Windows popped and the metal and wood started to wad up together, but that sound didn't seem to carry as much as the voices did.

Old Jack just sat right in the middle of all that screaming, agrindin those gears and pushin that house into the fire. I didn't know how much of that thing would burn, but Jack has an idea, and he was actin on it, and he was ridin it out to the very end. He was lettin it burn, and all the voices pecking away at him as he was doing it were more dry wood for the fire. That caterpillar was running fine, like a sewing machine, as he knew it would because he was a damn good mechanic.

I shut the gate and snapped the chain around the post. My horse can open just about any gate there is. I walked back to my house. I still had to mow the lawn one last time and put the mower up for the winter. I needed to get the storm windows out and clean them, haul the dead vines and stalks out of the garden. There was a little breeze, and I was glad because the smoke was all going east and I didn't have to smell it.

It wasn't but a couple of days later when I read in the paper, in the blotter, where Mae had called the police about the damage done to her property and they were looking for Jack to ask him some questions. Now that yellow trailer probably wasn't worth three hundred dollars in parts, as old and beat-up and used as it was. But all crumpled up and burned it was worth a whole lot more to Mae. At the time, I thought, go for it, Jack, one less eyesore I had to look at, and they sure had it coming.

All that work going up in smoke is what I been thinking all week, years of stretching days out like calves to be branded, and a good brandin's all he got out of it in the end. Mae'd say he deserved it, and maybe he did. It was ridiculous, a sixty-plus man in pink glasses, a new tattoo, pot-bellied as a stove, grease-stained, with an orange stockingcap, thinking he's got something left to say to anybody who'd listen.

What I can't get out of my mind is his standing there, a thumbin that barbed-wire, just a pettin those points, before cranking up that cat of his and then pushing that Half-Way House into the fire. Hell's bells, work all your life and this is what it comes to, a couple of bachelors puttin up storm windows for a storm that's already done come and gone.

RED GEESE

As the dark settled over the neighborhood, Evelyn was comforted by the blue of the television. She didn't particularly care which programs were on, though the game shows inspired a certain allegiance. She sat at the edge of the sofa, her hands gripped around her glass, trying to answer the questions before the contestants did. She thought she was especially good with geography and famous names. As a child, memorizing at St. Anthony's grade school had been easy. The names of states and capitals, mountain ranges, rivers, regions, and provinces. And she remembered word and geography flashcard games, her thin legs stepping closer and closer to the prizes of holy cards and rosaries. She still had them tucked away in a shoebox in her attic, including the blue rosary whose cross was filled with water from Lourdes. The secret thrill of these competitions still seized her as she tried to answer as fast as she could. She rarely beat the contestants, but she remembered so swiftly after the answer was given that she could almost persuade herself that she had gotten it. In fact, hours later, she thought she had.

She liked to think of herself as the salt of the earth and read the tabloids with a concerned conviction. Whenever she was at the doctor's or dentist's office, she read *People* magazine or thumbed through *National Geographic* testing her memory of the map.

When asked, she gave freely to her church or any relief fund drive. It was her Christian duty, and she was serious about her religious obligations, or "opportunities" as she liked to call them. The pure simple logic of her religion made it hard for her to understand unbelievers. They were like cartoon people leading a life of obvious delusion. She felt sorry for them and prayed that one day they would see the error of their ways. Touched to tears by the starving children in Ethiopia, she gave as much as she could. Their skinny arms and sallow sunken faces, their black glazed eyes, the flies that crawled like miniature buzzards over their faces, made her dinner-toast stick in her throat and water stream from her eyes. She wanted to shoo the flies and unconsciously waved them away in the blue-dark of her own house. All that night her check waited impatiently in its envelope to get to those poor children.

Sometimes she would lie in bed staring into the dark as if it were the soul of Africa loosened to fly around the world. It was sad and sinister and everywhere. When a dog in the neighborhood barked, it seemed like the lonely sound-track of the dead. It occurred to her that death might be a condition in which the entire body closed down except for sound, and she would lie there in the dark unable to move or respond, hearing familiar voices, tires on pavement, the chipping of chickadees under their black hoods. This spectral dream or vision which came to her as she stared into the dark scared her so much that she would fling on the light and play a Sousa march, so those sinful, visionary fears would get tangled in the rousing music.

It was after nights like these that she would call her daughter, Mindy, who lived with her husband and young son in Puyallup, almost thirty miles south of her house. Mindy was a quiet patient woman who had grown up during the Vietnam War which left a firm pessimism that invaded both her political and religious opinions. This pessimism created a tension that often ended conversations with her mother, but after two or three days Mindy would send a mitigating note, usually a brisk, self-critical, understated wisecrack below a quaint drawing. The drawings took their inspiration from typical 19th century cartoons of politicians with huge encephalitic heads on stick-bodies. They were decorated with peace insignias, victory signs, headbands, strange hats, feathers, or birds in various stages of flight. These things were part of the image residue from the war years when the fighting between Evelyn and Mindy was also fierce. Evelyn could not abandon her president in time of war, but Mindy would not relent and made an issue of Mylai, the Phoenix Program, nightly body counts, and Johnson's ear-stretched beagles. Evelyn's natural sympathy brought her great confusion and sorrow. She did not know how to appease her daughter, and her husband had been no help. At his gravesite, she remembered his helplessness during this time with a deep regret.

One Wednesday morning Evelyn sat in her kitchen drinking coffee, twirling her jade cross necklace, and occasionally listening to the disc jockey on the radio. She was thinking about her husband. The statue of Our Lady of the Snows on her windowsill was usually a consolation because of Our Lady's benign resignation as if she could endure the very fires of hell without so much as a frown. But today this only made Evelyn's house more lonely, and the radio voice didn't seem to help. She decided to call Mindy.

"Mindy, this is Mom. I picked up a few things for Scott the other day and was wondering what you were doing this afternoon."

"I'm just washing clothes and waiting for him to get home from school. If you want to come down now, now is a good time, before the traffic gets bad."

"Well, I have to go to Southgate, so I think I will. Is there anything you want from home?"

"No, I don't need anything, thanks. I'll see you soon, then."

Although Mindy had been married to her husband, Keith, for over ten years, Evelyn still thought of her house as Mindy's home. Keith had once complained to Mindy about it, but Mindy only shrugged and said, "Well, that's Mom" and let the subject drop. She knew that her mother had a hard time giving up that part of her past from which she derived some identity, regardless of how far removed or violated that past was.

During the drive to Puyallup, Evelyn couldn't help thinking about her husband, Carl. She was remembering times when they had just met. He was a large muscular man who worked at Weyerhaeuser. He had played football for Renton High School and was an all-state tackle. For such a big man, he had a soft touch and she remembered the way he used to put suntan oil on her back. Sometimes she imagined that she could almost feel it—the light, smooth circles his fingertips made over her naked shoulders. Or in bed, lost in thought, he would rub her back and neck, down and up like an elegant skater over a small pond. She would drift into sleep, paralyzed by the steady purr of sensation.

When they had been married for three years, Evelyn had grown jealous of his past. It was not that he talked of it much, but Evelyn began sitting up at night worrying about the women and friends in his past as if they would all suddenly appear and take him away. She burned his old pictures and letters. She was afraid of losing his hands.

Yet, even when he was young his fingers were stained yellow from the cigarettes that would eventually kill him. She used to tease him about breathing more smoke than air. He didn't talk much, and they never said anything about sex, but she could count on his faithfulness and willingness to help around the house which meant more to her anyway. Not that she thought about their sex life, for to have impure thoughts was a sin and she didn't know where God would draw the line—it could be right down the middle of the marriage bed. So, she always pushed those thoughts to one side and chose cheerier subjects. Like his fishing. It seemed oddly incongruous that such a large man would love to sit by a lake with a tiny pole, smoking cigarettes. She liked to watch his concentration as he threw the lure in a long looping arc, let it sink, and slowly reeled it in. He did this for hours and his patience seemed to contradict his impatience with Mindy as a child and made Evelyn think that perhaps something she had done caused his outbursts. But, of course, when Mindy was older, he would have given the world to her if he had much of it to give. His job at Weyerhaeuser was always fraught with layoffs and run-ins with his bosses until he took an early retirement and died six months later.

Somehow, every time she started to think about her husband it worked around to his death. She tried to think of something nice. The tip of Mount Rainier was just visible through the clouds and the afternoon sun gave it a gold radiance like a mountain in the background of a holy picture. She smiled at it as if she had a secret pact with beauty. Finally, she let the steady thrum of her car envelop her body and mind.

When she got to Puyallup, she passed a Snowball produce truck and decided to take a watermelon to Scott. She drove to the Safeway store that was three blocks from Mindy's and was about to get out of her car when an enormous woman came out of the store. She wore a floral print dress and her black purse swung beside her like a weapon. Her hair was dyed black, her cheeks bright red, and her lips smeared with an even brighter red. With each laborious step her whole body rippled. She was followed by a thin haggard man pushing a cart of plastic sacks. He was wearing a blue straw hat with a little brown feather in the band. His suit was worn slick and his zipper was half-down. They were coming right towards her. Evelyn glanced away, fumbling for something in her purse. She looked out the window at the car next to her and watched a sparrow fly up into the radiator and knock dead grasshoppers and moths to the pavement. It then flew down and ate them, then up into the radiator again. The pink floral print passing her window startled her, and she again looked into her purse. When they were safely behind her, she got out, straightened her dress, drew in her stomach, and walked towards the store.

She passed through the electric swinging door and took a deep breath of the refrigerated air. Huge green vegetables and "P-R-O-D-U-C-E" were painted on the east wall above the shelves, as if for some elementary school pageant. A dirty-faced child with long black hair sucked her thumb on the floor of aisle 15b. Evelyn looked around but couldn't see the child's mother. She had no patience for negligent mothers, but she kept walking toward the watermelon bin. Trying to find one that she could carry easily and was perfectly ripe, she thumped each melon, listening for that taut, drum-like resonance. She wanted one that would zag open ahead of the knife. Thumping and sorting through them until her finger was sore, she finally found one that would do. It wasn't perfect, but it would be very nice just the same.

When she walked out the door, she was feeling a little better. A beautiful child squatted beside a box with four kittens in it. One was a calico with lots of orange and black; one was gray with a white mustache and bright blue eyes; one was a tabby; one was solid black with four white paws and a white mouth as if he had walked into a puddle of white paint expecting milk. Evelyn bent down and stroked the black one's head. It meowed and looked up at her. The little girl said, "They're free if you'd like one."

"No thanks, dear, I was just looking. They're all different colors."

"There's lots of tomcats in our neighborhood. Daddy says we have to get our cat spayed or else we'll be running a cat house. This is her third litter in a year and a half."

"Oh, dear, child, your father shouldn't tell you such things," said Evelyn, wagging her finger.

When she got back to her car, there was a black boy and a white girl kissing in the car next to hers. She tried looking away, but she couldn't help taking furtive peeks as she started her engine and pulled out of her parking spot. The girl was very pretty with long blonde hair and a perfect complexion. She looked no more than fourteen and wore expensive clothes, what there were of them. Evelyn couldn't believe it, and in broad daylight. She began to think of the girl's mother and the torment she had to endure. Mothers with teenage daughters had to be living saints, worry and prayer being so closely related. If only these young girls had been steeped in the proper values, but then living in the city is not an easy thing.

Evelyn was from the dry country of eastern Washington, and for solace, it was the country she turned to. Her father had owned a small orchard and taught in high school. The town itself was no bigger than a whistle, but her years on their small farm blurred into an image of uncomplicated peace. There had been forty-eight students in her graduating class, and the school had no racial problems. There were only two old black men in the whole town: George-the-junk-man who owned acres of dead cars, bed frames, engine parts, bird cages, batteries, cable, and any other assorted what-not you might need; and a man who walked a red-dyed goose through the annual parade. This was always Evelyn's favorite part of the parade, and until she was thirteen she thought the goose was some magical creature he had brought from another country.

She remembered her teenage years as being full of horseback riding, apple picking, tree climbing, fishing with her brother, and long walks down dusty roads where magpies, meadowlarks, and grasshoppers sprang out of the roadside grass into the dry blue air. She was thinking about home when she pulled into Mindy's driveway.

Mindy was in a good mood—she genuinely seemed to appreciate the things Evelyn had brought for Scott. The watermelon was deeply sweet with a small white rind, and Scott loved sitting on the swing, spitting the seeds at the cat. Keith was gone, and she and Mindy were able to talk for the first time about Carl. The ice broke when they discussed vacations, especially the one in 1962 to Disneyland. Carl insisted that because he had been through California when he was in the Navy he knew the exact roads to take, regardless of what any map might say. When he finally acknowledged that they were lost, he just knew the state highway department must have rerouted the roads. They spent the night in a motel that smelled of mildew and lilac air-freshener. There were rusted flamingoes in the withered grass and the pool was closed and scummed chartreuse. A man with black stubble, butchwaxed hair, and a toothy grin came by to give them towels. Mindy remembered his hairy belly-button that showed through a hole in his shirt. She also remembered the pink bubblegum stuck to the edge of her father's shoe and how she was afraid to tell him.

"I haven't thought about that trip in years," Mindy said. "Do you remember that place we ate the next morning? Daddy ordered biscuits and gravy but got an old dinner roll with a thin brown sauce over the top. He was so mad he asked to see the manager. When she came out, and he told her that it was the poorest excuse for biscuits and gravy he had ever seen. Remember that? And her trying to make it up to him with something else, but he kept saying, 'No thanks, I lost my appetite.' Remember? I was so embarrassed I about choked on my poached egg. I don't even remember what you had."

"I don't either, come to think of it. He had a way of making you forget what you were eating. Our vacations never did seem to work out like they were supposed to. But Carl was a determined man and we took them whether we liked them or not."

"Do you ever miss Daddy?"

"Of course I do. What kind of question is that? I was only saying that he was a very determined man, a complex man. Sometimes I think the War was to blame for that stubbornness in him. War cheats people out of normal things. I just think I realized that too late. Your father was really a fine man and I loved him very much. Do you have any idea how lonely it is by yourself? It's not an easy thing." Evelyn's voice trailed off. Mindy reached out and squeezed her hand.

Scott blurted through the door waving his watermelon rind, "What do I do with this?" His face was splotched with red and a black pit was stuck to his chin.

"The compost pile," Mindy said, putting it on her plate, "and you had better go wash your face and hands. You're all sticky."

Scott ran down the hall to the bathroom, stomping his feet.

"Is there anything I can do for you, Mom? Would you like to stay here for a few days?"

"Oh, no. I'll be fine. Fact is, I'd better be going."

They hugged and kissed goodbye. Scott gave her a wet kiss and thanked her for the watermelon. It was almost dark when Evelyn got in her car to drive home.

Evelyn didn't really mind driving at night, but the early dusk when the landscape blurred and the car's lights didn't help was very difficult for her, especially in her left eye where a cataract was beginning to form. If she had to drive during these hours, she cupped her left hand around her eye like a horse's blinder. The Olympic Range floated in the last light like a red and ragged fleet of sails, but she was only able to turn and catch a glimpse during a lull in traffic. She got off the Interstate and sat patiently waiting for the light to change.

Ahead of her, a priest jumped off the curb and waved. She pulled over and watched him trot towards her in the rearview mirror, the heavy black cross swinging across his chest.

"God Bless you, ma'am. My car finally gave out completely—the Bishop, God preserve him, doesn't believe in cars made in this decade."

"Oh, I'm only too glad to help. Where you going? I can take you wherever you want to go."

"Well, actually I'm on my way to Bellingham for a retreat that doesn't start until next Wednesday, but I thought I would see an old friend of mine first. We were high-school buddies, and we haven't seen each other for twenty years. Take me to an inexpensive motel, I'll call him tomorrow, arrange to do something with the car."

She had never before considered the private lives of priests, and the fact that he might have "high-school buddies" was strangely foreign to her. This news made her shy as if she had been let in on a great secret whose consequences were tantalizing but unimaginable. She fumbled with silence for a few minutes, trying to find a balance that wouldn't embarrass her. She was thrilled to be helping the clergy—it was like taking the hand of God.

"Well, you know, I have a spare room in my house. You're certainly welcome to sleep there tonight and call your friend in the morning."

"Oh my, what a generous offer. It would be a blessing, a real blessing."

Evelyn was enthralled by his voice. It had a full, measured, Irish rhythm that must have come out of a profound understanding of human misery. The stressed syllables lingered tremulously in the air like smoke after a gunshot.

She thought it unfortunate that he couldn't marry and have children because that voice, its almost divine surety and reassurance, would be so comforting and inspiring. It would be wonderful, she thought, to hear a whole mass, especially a Latin mass where that beautiful sound would be unimpeded by meaning and become a slow and lonely trumpet forged by the very breath of God.

He was balding slightly, grey at the temples, a neck that had been pocked by some childhood disease. He was slightly overweight, late middle-age settling above his belt. His teeth were misaligned. Yet there was a kindness in his eyes that overcame defects of appearance. As they drove along, his silence was a soothing emanation that calmed everything around him, even the St. Christopher medal gently swinging from the mirror.

When they pulled into the driveway, the night was completely dark and her porchlight cast a yellow umbrella over the steps. Moths flickered like fluorescent rain.

"My home isn't anything fancy, but it's comfortable."

"It looks fine. A home is always a mansion," the priest said, as he pushed the car door shut.

"I can see why you're a priest, you must be a great comfort to the sick."

Evelyn went in, turned on the lights. She had thawed a chicken breast for dinner, so she chopped it and made chicken and noodles. While she cooked, the priest read the newspaper and had a drink of whiskey from a bottle that had been sitting on the liquor shelf since her husband died. She made a salad, set the table, and put out a loaf of bread and some butter. The notion of eating with a priest made her feel a little strange. How could you eat noodles in front of a man who had spent his life listening to the inner-most doubts and lies of the human heart? Wouldn't anything you said be misconstrued, a symptom, an evasion, a shameless calculation? And wasn't there something a little profane about it all, as if the food for the spirit weren't enough? These feelings were only a deep confusion, not questions she could form and answer. She decided to have him eat while she prepared his room. Once while she was putting on some fresh sheets, he asked her where the sugar was for his tea. She told him it was in the bowl next to the blue chicken in the left cupboard, but this was the only conversation they had had before it was time for bed. They knelt in the living room to say their prayers. The priest bowed his head over the black beads in his hands and the large gold cross that hung around his neck. He began to recite a psalm: "Be not far from me; for there is none to help. ...Deliver my soul from the sword; save me from the lion's mouth: for thou hast heard me from the horns of the unicorns... The meek shall eat and be satisfied; they shall praise the Lord that seek him: your heart shall live forever." The soft murmur of his voice as he recited the prayers was a spiritual massage that went deep into her body too. It didn't matter that she couldn't hear all the words, they soothed her, the steady rhythm was like a heartbeat magnified so that it resounded through the hollowness of the night.

Because she was a little light-headed when she tried to stand, he took her by the arm and steadied her.

"That's a beautiful necklace you have, Evelyn. Where did it come from?"

It was slightly hidden in her blouse and the priest picked it up and turned it over, but when he withdrew his hand it brushed her left nipple.

"My daughter gave it to me. She brought it back from Europe."

Although he went right on praising the fine engraving on the crucifix, Evelyn was startled by the incongruity and the electric buzz that went through her body. She was also amazed that he didn't even seem to notice.

As she lay in bed, her thoughts skipped along, one hardly touching the other. She hadn't asked him much at all, like where his parish was, the name of his church, the size of the congregation. She thought, too, of him—the way he lived, who looked after him, where he was from, if he had brothers and sisters or high-school sweethearts. She had never thought about the personal lives of priests and the subject seemed endless, and why had it never occurred to her before? She had always been against priests marrying, but now she didn't know why. They were, after all, marriage counselors, wouldn't this help their counseling? A few cars passed, dogs barked, and the thin fingers of the moon roved across the room before she finally closed her eyes. Just as she was dozing off, she thought she heard a door shutting somewhere in the night.

The next morning when she got up, she put the kettle on and busied herself with breakfast. She made apple-pancakes, fried bacon, and scrambled some eggs. She went to his door and knocked, but there was no answer. The bed was made and the spread was slightly wrinkled as if he had only rested on top. She knocked at the bathroom door, but he wasn't there, nor in the backyard, nor in the garage. As she mounted the steps to go back into the house, she realized that her car was gone. She walked to where it had been parked the night before and looked down the driveway and into the street. She tried to think of where he had gone. Perhaps he got up very early and went to mass? But why wouldn't he have taken her or asked the night before? It just didn't seem like him to leave without any warning. Maybe he went to breakfast? What should she do?

She went back into her house and poured a cup of coffee. She couldn't eat, so she wrapped her breakfast in foil and put it in the oven. She waited for two hours, then a third. She watched the second-hand move around and around. By mid-afternoon, the word "impostor" leapt into her mind. But how could he have done it? Where did he get those clothes, that white collar, the rosary around his neck? She imagined him stealing the clothes from a dry cleaners while the clerk wasn't looking, but that still didn't explain the crucifix, the trained voice, his eyes. Nothing made sense. She wanted to call Mindy, but she knew Mindy would be aghast that she had taken in a total stranger, even if he was supposed to be a priest. And what if she was wrong and he had only borrowed the car and then gotten stuck or lost on the way back. Surely he would have marked the house number and street as he left? But perhaps a man preoccupied by the world of the spirit might not have thought about it.

She waited some more. It was getting to be late afternoon when another thought occurred to her. She went to the cupboard and pulled down her blue ceramic chicken that held her grocery money. It was empty. So, that was it, that's where things stood. She couldn't believe it and put her hand into the empty chicken as if her sight couldn't be trusted.

Finally, she went to the phone and called the police to report a stolen car, but she realized she hadn't even asked the priest's name. When they arrived just before dark, they asked a lot of embarrassing questions, but Evelyn answered them straightforwardly as if she were filling out a neighborhood questionnaire. They lectured her about trust and the times and told her that maybe she should have someone stay with her for a few days because she looked a little "disoriented."

That night she went to bed early. The TV in her bedroom was on but she didn't watch it. She wanted other voices in her house just then. She felt like such a fool, as if God Himself had slapped her. Tears welled up and bleared the blue-dark. She felt naked. When she looked into the mirror on her dressing-table, the darkness and her tears made her seem very, very fat. She felt swollen and ugly, some of her hair was stuck to the side of her face. She pressed her hands against her head until her mind stopped thinking for a second, and she forced herself to concentrate on something good.

She shut her eyes and saw a hot dusty road. The sun was like a warm hand on her head. With long skinny legs, she was walking toward town, and brown grasshoppers clicked their castanets, black ones spread fiery wings that drifted off like sparks. Yellow meadowlarks with black bibs warbled from fenceposts. She breathed in the sweet green smell of roadside mint. The whole world seemed alive, capable of flying off in any direction at any minute. Then she was in town looking up at all the people that lined both sides of Pearl Street. A high school band in blue coats, gold epaulets, and stiff hats marched by blaring their instruments. Then the mounted posse in yellow-green shirts and handkerchief ties. Their horses were all the same color with the same blankets and saddles. A clown with giant shoes flapped by throwing candy. Then, there it was, beautiful, exotic, waddling and honking down the center of the street. It padded past her, its regal head in the air, its red shining from another country.

THE NIGHT CLERK

Simon Ortega was in Howard's office when I arrived. A young policeman sat in a chair beside the door, his hands folded in his lap. The office had a consuming spareness: white walls, a fake window and sill, brushed green carpet, a desk with synthetic oak veneer, but no pictures, posters, or memorabilia of any kind. He has been here for ten years but could pack up and leave in ten minutes.

"Sit down, please," Howard motioned toward the black leather chair with chrome legs. Simon looked at me, but with an expressionless face, like he was watching a movie, a self-contained observer in the dark.

"I came in early this morning," Howard continued, "and found this in the desk drawer. Simon says he doesn't know how it got there. Your shift ended at eleven o'clock. We'd like to know what you know about this." After a preliminary glance at me, he watched Simon's face as he said this, but Simon remained expressionless.

On the desk between the phone and the rolodex was an orange vial. The prescription label had been torn off, and it was half full of white powder. I sat down.

"We believe," the policeman said gravely, "that the hotel has been used for months as a dropping point for little 'packages' just like this. We have seen people who don't look like they're interested in a room stopping by and leaving." As he talked he slowly spun his watch band around his white wrist like a platinum handcuff. He gazed solemnly into the empty space between Howard and Simon.

"I am not aware of any. . .commerce of this sort going on here," I said.

"Was this in the desk when you left last night?" Howard asked, stroking his bald head with his ringed hand.

Simon's face was coldly reserved. I imagined the same look passing across his face when he and his friends executed the cats and dogs of his neighborhood. He had told me that story one night when there was very little to do at the hotel. His neighborhood was the line of houses adjacent to the mobile home park bordering the freeway. Old couches and car parts and plastic toys in the yards, broken picket fences, peeling paint. The kids raised themselves because their parents worked two or three jobs as waitresses, field-hands, furniture movers, frozen food packers, hotel maids, and babysitters. If the executions had begun out of some vague sense of powerlessness and racial confusion, the bloodletting would have ended like this meeting, with no real vengeance, no hint of triumph as the blood dripped to the ground and the twitches ebbed into silence.

"It's mine," I said, looking fully into the face of the policeman who sat up and seemed to square his shoulders.

I was arrested and spent the night in jail. My son bailed me out the next day. When the story hit the papers with its quoted suspicions from the policeman about my using the hotel to sell cocaine, the phone calls from parents whose children I had taught, from church groups, from concerned citizens, came several times each hour until I finally unplugged the phone. They shouted their hate across the wires. There were letters to the editor in the local paper, angry denunciations, bitter calls for a swift justice. Perhaps the one that hurt the most was from a former student who said she suspected it all along by the way I acted in classes. It was from a girl, a woman now, who was convinced I had "narked" on her own use of marijuana in high school. One of my illustrious colleagues had read the girl's English journal and reported her to the Vice-Principal. She blamed me because one day a crumpled baggie had dropped from her coat pocket onto the floor, and she knew I had seen it. I thought the issue had been clarified, but it is always a mystery how suspicion and resentment grow.

My job at the hotel was part of a pattern of less and less working out more and more as time went on. When the stock market dove, I stepped out of retirement and cast my applications about town. I was not altogether unhappy about doing this. My wife died of uterine cancer two years ago, and I was driving myself crazy wandering around our empty house. I taught math to eighth-graders for thirty-two years and had had enough of other people's children, not to mention other people, so it was with a detached and cynical curiosity that I set out looking for a job at the age of sixty-eight. And I must say my expectations were met.

Employers like Howard looked at me like their embarrassing drunk uncle who just asked for a loan. I enjoyed their ambivalence, for the money was not exactly a necessity, more like the difference between a steak or hamburger life. I believe they wanted me to be a little more desperate, but if I'd been more desperate I wouldn't have gotten the job. An aloof take-it-or-leave it attitude goes a long way with most businessmen; they'll hire you just to conquer that indifference, to give it a paycheck with a signature.

Ours is not a grand hotel, but it is clean, has a restaurant with a few good dishes, an exercise room and spa with a pool, a fairly polite and hard-working staff. People come in from traveling, kids run and scream to the pool, their parents following them with towels. The most interesting things happen when it is late. Some are drunk, some bored, some released from the bonds of their own homes and needing to dip their toes in possibilities or to take a plunge. It is all very curious and the night shift is best.

My wife, Eva, was a very conventional woman, not given to experimentation of any kind. But a good woman who believed in goodness in a vague abstract way, like an athlete believes in her good health. She regarded aberration like one does a country never visited, only a place on a map, uninhabited by real people or any people she thought she could know. My background was not as middle class as hers. Poverty and the thumb of Catholicism carried with it, for all its outward conventionality and incensed decorum, a need for wild counter-measures, some alley-dark release. I was only on the fringes of that, for my parents' thumbs pressed lightly, but I saw it in my friends, the bleak spaces they could drift toward. So I always thought I was more worldly, more attuned to the echo of the trapdoors we cross as we go through the world. When I taught school, I could hear this hollow sound in the voices of some of my students, the ones who came unwashed, clothes rumpled, cereal milk still on their faces, anarchy in their hair.

At the hotel, cheaters were easy to spot. We soon attune ourselves to the delicate nuances of liars. It is not in the way they sign their false names, as you might expect, for that is something they practice (we have found notepads of signatures crumpled in the trash), but in the way they clutch their luggage—whether deliberately carefree or vigorously business-like; it is in the small gestures, the way the woman needs to run fingers through her hair, flip her bangs, or push her hair behind her ears; the way the man carefully places the pen on the paper when he is done, or the way he pushes the registration form back to us; how they scan the lobby as they leave, the way their shoulders touch lightly in the elevator before the door closes.

But after a month, they are not any more interesting than the parents who sneak their children in through the back door or carry them under clothing. I pretend to look the other way. But there were surprises. Two nuns with very little luggage came in wearing navy-blue veils over white coifs, and I thought it right that brides of Christ should travel light. Now, I did not see this, but Simon was one of our most reliable waiters who also does our early or mid-week room service. When he brought a bottle of chardonnay, a Clos du Bois, to room 318, no one answered, so he went in, the door was unlocked. The black suitcase on the luggage rack was open. The shower was running. He put the wine on the table and left. He told me that the suitcase was full of multi-colored sex equipment—vibrators, penises, bright neatly folded lingerie. In my heart, I do not believe they were nuns, but impersonators, maybe transvestites experimenting, crass cross-dressers. Yet I would not be shocked if they were nuns, Boniface's bonafides in the flesh. Simon's was a glimpse into the subtext, the shadowlands of desire and deceit, but perhaps I am assuming this.

The things forgotten in the rooms are also a catalog of shadows: a gun under the bed, photos of naked children, baggies with the residue of pills and herbs and white dust, razors wrapped in bloody Kleenexes, leather straps and chains, Rorschach's of blood-spotted sheets. Not to mention the lists of conventioneers: Leather & Lace selling bondage equipment in the hallways or door to door like Fuller Brush, the Mirth & Girth group of gay men over 250 pounds, coffin makers and distributors, scat biologists, out-of-body travelers, deaf musicians, experts on chicken lice and liverfluke, support groups for men with small penises and women with big breasts, people who have talked with God or aliens, puzzlemasters and liontamers. The list of our odd passions is surprisingly long.

What keeps most of us harnessed to the plow of convention despite these yearnings? What keeps us doing laundry, sweeping floors, sleeping in the same beds until the sheets wear out, taking out the same garbage can day after day? Some, like Eva, have inside them a zone of comfort and satisfaction beyond which they do not care to venture. When the shadows leak into the room from the newspaper or the blue shade of the television, they shake their heads at the wonder and pity of it all, at the savages from a dark country or century. Others, like me, pull steady because of the furrow we leave behind us. We do not want others to say it is crooked, that it runs wide of its fellows or into them. We stay in line for fear that others may snicker. We go to war and kill people for the same reasons. I went to Korea without ever having met a Korean.

One night Simon, who would occasionally "party" with one of the women in housekeeping, produced a small vial of white powder in an orange prescription bottle with the label torn off. He held it as if I should know what it was—his eyebrow arched, a deliberate dimple showing on his left cheek. In that moment of uncertainty, my mind retracted. I didn't know if he was showing me something novel, inviting me into something illicit, or exhibiting somebody's foolishness. He made no immediate move to resolve the ambiguity. The moment magnified.

"So, what have we here?" I asked, finally, as casually as I could.

"Rosie found it in one of the rooms, behind a lamp on the nightstand."

"What is it?"

"Coke. What pumpkin patch are you from, man? I thought you taught in high school. You skip the drug awareness assemblies?"

In the winter we had many late nights with little to do. He was in most aspects a beautiful boy. His face had an open trusting quality like an altar boy now in his early twenties. He had few whiskers and his skin was a buffed bronze. He revealed his specialized knowledge in pill-sized increments. first, he showed me how to use the Internet, something I had heard of but never used. Then, it was a few sites that were sexually suggestive but not beyond the bounds of adult decency. I'm not sure why I went along with this. I know I wanted him to trust me so that I might more completely understand the paradoxes I was seeing, to help him get beyond the row of defenses he had so carefully set up. But that was only half of it, the good half. I know, too, that there is an absolved pleasure in being led into temptation, that arousal seems to hanker after glimpses, and there is an excitement in the blood that rides in and hums inside us at such moments. Risk and arousal open the same doors. And the further we go in, the wider and darker the room. How do we know we have gone too far until we flip on the light?

When Simon brought in a baggie or a tiny folded envelope of coke found in rooms, I told him to dispose of them quickly. He knew more about drugs than a pharmacist. I cannot really explain my attachment to him. He was confident, oddly curious, extremely generous, yet had the capacity to be cruel, to be completely untouched by conventional standards or emotions, to smile warmly at a man carrying a gun.

He showed me drug magazines like High Times someone found on a table or in a drawer. Then the Internet stores and their "shopping carts" full of videos and sex toys. Then pornography itself: bondage, fetishes, hirsute honeys, soul fucking, chicks with animals, aged ladies, racial and inter-racial mating. When he showed me these things, we did not linger on them. It was more like a professor outlining a syllabus or an air hostess demonstrating oxygen masks and exits. This exposé took about six months, as one revelation after another slowly dropped into my hands. At first I felt my role was fatherly, and he was seeing how far I would enter this world with him, whether I had the nerve. It was like a game of poker: could I see bluff and call it, or hit something inside and show him up. When I felt that he had pushed a little too far, one glance would end it. And it was back to business as usual. I began to feel like his white neighbors must have as the stories of the pet deaths circulated, that he was incorrigible in some way I didn't completely understand.

Simon had a curious intelligence with areas of competence that were surprising. He read novels by Gabriel Marquez and Isabelle Allende, poetry by Octavio Paz and

Pablo Neruda, and others whose names I didn't recognize. He had more than a passing interest in a family of moths called saturniidae. When I pushed a little to see if he really knew what he was talking about, he made references to Riley and Dyar and used words like frenulum and bipectination and anastomose which were not even in my dictionary. He was interested in the grains of different wood and what they indicated about where and how the trees lived, the stresses they endured. About politics, he knew almost nothing and couldn't name our Secretary of State. He knew little about math, and when I tried to explain its value, he seemed indifferent to both its practical properties and its elegance.

Howard's phone call asking me to come to the office occurred on a Tuesday morning. The sun was out and the trees had lost that pastel green of spring. I remember that very clearly. I was watering Eva's roses, pruning off some of the winter-killed branches. The answering machine took the message: "This is Howard Michaelson, and I would like to see you immediately, if not sooner." He is a thin man who wears gray polyester suits, white shirts, and black ties every day. His smile has a perfectly inert intimacy like his limp handshake. Perhaps it is the nature of the hotel business and the turnover of "personnel" that sponsors his reserve, yet in his phone message was a hushed note of urgency, a calm pressed tightly.

I drove to the hotel thinking about Simon and what he must have done, his arrogant flippancy which hid so much. When I walked into Howard's office, I felt like I had stepped into a line-up. I could feel their accusations, the way they were aligned against him, and I was to be their star witness.

A night in jail was nothing to me. And I knew that for a

first offense and the scant evidence they would have against me, the real cost to me would be slight. Yet, how swiftly, almost inadvertently, certainly without much premeditation, do we enter the house of shame. Since that day, I have had garbage dumped into my lawn, my garage spray painted with red obscenities, vile notes put in my mailbox, had "Dealers Die" and "Kid Killer" written into the dust on my car's rear-window, and donations for masses to be said for my swift reformation. My son stopped calling me when I told him I could not talk about this issue, that there were things I needed to work out first. I have not seen nor heard from Simon. I heard that he quit working at the hotel.

I am writing this not because I'm cynical but because one night about two weeks before my arrest I had a vision. It was late, about 1:00 in the morning. I was reading the paper. I, as you could probably guess, did not think I was one capable of visions. The spiritual life had long since become the fantasy of fools, a church's or a hotel's monetary opportunity.

At first I saw nothing extraordinary. The man came in to see if rooms were available. In that rotating wheel of style, he wore black hair to his shoulders and was unshaven. A dark green shirt under a black jacket, jeans. There was a slight hesitancy in his walk, weariness or perhaps the residue of that nagging belief we do not belong in clean polished places. It was not until the woman came in that it hit me. Her blonde hair was pulled back, but loose strands floated freely around her face. The freckles were in the same pattern, clustering at her nose and sprinkled across her forehead and cheeks. It was also the way her canine tooth on the left side pushed forward and curved like an ax-blade. Most astonishing were the green earrings set in gold. Across the wastes of time many things are altered, but I remember the green light from her ears on that first afternoon we met. Eva rode in the front seat, her father was driving, and I, who worked for him at the warehouse, was in the backseat. Not having much to say, a mere passenger, I watched the sway of her green earrings, the freckle pattern, the curves of her nose, the light in her hair and on her white pink-striped collar. The first stirrings of love are always a mystery and the images that cling to those feelings are just as odd and mysterious. And they fade very little over time even if the love has altered irrevocably.

I do not know the name of the woman who walked into our hotel. His name was William Halladay, but that neither revealed nor suggested anything. When I looked closely at him, I saw myself, forty years earlier. His hair was cut much differently, but there were astonishing similaritiesthe arc of the eyebrows, the full lips, the curve of the nose, the way he walked. In this couple, I saw me and Eva before we had children, before mortgages and life insurance and tax forms, before we became what we had become, what we were. And it was in that moment the human sounds awoke in me, echoed, and I saw and felt so deeply the arc of our trajectory, our trajectories. The couple stood in front of the elevator, and he reached out and curled his little finger around hers as they watched the light ascend and descend again. It was an unconscious gesture of ease and comfort, of assurance and reassurance, and had nothing in it of the fraudulent, the liars and reprobates I had spent my first months observing. I stood there and could actually feel Eva's fingers interlocked with mine.

I now spend most of my time in the basement, the lowest room, out of view. I have taken up painting and have discovered a certain freedom in the mind of the pariah, a tiny icy center that hardens and protects. Perhaps it is my age or the deaths of Eva and my parents, but the daily world and its lust for news, for blame, for fixed objects of our wrath, and all our eager sincerities seem so overlaid with a patronizing indulgence, with a misguided love, that silence is the one incontrovertible truth, the one holiness left us at the end of our days. So I paint and water and fertilize the roses, trying to learn names like Autumn Splendor, Perdita, Angelface, Playboy, Hawkeye Belle, and the Hybrid Tea Rose. I have taken my name off our mailbox, sent in initials for next year's phone book. I lock my doors at night, all small changes, small adjustments to the life within.